CHRISTMAS MIRACLES

One little miracle—that's all it takes to make
Christmas special for each couple in these
three original stories. An unexpected marriage
proposal, a new wife for a father with three
young children, and a little boy reunited with
his daddy for the holidays…

Christmas is a time for romance, for falling in
love and for wishes to come true. We hope you
enjoy these heartwarming stories—and who
knows? Maybe your own Christmas
miracle is right around the corner!

Betty Neels, Carole Mortimer and Rebecca Winters
send you their warmest best wishes for the
holiday season...

*Happy Christmas
and all best wishes*

*With love from
Betty Neels*

*Season's
Greetings
and warmest
wishes for
the holidays*

Rebecca Winters

*Wishing you all a
wonderful Christmas
and a happy
New Year!*

Carole Mortimer

BETTY NEELS
CAROLE MORTIMER
REBECCA WINTERS

CHRISTMAS MIRACLES

Harlequin Books

TORONTO • NEW YORK • LONDON
AMSTERDAM • PARIS • SYDNEY • HAMBURG
STOCKHOLM • ATHENS • TOKYO • MILAN
MADRID • WARSAW • BUDAPEST • AUCKLAND

HARLEQUIN BOOKS
225 Duncan Mill Road, Don Mills,
Ontario, Canada M3B 3K9

ISBN 0-373-15265-5

CHRISTMAS MIRACLES
Copyright © 1997 by Harlequin Books S.A.

The publisher acknowledges the copyright holders
of the individual works as follows:

A CHRISTMAS PROPOSAL
Copyright © 1996 by Betty Neels

HEAVENLY ANGELS
Copyright © 1996 by Carole Mortimer

A DADDY FOR CHRISTMAS
Copyright © 1996 by Rebecca Winters

CONTENTS

CONTENTS

A CHRISTMAS PROPOSAL
Betty Neels

Dear Reader,

Isn't it a comforting thought that whatever happenings the year has brought with it, Christmas is the time we all look forward to? Families gather together, small differences are forgotten, friends send their yearly letters and the children are in their own little seventh heaven.

And as for romance, there must be many of you who remember being kissed under the mistletoe—a kiss that may have led to your own romance and, even if it didn't, is a memory never quite forgotten.

I do hope that this Christmas—with or without the mistletoe—will be a romantic one for you.

A very happy Christmas.

Betty Neels

CHAPTER ONE

THE girl standing in a corner of the crowded room hardly merited a second glance; she was small, with light brown hair strained back into an unfashionable bun, a face whose snub nose and wide mouth did nothing to redeem its insignificance, and she was wearing an elaborate shrimp-pink dress. But after his first glance the man standing across the room from her looked again. Presently he strolled over to stand beside her. His 'Hello' was pleasant and she turned her head to look at him.

She answered him politely, studying him from large brown eyes fringed by curling lashes. Looking at her eyes, he reflected that one soon forgot the nose and mouth and dragged-back hair. He smiled down at her. 'Do you know anyone here? I came with friends—I'm staying with them and was asked to come along with them. A birthday party, isn't it?'

'Yes.' She looked past him to the crowded room, the groups of laughing, gossiping people waving to each other with drinks in their hands, the few couples dancing in the centre. 'Would you like me to introduce you to someone?'

He said in his friendly way, 'You know everyone here? Is it your birthday?'

'Yes.' She gave him a quick surprised look and bent her head to examine the beaded bodice of her dress.

9

'Then shouldn't you be the belle of the ball?'

'Oh, it's not my party. It's my stepsister's—that pretty girl over by the buffet. Would you like to meet Clare?'

'The competition appears too keen at the moment,' he said easily. 'Shouldn't you be sharing the party, since it's your birthday too?'

'Well, no.' She had a pretty voice and she spoke matter-of-factly. 'I'm sure you'd like to meet some of the guests. I don't know your name...'

'Forgive me. Hay-Smythe—Oliver.'

'Bertha Soames.' She put out a small hand and he shook it gently.

'I really don't want to meet anyone. I think that perhaps I'm a little on the old side for them.'

She scrutinised him gravely—a very tall, strongly built man, with fair hair thickly sprinkled with grey. His eyes were grey too, and he had the kind of good looks which matched his assured air.

'I don't think you're in the least elderly,' she told him.

He thanked her gravely and added, 'Do you not dance?'

'Oh, I love to dance.' She smiled widely at him, but as quickly the smile faded. 'I—that is, my stepmother asked me to see that everyone was enjoying themselves. That's why I'm standing here—if I see anyone on their own I make sure that they've got a drink and meet someone. I really think that you should...'

'Definitely not, Miss Soames.' He glanced down at her and thought how out of place she looked in the noisy room. And why, if it was her birthday, was she not wearing a pretty dress and not that ill-fitting, over-elaborate garment? 'Are you hungry?'

'Me? Hungry?' She nodded her head. 'Yes, I missed lunch.' Her eyes strayed to the buffet, where a number of people were helping themselves lavishly to the dainties upon it. 'Why don't you...?'

Dr Hay-Smythe, hard-working in his profession and already respected by older colleagues, a man who would never pass a stray kitten or a lost dog and who went out of his way to make life easy for anyone in trouble, said now, 'I'm hungry too. Supposing we were to slip away and have a meal somewhere? I don't imagine we should be missed, and we could be back long before this finishes.'

She stared at him. 'You mean go somewhere outside? But there isn't a café anywhere near here—besides...'

'Even Belgravia must have its pubs. Anyway, I've my car outside—we can look around.'

Her eyes shone. 'I'd like that. Must I tell my stepmother?'

'Certainly not. This door behind you—where does it lead? A passage to the hall? Let us go now.'

'I'll have to get my coat,' said Bertha when they were in the hall. 'I won't be long, but it's at the top of the house.'

'Haven't you a mac somewhere down here?'

'Yes, but it's very old...'

His smile reassured her. 'No one will notice in the pub.' He reflected that at least it would conceal that dreadful dress.

So, suitably shrouded, she went out of the house with him, through the important front door, down the imposing steps and onto the pavement.

'Just along here,' said the doctor, gesturing to where a dark grey Rolls-Royce was parked. He unlocked the door, popped her inside and got in beside her. As he drove off he asked casually, 'You live here with your parents?'

'Yes. Father is a lawyer—he does a lot of work for international companies. My stepmother prefers to live here in London.'

'You have a job?'

'No.' She turned her head to look out of the window, and he didn't pursue the subject but talked idly about this and that as he left the quiet streets with their stately houses and presently, in a narrow street bustling with people, stopped the car by an empty meter. 'Shall we try that pub on the corner?' he suggested, and helped her out.

Heads turned as they went in; they made an odd couple—he in black tie and she in a shabby raincoat—but the landlord waved them to a table in one corner of the saloon bar and then came over to speak to the doctor.

'Ain't seen yer for a while, Doc. Everything OK?'

'Splendid, thank you, Joe. How is your wife?'

'Fighting fit, thanks to you. What'll it be?' He glanced at Bertha. 'And the little lady here? A nice drop of wine for her?'

'We're hungry, Joe...'

'The wife's just this minute dished up bangers and mash. How about that, with a drop of old and mild?'

Dr Hay-Smythe raised an eyebrow at Bertha, and when she nodded Joe hurried away, to return presently with the beer and the wine and, five minutes later, a laden tray.

The homely fare was well cooked, hot and generous. The pair of them ate and drank in a friendly silence until the doctor said quietly, 'Will you tell me something about yourself?'

'There's nothing to tell. Besides, we're strangers; we're not likely to meet again.' She added soberly, 'I think I must be a little mad to be doing this.'

'Well, now, I can't agree with that. Madness, if at all, lies with people who go to parties and eat too much and drink too much and don't enjoy themselves. Whereas you and I have eaten food we enjoy and are content with each other's company.' He waited while Joe brought the coffee he had ordered. 'Being strangers, we can safely talk knowing that whatever we say will certainly be forgotten.'

'I've never met anyone like you before,' said Bertha.

'I'm perfectly normal; there must be thousands exactly like me.' He smiled a little. 'I think that perhaps you haven't met many people. Do you go out much? The theatre? Concerts? Sports club? Dancing?'

Bertha shook her head. 'Well, no. I do go shopping, and I take my stepmother's dog out and help when people come for tea or dinner. That kind of thing.'

'And your sister?' He saw her quick look. 'Stepsister Clare—has she a job?'

'No—she's very popular, you see, and she goes out a great deal and has lots of friends. She's pretty—you must have seen that...'

'Very pretty,' he agreed gravely. 'Why are you

unhappy, Bertha? You don't mind my calling you Bertha? After all, as you said, we are most unlikely to meet again. I'm a very good listener. Think of me as an elder brother or, if you prefer, someone who is going to the other side of the world and never returning.'

She asked, 'How do you know that I'm unhappy?'

'If I tell you that I'm a doctor, does that answer your question?'

She smiled her relief. 'A doctor! Oh, then I could talk to you, couldn't I?'

His smile reassured her.

'You see, Father married again—oh, a long time ago, when I was seven years old. My mother died when I was five, and I suppose he was lonely, so he married my stepmother.

'Clare was two years younger than I. She was a lovely little girl and everyone adored her. I did too. But my stepmother—you see, I've always been plain and dull. I'm sure she tried her best to love me, and it must be my fault, because I tried to love her, but somehow I couldn't.

'She always treated me the same as Clare—we both had pretty dresses and we had a nice nanny and went to the same school—but even Father could see that I wasn't growing up to be a pretty girl like Clare, and my stepmother persuaded him that it would be better for me to stay at home and learn to be a good housewife...'

'Was Clare not a partner in this, too?'

'Well, no. She has always had lots of friends—I mean, she hadn't time to be at home very much. She's really kind to me.' She laid a hand on a glimpse of pink frill which had escaped from the raincoat. 'She gave me this dress.'

'You have no money of your own?'

'No. Mother left me some, but I—I don't need it, do I?'

The doctor didn't comment on that. All he said was, 'There is a simple solution. You must find a job.'

'I'd like that, but I'm not trained for anything.' She added anxiously, 'I shouldn't have said all that to you. Please forget it. I have no right to complain.'

'Hardly complaining. Do you not feel better for talking about it?'

'Yes, oh, yes. I do.' She caught sight of the clock and gave a little gasp. 'Heavens, we've been here for ages...'

'Plenty of time,' said the doctor easily. 'I dare say the party will go on until midnight.' He paid the bill and stowed her in the Rolls once more, then drove her back and went with her into the house. Bertha shed the raincoat in the hall, smoothed the awful dress and went with him into the vast drawing room. The first person to see them was her stepmother.

'Bertha, where have you been? Go at once to the kitchen and tell Cook to send up some more vol-au-vents. You're here to make yourself useful—'

Mrs Soames, suddenly aware of the doctor standing close by, became all at once a different woman. 'Run along, dear.' She spoke in a quite different voice now, and added, 'Don't be long—I'm sure your friends must be missing you.'

Bertha said nothing, and slipped away without a glance at the doctor.

'Such a dear girl,' enthused Mrs Soames, her massive front heaving with pseudo maternal feelings, 'and such a companion and help to me. It is a pity that she is so shy and awkward. I have done my best—' she managed to sound plaintive '—but Bertha is an intelligent girl and knows that she is lacking in looks and charm. I can only hope that some good man will come along and marry her.'

She lifted a wistful face to her companion, who murmured the encouraging murmur at which doctors are so good. 'But I mustn't bother you with my little worries, must I? Come and talk to Clare—she loves a new face. Do you live in London? We must see more of you.'

So when Bertha returned he was at the other end of the room, and Clare was laughing up at him, a hand on his arm. Well, what did I expect? reflected Bertha, and went in search of Crook the butler, a lifelong friend and ally; she had had a good supper, and now, fired by a rebellious spirit induced by Dr Hay-Smythe's company, she was going to have a glass of champagne.

She tossed it off under Crook's fatherly eye, then took a second glass from his tray and drank that too. Probably she would have a headache later, and certainly she would have a red nose, but since there was no one to mind she really didn't care. She wished suddenly that her father were at home. He so seldom was...

People began to leave, exchanging invitations and greetings, several of them saying a casual goodbye to Bertha, who was busy finding coats and wraps and mislaid handbags. Dr Hay-Smythe was amongst the first to leave with his party, and he came across the hall to wish her goodbye.

'That was a splendid supper,' he observed, smiling down at her. 'Perhaps we might do it again some time.'

Before she could answer, Clare had joined them. 'Darling Oliver, don't you dare run off just as I've discovered how nice you are. I shall find your number in the phone book and ring you—you may take me out to dinner.'

'I'm going away for some weeks,' he said blandly. 'Perhaps it would be better if I phoned you when I get back.'

Clare pouted. 'You wretched man. All right, if that's the best you can do.'

She turned her head to look at Bertha. 'Mother's looking for you...'

Bertha went, but not before putting out a small, capable hand and having it shaken gently. Her, 'Goodbye Doctor,' was uttered very quietly.

It was after Bertha had gone to her bed in the modest room on the top floor of the house that Mrs Soames went along to her daughter's bedroom.

'A successful evening, darling,' she began. 'What do you think of that new man—Oliver Hay-Smythe? I was talking to Lady Everett about him. It seems he's quite well-known—has an excellent practice in Harley Street. Good family and plenty of money—old money...' She patted Clare's shoulder. 'Just the thing for my little girl.'

'He's going away for a while,' said Clare. 'He said he'd give me a ring when he gets back.' She looked at her mother and smiled. Then she frowned.

'How on earth did Bertha get to know him? They seemed quite friendly. Probably he's sorry for her—she did look a dowd, didn't she?'

Clare nibbled at a manicured hand. 'She looked happy—as though they were sharing a secret or something. Did you know that he has a great deal to do with backward children? He wouldn't be an easy man... If he shows an interest in Bertha, I shall encourage him.' She met her mother's eyes in the mirror. 'I may be wrong, but I don't think he's much of a party man—the Paynes, who brought him, told me that he's not married and there are no girlfriends—too keen on his work. If he wants to see more of Bertha, I'll be all sympathy!'

The two of them smiled at each other.

Dr Hay-Smythe parted from his friends at their house and took himself off to his flat over his consulting rooms. Cully, his man, had gone to his bed, but there was coffee warm on the Aga in the kitchen and a covered plate of sandwiches. He poured himself a mug of coffee and sat down at the kitchen table, and the Labrador who had been snoozing by the Aga got up sleepily and came to sit beside him, ready to share his sandwiches. He shared his master's thoughts too, chewing on cold roast beef and watching his face.

'I met a girl this evening, Freddie—a plain girl with beautiful eyes and wearing a truly awful frock. An uninteresting creature at first glance, but somehow I feel that isn't a true picture. She has a delightful voice—very quiet. She needs to get away from that ghastly stepmother too. I must think of something...'

*   *   *

Bertha, happily unaware of these plans for her future, slept all night, happier in her dreams than in her waking hours.

It was two days later that the doctor saw a way to help Bertha. Not only did he have a private practice, a consultancy at two of the major hospitals and a growing reputation in his profession, he was also a partner in a clinic in the East End of London, dealing with geriatrics and anyone else who could not or would not go to Outpatients at any of the hospitals.

He had spent the evening there and his last patient had been an old lady, fiercely independent and living on her own in a tiny flat near the clinic. There wasn't a great deal he could do for her; a hard working life and old age were taking their toll, but she stumped around with a stick, refusing to go into an old people's home, declaring that she could look after herself.

'I'm as good as you, Doctor,' she declared after he had examined her. 'But I miss me books—can't read like I used to and I likes a good book. The social lady brought me a talking book, but it ain't the same as a real voice, if yer sees what I mean.' She added, 'A nice, quiet voice...'

He remembered Bertha then. 'Mrs Duke, would you like someone to come and read to you? Twice or three times a week, for an hour or so?'

'Not if it's one of them la-de-da ladies. I likes a nice bit of romance, not prosy stuff out of the parish mag.'

'The young lady I have in mind isn't at all like that. I'm sure she will read anything you like.

Would you like to give it a try? If it doesn't work out, we'll think of something else.'

'OK, I'll 'ave a go. When'll she come?'

'I shall be here again in two days' time in the afternoon. I'll bring her and leave her with you while I am here and collect her when I've finished. Would that suit you?'

'Sounds all right.' Mrs Duke heaved herself out of her chair and he got up to open the door for her. 'Be seeing yer.'

The doctor went home and laid his plans; Mrs Soames wasn't going to be easy, a little strategy would be needed...

Presently he went in search of Cully. Cully had been with him for some years, was middle-aged, devoted and a splendid cook. He put down the silver he was polishing and listened to the doctor.

'You would like me to telephone now, sir?'

'Please.'

'And if the lady finds the time you wish to visit her unacceptable?'

'She won't, Cully.'

Cully went to the phone on the wall and the doctor wandered to the old-fashioned dresser and chose an apple. Presently Cully put back the receiver.

'Five o'clock tomorrow afternoon, sir. Mrs Soames will be delighted.'

The doctor took a bite. 'Splendid, Cully. If at any time she should ring me here, or her daughter, be circumspect, if you please.'

Cully allowed himself to smile. 'Very good, sir.'

The doctor was too busy during the next day to give much thought to his forthcoming visit; he would have liked more time to think up reasons for his request, but he presented himself at five o'clock at Mrs Soames' house and was shown into the drawing room by a grumpy maid.

Mrs Soames, encased in a vivid blue dress a little too tight for her ample curves, rose to meet him. 'Oliver, how delightful to see you—I'm sure you must be a very busy man. I hear you have a large practice.' She gave rather a shrill laugh. 'A pity that I enjoy such splendid health or I might visit your rooms.'

He murmured appropriately and she patted the sofa beside her. 'Now, do tell me why you wanted to see me—' She broke off as Clare came into the room. Her surprise was very nearly real. 'Darling, you're back. See who has come to see us.'

Clare gave him a ravishing smile. 'And about time, too. I thought you were going away.'

'So did I.' He had stood up when she'd joined them, and he now took a chair away from the sofa. 'A series of lectures, but they have been postponed for a couple of weeks.'

Clare wrinkled her nose enchantingly. 'Good; now you can take me out to dinner.'

'A pleasure. I'll look in my appointments book and give you a ring, if I may. I was wondering if you have any time to spare during your days? I'm looking for someone who would be willing to read aloud for an hour or two several times a week to an old lady.' He smiled at Clare. 'You, Clare?'

'Me? Read a boring book to a boring old woman? Besides, I never have a moment to myself. What kind of books?'

'Oh, romances...'

'Yuk. How absolutely grim. And you thought of me, Oliver?' She gave a tinkling laugh. 'I don't even read to myself—only *Vogue* and *Tatler*.'

The doctor looked suitably disappointed. 'Ah, well, I dare say I shall be able to find someone else.'

Clare hesitated. 'Who is this old woman? Someone I know? I believe Lady Power has to have something done to her eyes, and there's Mrs Dillis—you know, she was here the other evening—dripping with diamonds and quite able to afford half a dozen companions or minders or whatever they're called.'

'Mrs Duke lives in a tiny flat on her own and she exists on her pension.'

'How ghastly.' Clare looked up and caught her mother's eye. 'Why shouldn't Bertha make herself useful? She's always reading anyway, and she never does anything or goes anywhere. Of course—that's the very thing.'

Clare got up and rang the bell, and when the grumpy maid came she told her to fetch Miss Bertha.

Bertha came into the room quietly and stopped short when she saw Dr Hay-Smythe.

'Come here, Bertha,' said Mrs Soames. 'You know Dr Hay-Smythe, I dare say? He was at Clare's party. He has a request to make and I'm sure you will agree to it—something to keep you occupied from time to time. Perhaps you will explain, Oliver.'

He had stood up when Bertha had come into the room, and when she sat down he came to sit near her. 'Yes, we have met,' he said pleasantly. 'I came to ask Clare to read to an old lady—a patient of mine—whose eyesight is failing, but she suggested that you might like to visit her. I believe you enjoy reading?'

'Yes, yes, I do.'

'That's settled, then,' said Mrs Soames. 'She's at your disposal, Oliver.'

'Would you like to go to this lady's flat—say, three times a week in the afternoons—and read to her for an hour or so?'

'Yes, thank you, Doctor.' Bertha sounded politely willing, but her eyes, when she looked at him, shone.

'Splendid. Let me see. Could you find your way to my rooms in Harley Street tomorrow afternoon? Then my secretary will give you her address. It is quite a long bus ride, but it won't be too busy in the afternoon. Come about two o'clock, will you? And thank you so much.'

'You'll have a drink, won't you?' asked Mrs Soames. 'I must make a phone call, but Clare will look after you. Bertha, will you go and see Cook and get her list for shopping tomorrow?'

The doctor, having achieved his purpose, sat for another half-hour, drinking tonic water while Clare drank vodka.

'Don't you drink?' She laughed at him. 'Really, Oliver, I should have thought you a whisky man.'

He smiled his charming smile. 'I'm driving. It would never do to reel into hospital, would it?'

'I suppose not. But why work in a hospital when you've got a big practice and can pick and choose?'

He said lightly, 'I enjoy the work.' He glanced at his watch. 'I am most reluctant to go, but I have an appointment. Thank you for the drink. I'll take you out to dinner and give you champagne at the first opportunity.'

She walked with him to the door, laid a pretty little hand on his arm and looked up at him. 'You don't mind? That I don't want to go to that old woman? I can't bear poverty and old, dirty people and smelly children. I think I must be very sensitive.'

He smiled a little. 'Yes, I am sure you are, and I don't mind in the least. I am sure your stepsister will manage very well—after all, all I asked for was someone to read aloud, and she seems to have time on her hands.'

'I'm really very sorry for her—her life is so dull,' declared Clare, and contrived to look as though she meant that.

Dr Hay-Smythe patted her hand, removed it from his sleeve, shook it and said goodbye with beautiful manners, leaving Clare to dance away and find her mother and gloat over her conquest.

As for the doctor, he went home well pleased with himself. He found Clare not at all to his taste but he had achieved his purpose.

It was raining as Bertha left the house the following afternoon to catch a bus, which meant that she had to wear the shabby mackintosh again. She consoled herself with the thought that it concealed the dress she was wearing—one which Clare had bought on the spur of the moment and disliked as soon as she'd got home with it.

It was unsuitable for a late autumn day, and a wet one, being of a thin linen—the colour of which was quite brilliant. But until her stepmother decided that Bertha might have something more seasonal there was nothing much else in her wardrobe suitable for the occasion, and anyway, nobody would see her. The old lady she was to visit had poor eyesight...

She got off the bus and walked the short distance to Dr Hay-Smythe's rooms, rang the bell and was admitted. His rooms were elegant and restful, and the cosy-looking lady behind the desk in the waiting room had a pleasant smile. 'Miss Soames?' She had got up and was opening a door beside the desk. 'The doctor's expecting you.'

Bertha hadn't been expecting him! She hung back to say, 'There's no need to disturb him. I was only to get the address from you.'

The receptionist merely smiled and held the door wide open, allowing Bertha to glimpse the doctor at his desk. He looked up then, stood up and came to meet her at the door.

'Hello, Bertha. Would you mind waiting until I finish this? A few minutes only. Take this chair. You found your way easily?' He pushed forward a small, comfortable chair, sat her down and went back to his own chair. 'Do undo your raincoat; it's warm in here.'

He was friendly and easy and she lost her shyness and settled comfortably, undoing her raincoat to reveal the dress. The doctor blinked at its startling colour as he picked up his pen. Another of Clare's cast-offs, he supposed, which cruelly highlighted Bertha's nondescript features. Really, he reflected angrily, something should be done, but surely that was for her father to do? He finished his writing and left his chair.

'I'm going to the clinic to see one or two patients. I'll take you to Mrs Duke and pick you up when I've finished. Will you wait for me there?' He noticed the small parcel she was holding. 'Books? How thoughtful of you.'

'Well, Cook likes romances and she let me have some old paperbacks. They may please Mrs Duke.'

They went out together and the receptionist got up from her desk.

'Mrs Taylor, I'm taking Miss Soames with me. If I'm not back by five o'clock, lock up, will you? I've two appointments for this evening, haven't I? Leave the notes on my desk, will you?'

'Yes, Doctor. Sally will be here at six o'clock…'

'Sally is my nurse,' observed the doctor. 'My right hand. Mrs Taylor is my left hand.'

'Go on with you, Doctor,' said Mrs Taylor, and chuckled in a motherly way.

Bertha, brought up to make conversation when the occasion warranted it, worked her way painstakingly through a number of suitable subjects in the Rolls-Royce, and the doctor, secretly amused, replied in his kindly way, so that by the time he drew up in a shabby street lined with small terraced houses she felt quite at ease.

He got out, opened her door and led the way across the narrow pavement to knock on a door woefully in need of a paintbrush. It was opened after a few moments by an old lady with a wrinkled face, fierce black eyes and an untidy head of hair. She nodded at the doctor and peered at Bertha.

'Brought that girl, 'ave yer? Come on in, then. I

could do with a bit of company.' She led the way down the narrow hall to a door at the end. 'I've got me own flat,' she told Bertha. 'What's yer name?'

'Bertha, Mrs Duke.'

The doctor, watching her, saw with relief that she had neither wrinkled her small nose at the strong smell of cabbage and cats, nor had she let her face register anything other than friendly interest.

He didn't stay for more than a few minutes, and when he had gone Bertha, bidden to sit herself down, did so and offered the books she had brought.

Mrs Duke peered at their titles. 'Just me cup of tea,' she pronounced. 'I'll 'ave *Love's Undying Purpose* for a start.' She settled back in a sagging armchair and an elderly cat climbed onto her lap.

Bertha turned to the first page and began to read.

CHAPTER TWO

BERTHA was still reading when the doctor returned two hours later. There had been a brief pause while Mrs Duke had made tea, richly brown and laced with tinned milk and a great deal of sugar, but Bertha hadn't been allowed to linger over it. She had obediently picked up the book again and, with a smaller cat on her own knees, had continued the colourful saga of misunderstood heroine and swashbuckling hero.

Mrs Duke had listened avidly to every word, occasionally ordering her to 'read that bit again', and now she got up reluctantly to let the doctor in.

'Enjoyed yourselves?' he wanted to know.

'Not 'arf. Reads a treat, she does. 'Artway through the book already.' Mrs Duke subsided into her chair again, puffing a bit. 'Bertha's a bit of all right. When's she coming again?'

He looked at Bertha, sitting quietly with the cat still on her knee.

'When would you like to come again?' he asked her.

'Whenever Mrs Duke would like me to.'

'Tomorrow? We could finish this story...'

'Yes, of course. If I come about the same time?'

'Suits me. 'Ere, give me Perkins—like cats, do you?'

'Yes, they're good company, aren't they?' Bertha

got up. 'We'll finish the story tomorrow,' she promised.

In the car the doctor said, 'I'll bring you over at the same time and collect you later. I want to take a look at Mrs Duke; she's puffing a bit.'

'Yes—she would make tea and she got quite breathless. Is she ill?'

'Her heart's worn out and so are her lungs. She's turned eighty and had a very hard life. She refuses to go into hospital. You have made her happy reading to her—thank you, Bertha.' She smiled and he glanced at her. 'You didn't find the smells and the cats too much for you?'

'No, of course not. Would she be offended if I took a cake or biscuits? I'm sure Cook will let me have something.'

'Would you? I think she would be delighted; she's proud, but she's taken to you, hasn't she?'

He reflected with some surprise that he had rather taken to Bertha himself...

'Could we settle on which days you would like to visit Mrs Duke? I'll bring you tomorrow, as I've already said, but supposing we say three times a week? Would Monday, Wednesday and Friday suit you? Better still, not Friday but Saturday—I dare say that will help her over the weekend. I'll give you a lift on Wednesdays and Saturdays and on Mondays, if you will come to my rooms as usual, there will be someone to take you to Mrs Duke.'

'I'll go any day you wish me to, but I must ask my stepmother... And I can get a bus—there's no need...'

'I go anyway. You might just as well have a lift.

And on Mondays there is always someone going to the clinic—I'm one of several who work there.'

'Well, that would be nice, if you are sure it's no trouble?'

'None whatsoever. Is your stepmother likely to object to your going?'

'I don't think so.' Bertha paused. 'But she might not like me going with you...' She spoke matter-of-factly.

'Yes. Perhaps you are right. There is no need to mention that, is there?'

'You mean it will be a kind of secret between us?'

'Why not?' He spoke lightly and added, 'I'm taking your stepsister out to dinner tomorrow evening. She is a very popular girl, isn't she?'

Which somehow spoilt Bertha's day.

Two weeks went by and autumn showed signs of turning into winter. Mrs Soames had decided that Bertha, since she went out so seldom, needed no new dresses; Clare had several from last year still in perfect condition. A little alteration here and there and they would be quite all right for Bertha, she declared, making a mental note that she would have to buy something new for the girl when her father returned in a month's time.

So Bertha, decked out more often than not in a hastily altered outfit of Clare's—lime-green and too wide on the shoulders—went on her thrice-weekly visits to Mrs Duke: the highlights of her week. She liked Wednesdays and Saturdays best, of course, because then she was taken there by the doctor, but the young man who drove her there on Mondays was nice too. He was a doctor, recently qualified, who helped out at the clinic from time to time. They got on well together, for Bertha was a good listener, and he always had a great deal to say about the girl he hoped to marry.

It had surprised Bertha that her stepmother hadn't objected to her reading sessions with Mrs Duke, but that lady, intent on finding a suitable husband for Clare, would have done a good deal to nurture a closer friendship with Dr Hay-Smythe. That he had taken Clare out to dinner and accepted an invitation to dine with herself, Clare and a few friends she took as a good sign.

Clare had looked her best at the dinner party, in a deceptively simple white dress. Bertha had been there, of course, for there had been no good reason for her not to be, wearing the frightful pink frock again—quite unsuitable, but really, when the girl went out so seldom there was no point in buying her a lot of clothes.

Dr Hay-Smythe had been a delightful guest, Mrs Soames had noted, paying court to her darling Clare and treating Bertha with a friendly courtesy but at the same time showing no interest in the girl. Very satisfactory, Mrs Soames had reflected, heaving such a deep sigh that her corsets creaked.

It was at the end of the third week on the Saturday that Mrs Duke died. Bertha had just finished the third chapter of a novel that the old lady had particularly asked her to read when Mrs Duke gave a small sigh and stopped breathing.

Bertha closed her book, set the cat on her lap gently on the ground and went to take the old lady's hand. There was no pulse; she had known there wouldn't be.

She laid Mrs Duke's hands tidily in her lap and went into the tiny hall to where the doctor had left a portable phone, saying casually that she might need it and giving her a number to call. She hadn't thought much about it at the time, but now she blessed him for being thoughtful. She dialled the number—the clinic—and heard his quiet voice answer.

'Mrs Duke.' She tried to keep her voice steady. 'Please would you come quickly? She has just died...'

'Five minutes. Are you all right, Bertha?'

'Me? Yes, thank you. Only, please come...' Her voice wobbled despite her efforts.

It seemed less than five minutes until he opened the door and gave her a comforting pat on the shoulder as he went past her into the living room to examine Mrs Duke. He bent his great height over her for a few minutes and then straightened up.

'Exactly as she would have wished,' he said. 'In her own home and listening to one of her favourite stories.'

He looked at Bertha's pale face. 'Sit down while I get this sorted out.'

She sat with the two cats crouching on her lap—they were aware that something wasn't quite right—while he rang the clinic, and presently a pleasant elderly woman came and the doctor picked up Mrs Duke and carried her into her poky bedroom.

'I'll take you home,' he told Bertha. 'It's been a shock. I'm sorry you had to be here.'

'I'm not. I'm glad. If Mrs Duke didn't know any-thing about it... The cats—we can't just leave them.' She stroked their furry heads. 'I'd have them, only I don't think my stepmother...'

'I'll take them. There's room for them at my flat and Freddie will enjoy their company—my dog.'

'Mrs Duke would be glad of that; she loved them.' Bertha put the pair gently down and got to her feet. 'I could go by bus. I expect there's a lot for you to do.'

'Time enough for that. Come along.' He glanced at his watch. 'You need a cup of tea.'

'Please don't bother.' Two tears trickled slowly down her cheeks. 'It doesn't seem right to be talk-ing about tea...'

'If Mrs Duke were here it would be the first thing that she would demand. Be happy for her, Bertha, for this is exactly what she wished for.'

Bertha sniffed, blew her nose and mopped up her tears. 'Yes, of course. Sorry. I'll come now. You're sure about the cats?'

'Yes. Wait while I have a word with Mrs Tyler.' He went into the bedroom and presently came out of it again, and whisked Bertha into the car.

He stopped the car in a side-street close to Oxford Street and ushered her into a small café where he sat her down at a table, ordered a pot of tea and took a seat opposite her.

'There is no need to say anything to your step-mother for the moment. It so happens that a nursery school I know of needs someone to read to the chil-dren. Would you consider doing that? The times may be different, but I'm sure I can explain that to Mrs Soames. Will you leave it to me? You will want to come to the funeral, won't you? Will you phone my rooms—tomorrow evening? Can you do that?'

'Well, I take my stepmother's dog for a walk every evening—I could go to the phone box; it's not far…'

'Splendid.' His smile was kind. 'Now, drink your tea and I'll take you home.' He added casually, 'I don't think there is any need to say anything to your stepmother about your change of job or Mrs Duke's death, do you?' He gave her a sidelong glance. 'I can explain that it will suit everyone concerned if the times are changed.'

'If you wouldn't mind. I don't think my step-mother would notice. I mean…'

'I know what you mean, Bertha.' His quiet voice reassured her.

The funeral was to be on Wednesday, she was told when she telephoned the following evening on her walk, and if she went as usual to the doctor's rooms she would be driven to Mrs Duke's flat. 'And as regards Monday,' went on the doctor, 'come at the usual time and I'll take you along to the nursery school so that you can meet everyone and arrange your hours.'

As she went back into the house she met Clare in the hall, dressed to go out for the evening. She twirled round, showing off the short silky frock.

'Do you like it, Bertha? It shows off my legs very well, doesn't it? It's a dinner party at the Ritz.' She smiled her charming smile. 'I might as well have as much fun as possible before I settle down and become a fashionable doctor's wife.'

She danced off and Bertha took the dog to the kitchen. Was that why the doctor was being so kind to her, finding her work to fill her empty days? To please Clare, with whom he was in love? Well, who wouldn't be? reflected Bertha. Clare was so very pretty and such fun to be with.

She was surprised that her stepmother had had no objection to her changing the hours of her reading, but the doctor, driving her to the funeral, observed that there had been no trouble about it. 'Indeed, Mrs Soames seemed pleased that you have an outside interest.'

It was a remark which surprised Bertha, since her stepmother had evinced no interest in her comings and goings. It was a thought which she kept to herself.

A surprisingly large number of people were in the church. It seemed that Mrs Duke while alive had had few friends, but now even mere acquaintances crowded into the church and returned to her flat, filling it to overflowing while her nephew, a young man who had come from Sheffield with his wife, offered tea and meat-paste sandwiches.

Bertha, in the habit of making herself useful, filled the teacups and cut more bread and listened to the cheerful talk. Mrs Duke was being given a splendid send-off, and there had been a nice lot of flowers at the funeral.

'Aunty left her bits and pieces to me,' said her nephew, coming into the kitchen to make another pot of tea, 'as well as a bit in the Post Office. She 'as two cats too—I'll 'ave ter 'ave 'em destroyed. We've got a dog at home.'

'No need. Dr Hay-Smythe has taken them to his home.'

'Up ter 'im. 'E did a good job looking after Aunty.'

The doctor came in search of her presently. 'I think we might leave—I'll get someone to take over from you. Did you get a cup of tea?'

She shook her head. 'It doesn't matter.'

He smiled. 'It's a powerful brew. Wait there while I get someone…'

Mrs Tyler came back with him. 'Off you go, dearie. Everyone'll be here for another few hours and you've done more than your fair share. It was good of you and the doctor to come.'

'I liked Mrs Duke,' said Bertha.

'So did I. She'd have enjoyed this turn-out.'

'Are you expected home?' asked the doctor as he drove away.

'My stepmother and Clare are at a picture gallery and then going to have drinks with some friends. I expect you're busy—if you'd drop me off at a bus stop…'

'And then what will you do?' he wanted to know.

'Why, catch a bus, of course,' said Bertha in her practical way. 'And have a cup of tea when I get home.'

'Someone will have it ready for you?'

'Well, no. Crook's got the afternoon off and so has Daisy—she's the housemaid—and Cook will have her feet up—her bunions, you know.'

'In that case we'll have tea at my place.'

'It's very kind of you to ask me, but really you don't have to be polite. I've taken up a lot of your time, and you must have an awful lot to do.'

He spoke testily. 'Bertha, stop being so apologetic. If you don't wish to have tea with me say so. If not, come back with me and discuss the funeral over tea and toast.'

She said indignantly, 'I'm not being apologetic.' Her voice rose slightly. 'I don't care to be—to be...'

'Pitied? The last thing you can expect from me, my girl.'

He stopped outside his rooms and got out to open her door. She looked up at him as she got out and found herself smiling.

Cully had the door open before they had reached it. He was introduced to Bertha and offered her a dignified bow before opening the sitting-room door.

'We would like tea, Cully,' said the doctor. 'Earl Grey and hot buttered toast—and if you can find a few cakes?'

'Certainly, sir. Shall I take the young lady's coat?'

He shuddered inwardly at the sight of the garish dress, but his face was inscrutable; he had until now had a poor opinion of any young ladies his master had brought home from time to time for the occasional drink or lunch, but this one was different, never mind the horrible garment she was wearing. He glided away to arrange cakes on a plate. Made by himself, of course. He didn't trust cakes bought in a shop.

Bertha, happily unaware of Cully's thoughts, went into the sitting room with the doctor to be greeted by Freddie before he went to his master's side.

'How very convenient,' said Bertha, 'having

your home over your consulting rooms. I didn't know you lived here.'

She gently rubbed Freddie's head and looked around her. The room was very much to her taste—a pleasing mixture of comfortable chairs and sofas and antique wall cabinets, lamp-tables, a magnificent Georgian rent table under the window and a giltwood mirror over the fireplace. That was Georgian too, she was sure.

She gave a little sigh of pleasure. 'This is a beautiful room,' she told him gravely.

'I'm glad you like it. Do sit down.' He offered her a small bergère, with upholstery matching the mulberry brocade curtains, and took an armchair opposite her. When her eyes darted to the long-case clock as it chimed the hour of four, he said soothingly, 'Don't worry. I'll see that you get back home before anyone else.'

Cully came in then with a laden tray. He sat everything out on a low table between them and slid away, but not before he had taken a good look at Bertha—nicely contrived from under lowered lids. His first impressions had been good ones, he decided.

Bertha made a good tea; she was hungry and Cully's dainty sandwiches and little cakes were delicious. Sitting there in the quiet, restful room with the doctor, whom she trusted and thought of as a friend, she was content and happy, and if their conversation dealt entirely with the visits she was to make to the nursery school she had no quarrel with that. She had been reminded so often by her stepmother and Clare that she was a dull companion and quite lacking in charm that she would have been surprised if the doctor had been anything else but briskly businesslike.

She was to go each morning from eleven o'clock until half past twelve, if that suited her, he told her, and she agreed at once. It might be a bit awkward sometimes, if she was needed to take the dog out or to go to the shops on some errand for her step-mother, but she would worry about that if and when it happened; there was no need to tell him.

'There are any number of books there; the chil-dren are various ages—two years to around four or five. You do understand that you need only read to them? There are plenty of helpers to do the neces-sary chores.'

'I think I shall like it very much.' Bertha smiled. 'Every day, too...'

He took her home presently, waiting until she had gone inside and then poked her head round the front door to tell him that no one was home.

Beyond telling Bertha how fortunate she was that Dr Hay-Smythe had found her something to do, her stepmother asked no questions. It was inconvenient that Bertha had to go each morning, of course, but since he was almost a friend of the family—indeed, almost more than that—she complied. 'Clare is quite sure that he's in love with her, so of course we would wish to do anything to oblige him in any way.'

So on Monday morning Bertha set off to go to the doctor's rooms. She was to go there first, he'd told her. The nursery school wasn't far from them and she would be shown the way and introduced to the matron who ran the place. She wasn't to feel nervous about going, for Matron already knew that she would be coming.

Mrs Taylor was at the rooms and greeted her with a friendly smile. 'Just a minute while I get Dr Hay-Smythe—he's in the garden with that dog of his.' She picked up the phone as she spoke, and a few minutes later he came in.

'I'll walk round with you, Bertha.' He glanced at his watch. 'I've time enough.'

She went with him down into the street and skipped along beside him to keep up.

'You can take a bus to the corner,' he told her. 'Go straight there after today.'

He turned down a narrow street and then turned again into a cul-de-sac lined with narrow, rather shabby houses. Halfway down he mounted the steps to a front door, rang the bell and then walked in.

The hall was rather bare, but the walls were a cheerful yellow and there was matting on the floor and a bowl of flowers on a table against the wall. The woman who came to meet them was small and stout with a jolly face and small bright eyes. She greeted the doctor like an old friend and looked at Bertha.

'So you're to be our reader,' she said, and shook hands. 'We are so glad to have you—we need all the help we can get. Come and see some of the children.'

She opened the door into a large, airy room full of children and several younger women. 'Of course, you won't be reading to them all,' she explained, 'but I've picked out those who will understand you, more or less. They love the sound of a voice, you know...'

They were in the centre of the room now with children all around them. 'We have children with special needs—three who are blind, several who had brain damage at birth and quite a few physically disabled...'

The doctor was watching Bertha's face. It showed surprise, compassion and a serene acceptance. Perhaps it had been unkind of him not to have told her, but he had wanted to see how she would react and she had reacted just as he had felt sure she would—with kindness, concern and not a trace of repugnance.

She looked at him and smiled. 'I'm going to like coming here,' she told him. 'Thank you for getting me the job.' She turned to the matron. 'I do hope I'll do...'

'Of course you will, my dear. Come along and take your jacket off and we'll get you settled.'

Bertha put out a hand to the doctor. 'I dare say I shan't see you again—well, perhaps when you come to see Clare, but you know what I mean. I can't thank you enough for your kindness.'

The doctor shook her hand in his large, firm one. 'Probably we shall see each other here occasionally. I come quite often to see the children.'

He went away then, and Bertha was led away by the matron, introduced to the other helpers and presently began to read to the circle of children assembled round her chair. It was an out-of-date book—an old fairy tale collection—and she started with the first story.

It wasn't going to be straightforward reading; she was interrupted frequently by eager little voices wanting her to read certain parts again, and some of them needed to have parts of the story explained to them, but after a time she got the hang of it and by half past twelve she and the children understood each other very well. She would do better tomorrow, she promised herself, going home to a solitary lunch, since her stepmother and Clare were out.

Within a few days Bertha had found her feet. It was a challenging job but she found it rewarding; the children were surprisingly happy, though sometimes difficult and frequently frustrated. They were lovable, though, and Bertha, lacking love in her own home, had plenty of that to offer.

At the end of two weeks she realised that she was happy, despite the dull life she led at home. Her stepmother still expected her to run errands, walk the dog and fetch and carry for her, so that she had little time to call her own. She was glad of that, really, as it gave her less time to think about Dr Hay-Smythe, for she had quickly discovered that she missed him.

She supposed that if Clare were to marry him—and, from what her stepsister said occasionally, Bertha thought that it was very likely—she would see him from time to time. He had been to the house once or twice, and Clare would recount their evenings together at great length, making no attempt to hide the fact that she had made up her mind to marry him.

When Bertha had asked her if she loved him, Clare had laughed. 'Of course not, but he's exactly what I want. Plenty of money, a handsome husband, and a chance to get away from home. Oh, I like him well enough...'

Bertha worried a lot about that; it spoilt her happiness. Dr Hay-Smythe wasn't the right husband for Clare. On the other hand, being in love with someone wasn't something one could arrange to suit oneself, and if he loved Clare perhaps it wouldn't matter.

It was towards the middle of the third week of her visits to the nursery school that Clare unexpectedly asked her to go shopping with her in the afternoon. 'I've some things I simply must buy and Mother wants the car, and I hate taxis on my own. You'll have to come.'

They set out after lunch, and since it had been raining, and was threatening to do so again, Crook hailed a taxi. Clare was in good spirits and disposed to be friendly.

'It's time you had something decent to wear,' she said surprisingly. 'There's that jersey two-piece of mine—I never liked it; it's a ghastly colour—you can have that.'

'I don't think I want it if it's a ghastly colour, Clare. Thank you all the same.'

'Oh, the colour is ghastly on *me*. I dare say you'll look all right in it.' She glanced at Bertha. 'You'd better take it. Mother won't buy you anything until Father gets home, and he's been delayed so you'll have to wait for it.'

Bertha supposed that the jersey two-piece wouldn't be any worse than the lime-green outfits and there was no one to see her in it anyway. She wondered silently if there would ever be a chance for her to earn some money. She was a voluntary worker, but if she worked longer hours perhaps she could ask to be paid? She wouldn't want much.

The idea cheered her up, so that she was able to stand about patiently while Clare tried on dresses and then finally bought a pair of Italian shoes—white kid with high heels and very intricate straps. Bertha, watching them being fitted, was green with envy; she had pretty feet and ankles, and Clare's were by no means perfect. The shoes were on the wrong feet, she reflected in a rare fit of ill-humour.

The afternoon had cleared. Clare gave Bertha the shoes to carry and said airily that they would walk home. 'We can always pick up a taxi if we get tired,' she declared. 'We'll cut through here.'

The street was a quiet one, empty of traffic and people. At least, it was until they were halfway down it. The elderly lady on the opposite pavement was walking slowly, carrying a plastic bag and an umbrella, with her handbag dangling from one arm, so she had no hands free to defend herself when, apparently from nowhere, two youths leapt at her from a narrow alleyway. They pushed her to the ground and one of them hit her as she tried to keep a hand on her bag.

Clare stopped suddenly. 'Quick, we must run for it. They'll be after us if they see us. Hurry, can't you?'

Bertha took no notice. She pushed away Clare's hands clinging to her arm, ran across the street and swiped at one of the youths with the plastic bag containing Clare's new shoes. It caught him on the shins and he staggered and fell. She swung the bag again, intent on hitting the other youth. The bag split this time and the shoes flew into the gutter.

Confronted by a virago intent on hurting them, the pair scrambled to their feet and fled, dropping the lady's handbag as they went. Short of breath and shaking with fright, Bertha knelt down by the old lady.

'My purse—my pension…' The elderly face was white with fear and worry. It was bruised, too.

'It's all right,' said Bertha. 'They dropped your handbag. I'll get it for you. But, first of all, are you hurt?'

Before the old lady could answer, Clare hissed into Bertha's ear, 'My shoes—my lovely new shoes. You've ruined them. I'll never forgive you!'

'Oh, bother your shoes,' said Bertha. 'Go and bang on someone's door and get an ambulance.'

Just for once, Clare, speechless at Bertha's brisk orders, did as she was told.

She was back presently, and there were people with her. Bertha, doing her best to make the old lady as comfortable as possible, listened with half an ear to her stepsister's voice.

'Two huge men,' said Clare, in what Bertha always thought of as her little-girl voice. 'They ran at this poor lady and knocked her down. I simply rushed across the street and hit them with a shopping bag—one of them fell over and they ran away then.' She gave a little laugh. 'I've never been so scared in my life…'

'Very plucky, if I might say so,' said a voice.

Another voice asked, 'You're not hurt, young lady? It was a brave thing to do.'

'Well, one doesn't think of oneself,' murmured Clare. 'And luckily my sister came to help me once the men had gone.'

The old lady stared up at Bertha's placid face. 'That's a pack of lies,' she whispered. 'It was you;

I saw you...' She closed her eyes tiredly. 'I shall tell someone...'

'It doesn't matter,' said Bertha. 'All that matters is that you're safe. Here is your handbag, and the purse is still inside.'

She got to her feet as the ambulance drew up and the few people who had gathered to see what was amiss gave her sidelong glances with no sign of friendliness; she could read their thoughts—leaving her pretty sister to cope with those violent men... Luckily there were still brave girls left in this modern day and age of violence...

Bertha told herself that it didn't matter; they were strangers and never likely to see her again. She wondered what Clare would do next—beg a lift from someone, most likely.

There was no need for that, however.

By good fortune—or was it bad fortune?—Dr Hay-Smythe, on his way from somewhere or other, had seen the little group as he drove past. He stopped, reversed neatly and got out of his car. Clare, with a wistful little cry, exactly right for the occasion, ran to meet him.

CHAPTER THREE

'OLIVER!' cried Clare, in what could only be described as a brave little voice. 'Thank heaven you're here.' She waved an arm towards the ambulancemen loading the old lady onto a stretcher. 'This poor old woman—there were two enormous men attacking her. She's been hurt—she might have been killed—but I ran as fast as I could and threw my bag at them and they ran away.'

The onlookers, gathering close, murmured admiringly. 'Proper brave young lady,' said one.

'Oh, no,' Clare said softly. 'Anyone would have done the same.' She had laid a hand on the doctor's arm and now looked up into his face.

He wasn't looking at her. He was watching the stretcher being lifted into the ambulance. The old lady was saying something to Bertha, who had whipped a bit of paper and pencil from her bag and was writing something down.

He removed Clare's hand quite gently. 'I should just take a look,' he observed.

He spoke to the ambulance driver and then bent over the old lady, giving Bertha a quick smile as he did so. 'Can I help in any way? I'm told there's nothing broken, but you had better have a checkup at the hospital.'

The shrewd old eyes studied his face. 'You're a doctor? Don't you listen to that girl's tale. Not a word of truth in it. Seen it with my own eyes—tried

47

to run away, she did. It was this child who tackled those thugs—twice her size too.' She gave a weak snort of indignation. 'Mad as fire because her shoes had been spoilt. Huh!'

'Thank you for telling me. Do we have your name? Is there anyone who should be told?'

'This young lady's seen to that for me, bless her. Gets things done while others talk.'

'Indeed she does.' He took her hand. 'You'll be all right now.'

He went back to the driver and presently, when the ambulance had been driven away, he joined Bertha. 'Let me have her name and address, will you? I'll check on her later today. Now I'll drive you both home.'

Clare had joined them. 'What was all that about? You don't need to bother any more; she'll be looked after at the hospital. I feel awfully odd—it was a shock...'

'I'll drive you both back home. I dare say you may like to go straight to bed, Clare.'

Clare jumped into the car. 'No, no—I'm not such a weakling as all that, Oliver. I dare say Bertha would like to lie down for a bit, though—she was so frightened.' She turned her head to look at Bertha on the back seat, who looked out of the window and didn't answer.

The doctor didn't say anything either, so Clare went on uncertainly, 'Well, of course, it was enough to scare the wits out of anyone, wasn't it?'

No one answered that either. Presently she said pettishly, 'I had a pair of new shoes—wildly expensive—they've been ruined.' Quite forgetting her role of brave girl, she turned on Bertha. 'You'll have to pay for them, Bertha. Throwing them around like that—' She stopped, aware that she had let the cat out of the bag. 'What was the good of flinging the bag at those men when they had already run away?'

'I'm sure you can buy more shoes,' said the doctor blandly. 'And what is a pair of shoes compared with saving an old lady from harm?'

He glanced in his mirror, caught Bertha's eye and smiled at her, and lowered an eyelid in an unmistakable wink.

It gave her a warm glow. Never mind that there would be some hard words when she got home; she had long since learned to ignore them. He had believed the old lady and she had the wit to see that he wouldn't mention it—it would make it so much worse for her and would probably mean the end of her job at the nursery school. If any special attention from him were to come to Clare's or her stepmother's notice, they would find a way to make sure that she never saw him again...

The doctor stopped the car before their door, and Clare said coaxingly, 'Take me out to dinner this evening, Oliver? I do need cheering up after all I've just gone through. Somewhere quiet where we can talk?'

He had got out to open her door and now turned to do the same for Bertha. 'Impossible, I'm afraid. I've a meeting at seven o'clock which will last for hours—perhaps at the weekend...'

He closed the car door. 'I suggest that you both have an early night. If there is any news of the old lady I'll let you have it. I shall be seeing her later this evening. Bertha, if you will give me her address, I'll see that her family are told.'

She handed it over with a murmured thank-you, bade him goodbye and started up the steps to the door, leaving Clare to make a more protracted leavetaking—something which he nipped in the bud with apparent reluctance.

Clare's charm turned to cold fury as they entered the house. 'You'll pay for this,' she stormed. 'Those shoes cost the earth. Now I've nothing to wear with that new dress...'

Bertha said matter-of-factly, 'Well, I can't pay for them, can I? I haven't any money. And you've dozens of shoes.' She looked at Clare's furious face. 'Are they really more important than helping someone in a fix?' She wanted to know. 'And what a lot of fibs you've told everyone. I must say you looked the part.'

She stopped then, surprised at herself, but not nearly as surprised as Clare. 'How dare you?' Clare snapped. 'How dare you talk to me like that?'

'Well, it's the truth, isn't it?' asked Bertha placidly. 'But, don't worry, I shan't give you away.'

'No one would believe you...'

'Probably not.' Bertha went up to her room, leaving Clare fuming.

The full weight of her stepmother's displeasure fell upon her when she went downstairs presently. She was most ungrateful, careless and unnaturally mean towards her stepsister, who had behaved with the courage only to be expected of her. Bertha should be bitterly ashamed of herself. 'I had intended to take you to a charity coffee morning at

Lady Forde's, but I shall certainly not do so now,' she finished.

Bertha, allowing the harsh voice to wash over her head, heaved a sigh of relief; the last time she had been taken there she had ended up making herself useful, helping Lady Forde's meek companion hand round the coffee and cakes. She looked down at her lap and didn't say a word. What would be the use?

She would have been immensely cheered if she had known of the doctor's efforts on her behalf. There had to be a way, he reflected, sitting in his sitting room with Freddie at his feet, in which he could give Bertha a treat. It seemed to him that she had no fun at all—indeed, was leading an unhappy life.

'She deserves better,' he told Freddie, who yawned. 'Properly dressed and turned out, she might stand a chance of attracting some young man. She has beautiful eyes, and I don't know another girl who would have held her tongue as she did this afternoon.'

It was much later, after Cully had gone to his bed and the house was quiet, that he knew what he would do. Well satisfied, he settled Freddie in his basket in the kitchen and went to bed himself.

The doctor waited another two days before calling at Mrs Soames's house. He had satisfied himself that Bertha was still going to the nursery. Matron had been enthusiastic about her and assured him that there had been no question of her leaving, so he was able to dispel the nagging thought that her stepmother might have shown her anger by forbidding her to go.

He chose a time when he was reasonably sure that they would all be at home and gave as his excuse his concern as to whether the two girls had got over their unfortunate experience. All three ladies were in the drawing room—something which pleased him, for if Bertha wasn't there, there was always the chance that she would hear nothing of his plans.

Mrs Soames rose to meet him. 'My dear Oliver, most kind of you to call—as you see, we are sitting quietly at home. Dear Clare is somewhat shocked still.'

'I'm sorry to hear it,' said the doctor, shaking Clare's hand and giving Bertha a smiling nod. 'Perhaps I can offer a remedy—both for her and for Bertha, who must also be just as upset.'

Mrs Soames looked surprised. 'Bertha? I hardly think so. She isn't in the least sensitive.'

The doctor looked grave and learned. He said weightily, 'Nevertheless, I think that both young ladies would benefit from my plan.'

His bedside manner, reflected Bertha, and very impressive and effective too, for her stepmother nodded and said, 'Of course. I bow to your wisdom, Oliver.'

'Most fortunately I am free tomorrow. I should be delighted if I might drive them into the country for the day, away from London. To slow down one's lifestyle once in a while is necessary, especially when one has had a shock such as Clare had.' He looked at Bertha. 'And I am sure that Bertha must have been upset. I haven't had the opportunity to ask her—'

'There's no need,' Clare interrupted him hastily.

'I'm sure she needs a break just as I do. We'd love to come with you, Oliver. Where shall we go?'

'How about a surprise? Is ten o'clock too early for you?'

'No, no. Not a minute too early.' Clare was at her most charming, and then, as he got up to go, she said suddenly, 'But of course Bertha won't be able to go with us—she reads to old ladies or something every morning.'

'Tomorrow is Saturday,' the doctor reminded her gently. 'I doubt if she does that at the weekends.' He glanced at Bertha. 'Is that not so, Bertha?'

Bertha murmured an agreement and saw the flash of annoyance on Clare's face. All of a sudden she was doubtful as to whether a day spent in the company of Clare and the doctor would be as pleasant as it sounded.

After he had gone, Clare said with satisfaction, 'You haven't anything to wear, Bertha. I hope Oliver won't feel embarrassed. It's a great pity that you have to come with us. You could have refused.'

'I shall enjoy a day out,' said Bertha calmly, 'and I shall wear the jersey two-piece you handed down to me. I'll have to take it in...'

Clare jumped up. 'You ungrateful girl. That outfit cost a lot of money.'

'It's a ghastly colour,' said Bertha equably, and went away to try it on. It was indeed a garment which Clare should never have bought—acid-yellow, and it needed taking in a good deal.

'Who cares?' said Bertha defiantly to the kitchen cat, who had followed her upstairs, and began to sew—a tricky business since her eyes were full of tears. To be with the doctor again would be, she had to admit, the height of happiness, but she very much doubted if he would feel the same. He was far too well-mannered to comment upon the two-piece—probably he would be speechless when he saw it—but it would be nice to spend a day with him wearing an outfit which was the right colour and which fitted.

'I suppose I am too thin,' she observed to the cat, pinning darts and cobbling them up. The sleeves were a bit too long—she would have to keep pushing them up—and the neck was too low. Clare liked low necks so that she could display her plump bosom, but Bertha, who had a pretty bosom of her own, stitched it up to a decent level and hoped that no one would notice.

Dr Hay-Smythe noticed it at once, even though half-blinded by the acid-yellow. An appalling outfit, he reflected, obviously hastily altered, for it didn't fit anywhere it should and the colour did nothing for Bertha's ordinary features and light brown hair. He found that he was full of rage at her treatment, although he allowed nothing of that to show. He wished her good morning and talked pleasantly to Mrs Soames while they waited for Clare.

She came at last, with little cries of regret at keeping him waiting. 'I wanted to look as nice as possible for you, Oliver,' she said with a little laugh. And indeed she did look nice—in blue and white wool, simply cut and just right for a day in the country. She had a navy shoulder-bag and matching shoes with high heels. The contrast between the two girls was cruel.

The doctor said breezily, 'Ah, here you are at

last. I was beginning to think that you had changed your mind!' He smiled a little. 'Found someone younger and more exciting with whom to spend the day.'

This delighted Clare. 'There isn't anyone more exciting than you, Oliver,' she cooed, and Bertha looked away, feeling sick and wishing that the day was over before it had begun.

Of course Clare got into the seat beside Oliver, leaving him to usher Bertha into the back of the car where Freddie, delighted to have company, greeted her with pleasure.

Clare, turning round to stare, observed tartly, 'Oh, you've brought a dog.' And then said, with a little laugh, 'He'll be company for Bertha.'

'Freddie goes wherever I go when it's possible. He sits beside me on long journeys and is a delightful companion.'

'Well, now you have me,' declared Clare. 'I'm a delightful companion too!'

A remark which the doctor apparently didn't hear.

He drove steadily towards the western suburbs, apparently content to listen to Clare's chatter, and when he was finally clear of the city he turned off the main road and slowed the car as they reached the countryside. They were in Hertfordshire now, bypassing the towns, taking minor roads through the woods and fields and going through villages, peaceful under the morning sun. At one of these he stopped at an inn.

'Coffee?' he asked, and got out to open Clare's door and then usher Bertha and Freddie out of the car.

The inn was old and thatched and cosy inside. The doctor asked for coffee, then suggested, 'You two girls go ahead. I'll take Freddie for a quick run while the coffee's fetched.'

The ladies' was spotlessly clean, but lacked the comforts of its London counterparts. Clare, doing her face in front of the only mirror, said crossly, 'He might have stopped at a decent hotel—this is pretty primitive. I hope we shall lunch somewhere more civilised.'

'I like it,' said Bertha. 'I like being away from London. I'd like to live in the country.'

Clare didn't bother to reply, merely remarking as they went to join the doctor that the yellow jersey looked quite frightful. 'When I see you in it,' said Clare, 'I can see just how ghastly it is!'

It was an opinion shared by the doctor as he watched them cross the bar to join him at a table by the window, but nothing could dim the pleasure in Bertha's face, and, watching it, he hardly noticed the outfit.

'The coffee was good. I'm surprised,' said Clare. 'I mean, in a place like this you don't expect it, do you?'

'Why not?' The doctor was at his most genial. 'The food in some of these country pubs is as good or better than that served in some of the London restaurants. No dainty morsels in a pretty pattern on your plate, but just steak and kidney pudding and local vegetables, or sausages and mash with apple pie for a pudding.'

Clare looked taken aback. If he intended giving her sausages and mash for lunch she would demand to be taken home. 'Where are we lunching?' she asked.

'Ah, wait and see!'

Bertha had drunk her coffee almost in silence, with Freddie crouching under the table beside her, nudging her gently for a bit of biscuit from time to time. She hoped that they would lunch in a country pub—sausages and mash would be nice, bringing to mind the meal she and the doctor had eaten together. Meeting him had changed her life...

They drove on presently into Buckinghamshire, still keeping to the country roads. It was obvious that the doctor knew where he was going. Bertha stopped herself from asking him; it might spoil whatever surprise he had in store for them.

It was almost noon when they came upon a small village—a compact gathering of Tudor cottages with a church overlooking them from the brow of a low hill.

Bertha peered and said, 'Oh, this is delightful. Where are we?'

'This is Wing—'

'Isn't there a hotel?' asked Clare. 'We're not going to stop here, are we?' She had spoken sharply. 'It's a bit primitive, isn't it?' She saw his lifted eyebrows. 'Well, no, not primitive, perhaps, but you know what I mean, Oliver. Or is there one of those country-house restaurants tucked away out of sight?'

He only smiled and turned the car through an open wrought-iron gate. The drive was short, and at its end was a house—not a grand house, one might call it a gentleman's residence—sitting squarely amidst trees and shrubs with a wide lawn before it edged by flowerbeds. Bertha, examining it from the car, thought that it must be Georgian, with its Palladian door with a pediment above, its many paned windows and tall chimneystacks.

It wasn't just a lovely old house, it was a home; there were long windows, tubs of japonica on either side of the door, the bare branches of Virginia creeper rioting over its walls and, watching them from a wrought-iron sill above a hooded bay window, a majestic cat with a thick orange coat. Bertha saw all this as Clare got out, the latter happy now at the sight of a house worthy of her attention and intent on making up for her pettishness.

'I suppose we are to lunch here?' she asked as the doctor opened Bertha's door and she and Freddie tumbled out.

His 'yes' was noncommittal.

'It isn't a hotel, is it?' asked Bertha. 'It's someone's home. It's quite beautiful.'

'I'm glad you like it, Bertha. It is my home. My mother will be delighted to have you both as her guests for lunch.'

'Yours?' queried Clare eagerly. 'As well as your flat in town? I suppose your mother will live here until you want it for yourself—when you marry?' She gave him one of her most charming smiles, which he ignored.

'Your mother doesn't mind?' asked Bertha. 'If we are unexpected...'

'You're not. I phoned her yesterday. She is glad to welcome you—she is sometimes a little lonely since my father died.'

'Oh, I'm sorry.' Bertha's plain face was full of sympathy.

'Thank you. Shall we go indoors?'

The house door opened under his hand and he ushered them into the wide hall with its oak floor and marble-topped console table flanked by cane and walnut chairs. There was a leather-covered armchair in one corner too, the repository of a variety of coats, jackets, walking sticks, dog leads and old straw hats, giving the rather austere grandeur of the hall a pleasantly lived-in look. The doctor led the way past the oak staircase with its wrought-iron balustrade at the back of the hall and opened a small door.

'Mother will be in the garden,' he observed. 'We can go through the kitchen.'

The kitchen was large with a vast dresser loaded with china against one wall, an Aga stove and a scrubbed table ringed by Windsor chairs at its centre. Two women looked up as they went in.

'Master Oliver, good morning to you, sir—and the two young ladies.'

The speaker was short and stout and wrapped around by a very white apron. The doctor crossed the room and kissed her cheek.

'Meg, how nice to see you again.' He looked across at the second woman, who was a little younger and had a severe expression. 'And Dora—you're both well? Good. Clare, Bertha—this is Meg, our cook, and Dora, who runs the house.'

Clare nodded and said, 'hello,' but Bertha smiled and shook hands.

'What a heavenly kitchen.' Her lovely eyes were sparkling with pleasure. 'It's a kind of haven...' She blushed because she had said something silly, but Meg and Dora were smiling.

'That it is, miss—specially now in the winter of an evening. Many a time Mr Oliver's popped in here to beg a slice of dripping toast.'

He smiled. 'Meg, you are making my mouth water. We had better go and find my mother. We'll see you before we go.'

Clare had stood apart, tapping a foot impatiently, but as they went through the door into the garden beyond she slipped an arm through the doctor's.

'I love your home,' she told him, 'and your lovely old-fashioned servants.'

'They are our friends as well, Clare. They have been with us for as long as I can remember.'

The garden behind the house was large and rambling, with narrow paths between the flowerbeds and flowering shrubs. Freddie rushed ahead, and they heard his barking echoed by a shrill yapping.

'My mother will be in the greenhouses.' The doctor had disengaged his arm from Clare's in order to lead the way, and presently they went through a ramshackle door in a high brick wall and saw the greenhouses to one side of the kitchen garden.

Bertha, lingering here and there to look at neatly tended borders and shrubs, saw that Clare's high heels were making heavy weather of the earth paths. Her clothes were exquisite, but here, in this country garden, they didn't look right. Bertha glanced down at her own person and had to admit that her own outfit didn't look right either. She hoped that the doctor's mother wasn't a follower of fashion like her stepmother.

She had no need to worry; the lady who came to meet them as the doctor opened the greenhouse door was wearing a fine wool skirt stained with earth and with bits of greenery caught up in it, and her blouse, pure silk and beautifully made, was almost covered by a misshapen cardigan of beige cashmere as stained as the skirt. She was wearing wellies and thick gardening gloves and looked, thought Bertha, exactly as the doctor's mother should look.

She wasn't quite sure what she meant by this, it was something that she couldn't put into words, but she knew instinctively that this elderly lady with her plain face and sweet expression was all that she would have wanted if her own mother had lived.

'My dear.' Mrs Hay-Smythe lifted up her face for her son's kiss. 'How lovely to see you—and these are the girls who had such an unpleasant experience the other day?'

She held out a hand, the glove pulled off. 'I'm delighted to meet you. You must tell me all about it, presently—I live such a quiet life here that I'm all agog to hear the details.'

'Oh, it was nothing, Mrs Hay-Smythe,' said Clare. 'I'm sure there are many more people braver than I. It is so kind of Oliver to bring us; I had no idea that he had such a beautiful home.'

Mrs Hay-Smythe looked a little taken aback, but she smiled and said, 'Well, yes, we're very happy to live here.'

She turned to Bertha. 'And you are Bertha?' Her smile widened and her blue eyes smiled too, never once so much as glancing at the yellow jersey. 'Forgive me that I am so untidy, but there is always work to do in the greenhouse. We'll go indoors and have a drink. Oliver will look after you while I tidy myself.'

They wandered back to the house—Clare ahead with the doctor, his mother coming slowly with Bertha, stopping to describe the bushes and flowers that would bloom in the spring as they went, Freddie and her small border terrier beside them.

'You are fond of gardening?' she wanted to know.

'Well, we live in a townhouse, you know. There's a gardener, and he comes once a week to see to the garden—but he doesn't grow things, just comes and digs up whatever's there and then plants the next lot. That's not really gardening. I'd love to have a packet of seeds and grow flowers, but I—I don't have much time.'

Mrs Hay-Smythe, who knew all about Bertha, nodded sympathetically. 'I expect one day you'll get the opportunity—when you marry, you know.'

'I don't really expect to marry,' said Bertha matter-of-factly. 'I don't meet many people and I'm plain.' She sounded quite cheerful and her hostess smiled.

'Well, as to that, I'm plain, my dear, and I was a middle daughter of six living in a remote vicarage. And that, I may tell you, was quite a handicap.'

They both laughed and Clare, standing waiting for them with the doctor, frowned. Just like Bertha to worm her way into their hostess's good books, she thought. Well, she would soon see about that.

As they went into the house she edged her way towards Mrs Hay-Smythe. 'This is such a lovely house. I do hope there will be time for you to take me round before we go back.' She remembered that that would leave Bertha with Oliver, which would never do. 'Bertha too, of course...'

Mrs Hay-Smythe had manners as beautiful as her son's. 'I shall be delighted. But now I must go and change. Oliver, give the girls a drink, will you? I'll be ten minutes or so. We mustn't keep Meg waiting.'

It seemed to Bertha that the doctor was perfectly content to listen to Clare's chatter as she drank her gin and lime, and his well-mannered attempts to draw her into the conversation merely increased her shyness. So silly, she reflected, sipping her sherry, because when I'm with him and there's no one else there I'm perfectly normal.

Mrs Hay-Smythe came back presently, wearing a black and white dress, which, while being elegant, suited her age. A pity, thought Bertha, still wrapped in thought, that her stepmother didn't dress in a similar manner, instead of forcing herself into clothes more suitable to a woman of half her age. She was getting very mean and unkind, she reflected.

Lunch eaten in a lovely panelled room with an oval table and a massive sideboard of mahogany, matching shield-back chairs and a number of portraits in heavy gilt frames on its walls, was simple but beautifully cooked: miniature onion tarts decorated with olives and strips of anchovy, grilled trout with a pepper sauce and a green salad, followed by orange cream soufflés.

Bertha ate with unselfconscious pleasure and a good appetite and listened resignedly to Clare tell her hostess as she picked daintily at her food that she adored French cooking.

'We have a chef who cooks the most delicious food.' She gave one of her little laughs. 'I'm so fussy, I'm afraid. But I adore lobster, don't you? And those little tartlets with caviare…'

Mrs Hay-Smythe smiled and offered Bertha a second helping. Bertha, pink with embarrassment, accepted. So did the doctor and his mother, so that Clare was left to sit and look at her plate while the three of them ate unhurriedly.

They had coffee in the conservatory and soon the doctor said, 'We have a family pet at the bottom of the garden. Nellie the donkey. She enjoys visitors and Freddie is devoted to her. Shall we stroll down to see her?'

He smiled at Bertha's eager face and Freddie was already on his feet when Clare said quickly, 'Oh, but we are to see the house. I'm longing to go all over it.'

'In that case,' said Mrs Hay-Smythe in a decisive voice, 'you go on ahead to Nellie, Oliver, and take Bertha with you, and I'll take Clare to see a little of the house.' When Clare would have protested that perhaps, after all, she would rather see the donkey, Mrs Hay-Smythe said crisply, 'No, no, I mustn't disappoint you. We can join the others very shortly.'

She whisked Clare indoors and the doctor stood up. 'Come along, Bertha. We'll go to the kitchen and get a carrot…'

Meg and Dora were loading the dishwasher, and the gentle clatter of crockery made a pleasant background for the loud tick-tock of the kitchen clock and the faint strains of the radio. There was a tabby cat before the Aga, and the cat with the orange coat was sitting on the window-sill.

'Carrots?' said Meg. 'For that donkey of yours,

Master Oliver? Pampered, that's what she is.' She smiled broadly at Bertha. 'Not but what she's an old pet, when all's said and done.'

Dora had gone to fetch the carrots and the doctor was sitting on the kitchen table eating a slice of the cake that was presumably for tea.

'I enjoyed my lunch,' said Bertha awkwardly. 'You must be a marvellous cook, Meg.'

'Lor' bless you, miss, anyone can cook who puts their mind to it.' But Meg looked pleased all the same.

The donkey was in a small orchard at the bottom of the large garden. She was an elderly beast who was pleased to see them; she ate the carrots and then trotted around a bit in a dignified way with a delighted Freddie.

The doctor, leaning on the gate to the orchard, looked sideways at Bertha. She was happy, her face full of contentment. She was happily oblivious of her startling outfit too—which was even more startling in the gentle surroundings.

Conscious that he was looking at her, she turned her head and their eyes met.

Good gracious, thought Bertha, I feel as if I've known him all my life, that I've been waiting for him...

Clare's voice broke the fragile thread which had been spun between them. 'There you are. Is this the donkey? Oliver, you do have a lovely house—your really ought to marry and share it with someone.'

CHAPTER FOUR

THEY didn't stay long in the orchard—Clare's high-heeled shoes sank into the ground at every step and her complaints weren't easily ignored. They sat in the conservatory again, and Clare told them amusing tales about her friends and detailed the plays she had recently seen and the parties she had attended.

'I scarcely have a moment to myself,' she declared on a sigh. 'You can't imagine how delightful a restful day here is.'

'You would like to live in the country?' asked Mrs Hay-Smythe.

'In a house like this? Oh, yes. One could run up to town whenever one felt like it—shopping and the theatre—and I dare say there are other people living around here...'

'Oh, yes.' Mrs Hay-Smythe spoke pleasantly. 'Oliver, will you ask Meg to bring tea out here?'

After tea they took their leave and got into the car, and were waved away by Mrs Hay-Smythe. Bertha waved back, taking a last look at the house she wasn't likely to see again but would never forget.

As for Mrs Hay-Smythe, she went to the kitchen, where she found Meg and Dora having their own tea. She sat down at the table with them and accepted a cup of strong tea with plenty of milk. Not her favourite brand, but she felt that she needed something with a bite to it.

'Well?' she asked.

'Since you want to know, ma'am,' said Meg, 'and speaking for the two of us, we just hope that the master isn't taken with that young lady what didn't eat her lunch. High and mighty, we thought—didn't we, Dora?'

'Let me put your minds at rest. This visit was made in order to give the other Miss Soames a day out, but to do so it was necessary to invite her stepsister as well.'

'Well, there,' said Dora. 'Like Cinderella. Such a nice quiet young lady too. Thanked you for her lunch, didn't she, Meg?'

'That she did, and not smarmy either. Fitted into the house very nicely too.'

'Yes, she did,' said Mrs Hay-Smythe thoughtfully. Bertha would make a delightful daughter-in-law, but Oliver had given no sign—he had helped her out of kindness but shown no wish to be in her company or even talk to her other than in a casual friendly way. 'A pity,' said Mrs Hay-Smythe, and with Flossie, her little dog, at her heels she went back to the greenhouse, where she put on a vast apron and her gardening gloves and began work again.

The doctor drove back the way they had come, listening to Clare's voice and hardly hearing what she was saying. Only when she said insistently, 'You will take me out to dinner this evening, won't you, Oliver? Somewhere lively where we can dance afterwards? It's been a lovely day, but after all that rural quiet we could do with some town life...'

'When we get back,' he said, 'I am going straight to the hospital where I shall be for several hours, and I have an appointment for eight o'clock to-morrow morning. I am a working man, Clare.'

She pouted. 'Oh, Oliver, can't you forget the hospital just for once? I was so sure you'd take me out.'

'Quite impossible. Besides, I'm not a party man, Clare.'

She touched his sleeve. 'I could change that for you. At least promise you'll come to dinner one evening? I'll tell Mother to give you a ring.'

He glanced in the side-mirror and saw that Bertha was sitting with her arm round Freddie's neck, looking out of the window. Her face was turned away, but the back of her head looked sad.

He stayed only as long as good manners required when they reached the Soameses' house, and when he had gone Clare threw her handbag down and flung herself into a chair.

Her mother asked sharply, 'Well, you had Oliver all to yourself—is he interested?'

'Well, of course he is. If only we hadn't taken Bertha with us...'

'She didn't interfere, I hope.'

'She didn't get the chance—she hardly spoke to him. I didn't give her the opportunity. She was with his mother most of the time.'

'What is Mrs Hay-Smythe like?'

'Oh, boring—talking about the garden and the Women's Institute and doing the flowers for the church. She was in the greenhouse when we got there. I thought she was one of the servants.'

'Not a lady?' asked her mother, horrified.

'Oh, yes, no doubt about that. Plenty of money too, I should imagine. The house is lovely—it would be a splendid country home for weekends if we could have a decent flat here.' She laughed. 'The best of both worlds.'

Bertha, in her room, changing out of the two-piece and getting into another of Clare's too-elaborate dresses, told the kitchen cat, who was enjoying a stolen hour or so on her bed, all about her day.

'I don't suppose Oliver will be able to withstand Clare for much longer—only I mustn't call him Oliver, must I? I'm not supposed to have more than a nodding acquaintance with him.' She sat down on the bed, the better to address her companion. 'I think that is what I must do in the future, just nod. I think about him too much and I miss him...'

She went to peer at her face in the mirror and nodded at its reflection. 'Plain as a pikestaff, my girl.'

Dinner was rather worse than usual, for there were no guests and that gave her stepmother and Clare the opportunity to criticise her behaviour during the day.

'Clare tells me that you spent too much time with Mrs Hay-Smythe...'

Bertha popped a morsel of fish into her mouth and chewed it. 'Well,' she said reasonably, 'what else was I to do? Clare wouldn't have liked it if I'd attached myself to Dr Hay-Smythe, and it would

have looked very ill-mannered if I'd just gone off
on my own.'

Mrs Soames glared, seeking for a quelling reply.
'Anyway, you should never have gone off with the
doctor while Clare was in the house with his
mother.'

'I enjoyed it. We talked about interesting
things—the donkey and the orchard and the house.'

'He must have been bored,' said her stepmother
crossly.

Bertha looked demure. 'Yes, I think that some of
the time he was—very bored.'

Clare tossed her head. 'Not when he was with
me,' she said smugly, but her mother shot Bertha a
frowning look.

'I think you should understand, Bertha, that Dr
Hay-Smythe is very likely about to propose marriage to your stepsister...'

'Has he said so?' asked Bertha composedly. She
studied Mrs Soames, whose high colour had turned
faintly purple.

'Certainly not, but one feels these things.' Mrs
Soames pushed her plate aside. 'I am telling you
this because I wish you to refuse any further invitations which the doctor may offer you—no doubt
out of kindness.'

'Why?'

'There is an old saying—two is company, three
is a crowd.'

'Oh, you don't want me to play gooseberry. I
looked like one today in that frightful outfit Clare
passed on to me.'

'You ungrateful—' began Clare, but was silenced
by a majestic wave of her mother's hand.

'I cannot think what has come over you, Bertha. Presumably this day's outing has gone to your head. The two-piece Clare so kindly gave you is charming.'

'Then why doesn't she wear it?' asked Bertha, feeling reckless. She wasn't sure what had come over her either, but she was rather enjoying it. 'I would like some new clothes of my own.'

Mrs Soames's bosom swelled alarmingly. 'That is enough, Bertha. I shall buy you something suitable when I have the leisure to arrange it. I think you had better have an early night, for you aren't yourself... The impertinence...'

'Is that what it is? It feels nice!' said Bertha.

She excused herself with perfect good manners and went up to her room. She lay in the bath for a long time, having a good cry but not sure why she was crying. At least, she had a vague idea at the back of her head as to why she felt lonely and miserable, but she didn't allow herself to pursue the matter. She got into bed and the cat curled up against her back, purring in a comforting manner, so that she was lulled into a dreamless sleep.

Her mother and Clare had been invited to lunch with friends who had a house near Henley. Bertha had been invited too, but she didn't know that. Mrs Soames had explained to their hosts that she had a severe cold in the head and would spend the day in bed.

Bertha was up early, escorting the cat back to her rightful place in the kitchen and making herself tea. She would have almost the whole day to herself;

Crook was to have an afternoon off and Cook's sister was coming to spend the day with her.

Mrs Soames found this quite satisfactory since Bertha could be served a cold lunch and get her own tea if Cook decided to walk down to the nearest bus stop with her sister. The daily maid never came on a Sunday.

All this suited Bertha; she drank her tea while the cat lapped milk, and decided what she would do with her day. A walk—a long walk. She would go to St James's Park and feed the ducks. She went back upstairs to dress and had almost finished breakfast when Clare joined her. Bertha said good morning and she got a sour look, which she supposed was only to be expected.

It was after eleven o'clock by the time Mrs Soames and Clare had driven away. Bertha, thankful that it was a dull, cold day, allowing her to wear the lime-green which she felt was slightly less awful than the two-piece, went to tell Crook that she might be late for lunch and ask him to leave it on a tray for her before he left the house and set out.

There wasn't a great deal of traffic in the streets, but there were plenty of people taking their Sunday walk as she neared the park. She walked briskly, her head full of daydreams, not noticing her surroundings until someone screamed.

A young woman was coming out of the park gates pushing a pram—and running across the street into the path of several cars was a small boy. Bertha ran. She ran fast, unhampered by high heels and handbag, and plucked the child from the nearest car's wheels just before those same wheels bowled her over.

The child's safe, she thought hazily, aware that every bone in her body ached and that she was lying in a puddle of water, but somehow she felt too tired to get up. She felt hands and then heard voices, any number of them, asking if she were hurt.

'No—thank you,' said Bertha politely. 'Just aching a bit. Is that child OK?'

There was a chorus of 'yes', and somebody said that there was an ambulance coming. 'No need,' said Bertha, not feeling at all herself. 'If I could get up…'

'No, no,' said a voice. 'There may be broken bones…'

So she stayed where she was, listening to the voices; there seemed to be a great many people all talking at once. She was feeling sick now…

There were no broken bones, the ambulanceman assured her, but they laid her on a stretcher, popped her into the ambulance and bore her away to hospital. They had put a dressing on her leg without saying why.

The police were there by then, wanting to know her name and where she lived.

'Bertha Soames. But there is no one at home.'

Well, Cook was, but what could she do? Better keep quiet. Bertha closed her eyes, one of which was rapidly turning purple.

Dr Hay-Smythe, called down to the accident and emergency department to examine a severe head injury, paused to speak to the casualty officer as he left. The slight commotion as an ambulance drew up and a patient was wheeled in caused him to turn his head. He glanced at the patient and then looked again.

'Will you stop for a moment?' he asked, and bent over the stretcher. It was Bertha, all right, with a muddy face and a black eye and hair all over the place.

He straightened up. 'I know this young lady. I'll wait while you take a look.'

'Went after a kid running under a car. Kid's OK but the car wheel caught her. Nasty gash on her left leg.' The ambulanceman added, 'Brave young lady.'

Dr Hay-Smythe bent his great height again. 'Bertha?' His voice was quiet and reassuring. She opened the good eye.

'Oliver.' She smiled widely. 'You oughtn't to be working; it's Sunday.'

He smiled then and signalled to the men to wheel the stretcher away. It struck him that despite the dirt and the black eye nothing could dim the beauty of her one good eye, its warm brown alight with the pleasure of seeing him again.

There wasn't too much damage, the casualty officer told him presently—bruising, some painful grazes, a black eye and the fairly deep gash on one leg. 'It'll need a few stitches, and there's a good deal of grit and dirt in the wound. She'd better have a whiff of anaesthetic so that I can clean it up. Anti-tetanus jab too.'

He looked curiously at his companion; Dr Hay-Smythe was a well-known figure at the hospital, occasionally giving anaesthetics and often visiting the patients in his beds on the medical wards. He was well liked and respected, and rumour had it that he was much in demand socially; this small girl didn't seem quite his type...

Dr Hay-Smythe looked at his watch. 'If you could see to her within the next half-hour I'll give a hand. It'll save calling the anaesthetist out.'

Bertha, getting stiffer with every passing minute and aware of more and more sore places on her person, had her eyes closed. She opened the sound one when she heard his voice.

'You have a cut on your leg, Bertha,' he told her. 'I'm going to give you a whiff of something while it's seen to, then you will be warded.'

'No, no, I must go back home. Cook might wonder where I am.'

'Only Cook?' he gueried gently.

'Crook's got a half-day and my stepmother and Clare have gone to Henley to lunch with friends. There's no need to bother Cook; her sister's there.'

'Very well, but you are to stay here, Bertha. I'll see that your stepmother knows when she returns. Now, how long ago is it since you had your breakfast?'

'Why ever do you want to know? About eight o'clock.'

'Purely a professional question. No, close your eyes; I'm going to give you an injection in the back of your hand.' He turned away and spoke to someone she couldn't see and presently, eyes obediently shut, she felt a faint prick. 'Count up to ten,' he said, his voice reassuringly casual.

She got as far as five.

When she opened her eyes again she was in bed—a corner bed in a big ward—and the casualty officer and Dr Hay-Smythe were standing at the foot of it.

'Ah, back with us.' He turned away for a moment while two nurses heaved her up the bed, rearranged a cradle over her leg and disappeared again.

He studied her thoughtfully; anywhere else she would have minded being stared at like that, but here in hospital it was different; here he was a doctor and she was just another patient.

'Can I go home soon?' she asked.

It was the last place he wished her to go. She looked very small, engulfed in a hospital gown far too large for her, with her face clean now but pale and the damaged eye the only colour about her. Her hair, its mousy abundance disciplined into a plait, hung over one shoulder.

He said after a moment, 'No, you can't, Bertha. You're in one of my beds and you'll stay here until I discharge you.' He smiled suddenly. 'This is Dr Turner, the casualty officer who stitched you up.' And as another young man joined them he went on, 'And this is the medical officer who will look after you—Dr Greyson. I'll go and see your stepmother this afternoon and she will doubtless arrange to send in whatever you need.'

He offered a hand and she took it and summoned up a smile. 'Thank you for all your trouble. I hope I haven't spoilt your day.'

She closed her eyes, suddenly overcome by sleep.

Dr Hay-Smythe waited until the late afternoon before calling at the Soameses' house—too late for tea and too early for drinks—since he had no wish to linger there. He was admitted by Cook, since Crook was still enjoying his half-day, and ushered into the drawing room, where Mrs Soames and Clare were sitting discussing the lunch party. They greeted him eagerly, bored with each other's company.

'Oliver!' Clare went to meet him. 'How lovely—I was just wondering what I would do with the rest of this dull day, and you're the answer.'

He greeted her mother before replying, 'I'm afraid not. I have to return to the hospital very shortly. I have come to tell you that Bertha has had an accident—'

'The silly girl,' interposed Mrs Soames.

'She saved the life of a small boy who had run into the street in front of a car.' His voice was carefully expressionless. 'She is in hospital with a badly cut leg and severe bruising, so she must stay there for a few days at least. Would you take her whatever is necessary when you go to see her?'

'You've seen her?' Clare's voice was sharp.

'Yes. I happened to be in the accident and emergency department when she was admitted. She is in very good hands. I'll write down the name of the ward for you—there is no reason why you shouldn't visit her this evening.'

'Quite impossible, Oliver. I've guests coming for dinner.' Mrs Soames uttered the lie without hesitation. 'And I can't allow Clare to go. She is so sensitive to pain and distressing scenes; besides, who knows what foul germs there are in those public wards? She *is* in a public ward?'

'Yes. Perhaps you would ask one of your staff.' He paused, and then went on silkily, 'Better still, if you could give me whatever is needed, I will take it to Bertha.'

This suggestion met with the instant rejection he had expected. 'No, no!' cried Mrs Soames. 'Cook shall go with Bertha's things, and at the same time make sure that she has all she wants. The poor child!' she added with sickening mendacity. 'We must take good care of her when she comes home.'

She gave Clare a warning glance so that the girl quickly added her own sympathy. 'I hope she comes home soon.' Clare sounded wistfully concerned. 'I shall miss her.'

As indeed she would, reflected the doctor. There would be no one to whom she might pass on her unsuitable clothes. She was wearing a ridiculous outfit now, all frills and floating bits; he much preferred Bertha in her startling lime-green. Indeed, upon further reflection he much preferred Bertha, full-stop.

He took his leave presently and went back home to fetch Freddie and take him for a long walk in Hyde Park. And that evening, after he had dined, he got into his car once more and drove to the hospital. Visiting hours were long over and the wards were quiet, the patients drinking their milk or Ovaltine and being settled down for the night. Bertha was asleep when, accompanied by the ward sister, he went to look at her.

'Someone came with her nightclothes and so on?' he wanted to know.

'Oh, yes, Doctor. The family cook—a nice old soul. Gave her a large cake in a tin too, and said she would come again and that if she couldn't come someone called Crook would.'

'Ah, yes, the butler.'

'Has she no family?'

'A stepmother and a stepsister and a father who at present is somewhere in the States. He's a well-known QC.'

Sister looked at him. There was nothing to see on his handsome features, but she sensed damped-down rage. 'I'll take good care of her, Doctor,' she said.

He smiled at her then. 'Good—and will you be sure and let me know before she goes home?'

Bertha, after a refreshing sleep, felt quite herself in the morning. True, she was still stiff and sore, and it was tiresome only having the use of one eye, but she sat up and ate her breakfast and would have got out of bed armed with towel and toothbrush if she hadn't been restrained.

The leg must be rested, she was told. The cut had been deep and very dirty, and until it had been examined and re-dressed she would have to remain in her bed.

There was plenty to keep her interested, however. The elderly lady in the bed next to hers passed half an hour giving her details of her operation, most of them inaccurate, but Bertha listened enthralled until Sister came down the ward with a Cellophaned package.

'These have just come for you, Bertha. Aren't you a lucky girl?'

It was a delicate china bowl filled with a charming mixture of winter crocuses.

'There's a card,' prompted Sister.

Bertha took it from its miniature envelope. The

writing on it was hard to read. 'Flowers for Bertha', it said, and then the initials 'O.H-S.'

Sister recognised the scrawl. 'Just the right size for your locker top,' she said breezily, and watched the colour flood into Bertha's pale face. Who'd have thought it? the sister asked herself, sensing romance.

There were visitors later—the small boy whom she had saved led into the ward by his mother and bearing a bunch of flowers. The mother cried all over Bertha and wrung her hand and, very much to Bertha's embarrassment, told everyone near enough to listen how Bertha had saved her small son from being run over.

'Killed, he would have been—or crippled for life. A proper heroine, she is.'

That evening Crook came, bearing more flowers and a large box of chocolates from Cook and the daily and the man who came to do the garden each week.

'Is everything all right at home, Crook?' asked Bertha.

'Yes, Miss Bertha. I understand that there is a letter from your father; he hopes to return within the next few weeks. Mrs Soames and Miss Clare have been down to Brighton with friends; they are dining out this evening.'

'I'm not sure how long I am to stay here, Crook…'

'As long as it takes you to get quite well, Miss Bertha. You're not coming home before.'

He got up to go presently, with the promise that someone would come to see her again.

'Thank you for coming, and please thank the others for the chocolates and flowers. It's so kind of them and I know how busy you all are, so I won't mind if none of you can spare the time to visit. You can see how comfortable I am, and everyone is so friendly.'

On his way out, Sister stopped him. 'You come from Mrs Soames's household? Is she coming to see Miss Soames? She must wish to know about her injuries and I'd like to advise her about her convalescence.'

'Mrs Soames is most unlikely to come, Sister. If you will trust me with any details as to the care of Miss Bertha when she returns home, I shall do my utmost to carry them out,' said Crook.

When Dr Hay-Smythe came onto the ward later that evening, as she was going off duty, Sister paused to talk to him and tell him and the medical officer, who had come to do an evening round, what Crook had told her. 'I'll keep her as long as possible, but I'm always pushed for beds. And although I know you have beds in this ward, doctor, it is a medical unit and Bertha's a surgical case.'

'A couple more days, Sister?' He glanced at the young doctor with him. 'Turn a blind eye, Ralph? At least until the stitches come out. If she goes home too soon she'll be on that leg all day and ruin the CO's painstaking surgery. How is she, by the way?'

'A model patient; she's next to Mrs Jenkins—a thrombosis after surgery—and she's delighted to have such a tolerant listener.' She glanced at the doctor. 'She was delighted with your flowers, doctor.'

'Good. May I see Miss Arkwright for a moment? She wasn't too good yesterday.'

Miss Arkwright was at the other end of the ward from Bertha, but she could see Dr Hay-Smythe clearly as he went to his patient's bedside. She was feeling sleepy, but she kept her eye open; he would be sure to come and say goodnight presently. Only he didn't. After a few minutes he went away again without so much as a glance in her direction.

Bertha discovered that it was just as easy to cry with one eye as two.

The next few days were pleasant enough—the nurses were friendly, those patients who were allowed up came to sit by her, bringing their newspapers and reading out the more lurid bits, since her eye, now all the colours of the rainbow and beginning to open again, was still painful. Cook came too, this time with a bag of oranges.

Everything was much as usual, she told Bertha comfortably, omitting to mention that Mrs Soames's temper had been worse than usual and that Clare was having sulking fits.

'That nice doctor what she's keen on—always asking 'im ter take 'er out, she is, and 'im with no time to spare. 'E's taking 'er out to dinner this evening, though.'

Bertha stayed awake for a long time that night, listening to the snores and mutterings around her, the occasional urgent cry for a bedpan, the equally urgent whispers for tea. She closed her eyes each time the night nurse or night sister did her round and she heard the night sister say quietly, 'She'll have to go home in a couple of days; she's only here as a favour to Dr Hay-Smythe.'

Bertha lay and thought about going home. She had no choice but to do so for she had no money. It would mean seeing Clare and Oliver together, and she wasn't sure if she could bear that.

I suppose, she reflected, with the clarity of mind which comes to everybody at three o'clock in the morning, that I've been in love with him since he came over to me and asked me if it was my birthday. I'll have to go away... Once Father's back home, perhaps he'll agree to my training for something so that I can be independent. I'll have my own flat and earn enough money to be able to dress well and to go to the hairdresser and have lots of friends... She fell into an uneasy doze.

She was allowed out of bed now, and later the next day Staff Nurse took out alternate stitches.

'I'll have the rest tomorrow,' she said briskly. 'Don't run around too much; it's not quite healed yet. I expect you'll be going home in a day or two now.'

Bertha told Crook that when he came that afternoon. 'Please don't tell anyone, will you? I wouldn't want to upset any plans...'

They both knew Mrs Soames wasn't likely to change any plans she had made just because Bertha was coming home.

Dr Hay-Smythe came to see her that evening. 'You're to go home the day after tomorrow. I'll take you directly after lunch. You feel quite well?'

'Yes, thank you, I'm fine. Some of the stitches are out and it's a very nice scar—a bit red...'

'You won't see it in a few months. Will you be able to rest at home?'

'Oh, of course,' said Bertha airily. 'I can sit in the drawing room. But I don't need to rest, do I? I'm perfectly well. I know my eye's still not quite right, but it looks more dramatic than it is.'

He sat down on the side of the bed. 'Bertha, my mother would like you to go and stay with her for a week or two, perhaps until Christmas. How would you like that?'

Her eyes shone. 'Oh, how kind of her. I'd have to ask my stepmother first...'

He found himself smiling at her eager face. The few days in hospital had done her good; she had a pretty colour and she looked happy. He took her hand in his, conscious of a deep contentment. He had cautioned himself to have patience, to give her time to get to know him, but he had fallen in love with her when he had first seen her and his love had grown over the weeks. She was the girl he had been waiting for, and somehow or other he had managed to keep close to her, despite the dreadful stepmother and the tiresome Clare. He wouldn't hurry her, but after a few days he would go home and tell her that he loved her in the peace and quiet of the country.

He said now, 'We have to talk, Bertha. But not here.'

The ward was very quite and dim. He bent and kissed her gently and went away. Mrs Jenkins, feigning sleep and listening to every word, whispered, 'Now go to sleep, ducks. Nothing like a kiss to give you sweet dreams.'

*   *   *

The next day Oliver realized that he would have to see Mrs Soames before taking Bertha home. There was bound to be unpleasantness and he wanted that dealt with before she arrived. Not that he intended to tell her that he was in love with Bertha and was going to marry her, only that his mother had invited her to stay for a short time.

Mrs Soames gushed over him and then listened to his plans, a smile pinned onto her face. He was surprised at her readiness to agree with him that a week or so's rest was necessary for Bertha, but, thinking about it later, he concluded that it might suit her and Clare to have Bertha out of the way—she would be of no use to them around the house until her leg was quite healed. All the same, he had a feeling of unease.

CHAPTER FIVE

'OLIVER'S feeling of unease was justified. Mrs Soames, left to herself, paced up and down her drawing room, fuming. Bertha had gone behind her back and was doing her best to put a spoke in Clare's wheel. The wretched girl! Something would have to be done.

Mrs Soames, by now in a rage, spent some time thinking of the things she would like to do to Bertha before pulling herself together. Anger wasn't going to help. She must keep a cool head and think of ways and means. She heard Clare's voice in the hall and went to the door and called for her to come to the drawing room.

'Presently,' said Clare, who was halfway up the stairs. 'I've broken a fingernail and I must see to it at once...'

Something in her mother's voice brought her downstairs again.

'What's the matter?'

'Oliver has been here. Bertha is to come home tomorrow and his mother has invited her to stay with her for a couple of weeks.' Mrs Soames almost choked with fury as she spoke. 'The ungrateful girl—going behind our backs. She's cunning enough—she'll have him all to herself if she goes to his home.' She looked thoughtful. 'I wonder— Clare, get me the telephone directory.'

His receptionist was still at his rooms, and, in

answer to Mrs Soames's polite enquiry, said that she was afraid that Dr Hay-Smythe wouldn't be seeing new patients during the coming week. 'And he will be going on holiday the following week. But I could book you for an appointment in three weeks' time.'

Mrs Soames put down the phone without bothering to answer.

'He's going on holiday in a week's time—he'll go home, of course, and they'll have a whole week together. We have this week to think of something, Clare.'

Clare poured them each a drink and sat down. 'She'll have to go away—miles away. Now, who do we know...?'

'She'll have to go immediately—supposing he calls to see her?'

'We can say she's spending the weekend with friends.' Clare sat up suddenly. 'Aunt Agatha,' she said triumphantly. 'That awful old crow—Father's elder sister, the one who doesn't like us. We haven't seen her for years. She lives somewhere in the wilds of Cornwall, doesn't she?'

'Perfect—but will she have Bertha to stay? Supposing she refuses?'

'She doesn't need to know. You can send Bertha there—tell her that Aunt Agatha isn't well and has asked if she would go and stay with her.'

'What are we to say? Bertha may want to see the letter...'

'No letter. A phone call.' Clare crowed with laughter. 'I'd love to see her face when Bertha gets there.' She paused to think. 'We'll have to wait until Oliver has brought her home and then pack her off smartly. Do you suppose that he's interested in her? It's ridiculous even to think it. Why, Bertha's plain and dull—it's not possible. Besides, he's taken me out several times…'

'He will again, darling,' said Mrs Soames. She smiled fondly at her daughter; she could rest assured that Clare would get her way.

Bertha was ready and waiting when the doctor came for her. Her leg was still bandaged and her cheek under the black eye was grazed, but all he saw was the radiance of her smile when she saw him. He held down with an iron will a strong desire to gather her into his arms and kiss her, and said merely, 'Quite ready? The leg is comfortable? I can see that the eye is better.'

'I'm fine,' declared Bertha—a prosaic statement, which concealed her true feelings. 'It's very kind of you to take me home.'

He only smiled, waiting while she said goodbye to Sister and the nurses; she had already visited each bed to shake hands with its occupant.

He carried on a gentle, rambling conversation as he drove her home and as he drew up before the door he said, 'I'm coming in with you, Bertha.' Mrs Soames had seemed pleasant enough, but he still had an uneasy feeling about her.

Mrs Soames and Clare were both there, waiting for them. Clare spoke first.

'Bertha, are you quite better? Ought you to rest?' She gave a small, apologetic smile. 'I'm sorry I didn't come and see you—you know how I hate illness and dreary hospitals. But I'll make it up to you.'

Bertha, recognising this as a deliberate act to put her stepsister in a good light, murmured back and replied suitably to her stepmother's enquiries, which gave Clare the opportunity to take the doctor aside on the pretext of enquiring as to Bertha's fitness.

'Is she all right to walk about? Not too much, of course. We'll take good care of her.' She smiled up into his face. 'It is so kind of your mother to have her to stay. Will you be going to your home too?'

He looked down at her, his face bland. 'I shall do my best.' He got up from the sofa where they were sitting. 'I must go. I have several patients to see this afternoon.' He crossed the room to where Bertha was in uneasy conversation with her stepmother. 'I will come for you in three days' time, Bertha. Mrs Soames, I'm sure you'll take good care of her until then.' He shook hands then turned to Bertha. 'I hope to get away at half past twelve—will you be ready for me then?'

'Yes—yes, thank you.'

'Don't try and do too much for a few days.'

No one could fault the way in which he spoke to her—a detached kindness, just sufficiently friendly. Only his eyes gleamed under their lids.

Bertha's stepmother, once the doctor had gone, was so anxious to make sure that Bertha had everything she wanted, wasn't tired, wasn't hungry, or didn't wish to lie down on her bed that Bertha was at pains to discover what had brought about this change of heart.

She wasn't the only one. Crook, going back to the kitchen after he had served dinner, put down his tray and said darkly, 'Depend upon it, this won't last—there's madam begging Miss Bertha to have another morsel and is she comfortable in that chair and would she like to go to bed and someone would bring her a warm drink. Poppycock—I wonder what's behind it?'

Apparently nothing; by the end of the second day Bertha's surprise at this cosseting had given way to pleased relief, and Crook had to admit that Mrs Soames seemed to have had a change of heart. 'And not before time,' he observed.

Bertha went to bed early. She had packed her bag with the miserable best of her wardrobe, washed her hair and telephoned the nursery school to tell the matron that she would be coming back after Christmas if they still wanted her. Since her stepmother was showing such a sympathetic face, Bertha had told her that she was no longer reading to an old lady but to a group of children.

'Why didn't you tell me this?' Mrs Soames strove to keep the annoyance out of her voice.

'I didn't think that it was important or that you would be interested.'

Mrs Soames bit her tongue and summoned up a smile. 'Well, it really doesn't matter, Bertha. I'm sure it is very worthwhile work. Oliver arranged it for you, I expect?'

Bertha said that yes, he had, and didn't see the angry look from her stepmother.

Clare, when told of this, burst into tears. 'You see, Mother, how she has been hoodwinking us all this time. Probably seeing him every day. Well, she'll be gone when he comes. Is it all arranged?'

*   *   *

It was still early morning when Bertha was roused by her stepmother. 'Bertha, I've just had a phone call from your aunt Agatha. She's not well and asks for you. I don't think she's desperately ill, just needs someone there other than the servants. She has always been fond of you, hasn't she? She begged me to ask you to go as soon as possible, and I couldn't refuse.'

'I'm going to Mrs Hay-Smythe today, though...'

'Yes, yes, I know. But perhaps you could go to your aunt just for a day or two.'

'Why must I go? Why should she ask for me?'

'She's elderly—and she's always been eccentric.' Mrs Soames, sensing that she was losing the battle, said with sudden inspiration, 'Suppose you go today? I'll phone her doctor and see if he can arrange for someone to stay with your aunt, then you can come straight back. A day's delay at the most. Your father would want you to go.'

'Oliver expects me to be ready—'

'Write him a note and I'll explain. Believe me, Bertha, if Clare could go in your place she would, but you know how your aunt dislikes her.'

Bertha threw back the bed clothes. 'Very well, but I'm coming back, whatever arrangements are made.'

'Well, of course you are. Get dressed quickly and I'll find out about trains.'

Mrs Soames went away to tell Clare that their plan was working so far. 'I told her that I was finding out about the next train.' She glanced at the clock. 'I've just time to dress and drive her to Paddington. She can have breakfast on the train.' She turned at the door. 'Bertha's writing a note for

Oliver. Get rid of it before he comes—and not a word to the servants. I'll see them when I get back. I don't mean to tell them where she has gone.'

An hour later, sitting in the train, eating a breakfast she didn't want, Bertha tried to sort out the morning's happenings. It didn't occur to her that she had been tricked; she knew that her stepmother didn't like her, but that she would descend to such trickery never crossed her mind. She had written to Oliver—a careful little note, full of apologies, hoping that he wouldn't be inconvenienced and hoping to see his mother as soon as she could return.

Clare had read it before she'd torn it into little pieces.

The train journey was a lengthy one. Bertha, eating another meal she didn't want, thought about Oliver. He would have been to her home by now, of course, and been told about her sudden departure. She wished she could have written a longer letter, but there hadn't been time. She could think of nothing else, her head full of the whys and wherefores of something she couldn't understand. It was a relief when Truro was reached at last and she got out to change to a local train, which stopped at every station until it stopped, at last, at her destination.

The village was small and she remembered it well from visits when she was a child. Miss Soames lived a mile or two away from the narrow main street, and Bertha was relieved to see a taxi in the station yard. She had been given money for her expenses—just sufficient to get her to her aunt's house—and since her stepmother had pointed out that there was no point in getting a return ticket as she herself would drive down and fetch Bertha she had accepted the situation willingly enough. Her head full of Oliver, nothing else mattered.

Her aunt's house looked exactly the same as she remembered it—solid and rather bleak, with a splendid garden. Bertha toiled up the path with her suitcase and knocked at the door.

After a moment it was flung open and Miss Agatha Soames, majestic in a battered felt hat and old and expensive tweeds, stood surveying Bertha.

'Well, upon my word. Why are you here, gel?'

Bertha, not particularly put out by this welcome, for her aunt was notoriously tart, said composedly that her stepmother had sent her. 'She told me that you were ill and needed a companion and had asked for me urgently.'

Miss Soames breathed deeply. 'It seems to me from the look of you that it is you who needs a companion. Your stepmother is a vulgar, scheming woman who would be glad to see me dead. I am in the best of health and need no one other than Betsy and Tom. You may return home.' She bent a beady eye on Bertha. 'Why have you a black eye? She actually sent you here to me?'

'Yes, Aunt Agatha.' Awful doubts were crowding into Bertha's tired head.

Miss Soames snorted. 'Then she's up to something. Wants you out of the way in a hurry. Been upsetting the applecart, have you? Poaching on that Clare's preserves, are you?'

When Bertha's cheeks grew pink, she said, 'Took a fancy to you instead of her, did he? Well, if he's got any sense he will come after you.'

Bertha shook her head. 'No, I don't think so. He doesn't know where I am—I didn't tell him.'

'They won't tell him either. But if he's worth his salt he'll find you. Love him?'

'Yes, Aunt Agatha. But he doesn't think of me like that, though he's a kind man.'

'We will see.' Miss Soames thrust the door wide open and said belatedly, 'Well, come in. Now you're here you'd better stay. Where's your father?'

'I'm not exactly sure, but he's coming home soon.'

Aunt Agatha said, 'Pah!' and raised her voice. 'Betsy, come here and listen to this.' Betsy came so quickly that Bertha wondered if she had been standing behind the door.

'No need to tell, I heard it all. Poor lamb. I'll get the garden room ready and a morsel of food. The child looks starved—and look at that eye! A week or two here with good food and fresh air is what she needs.'

During the next few days that was what Bertha got. Moreover, her aunt ordered Tom to bring the elderly Rover to the front door and she and Bertha were driven into Truro, where she sailed in and out of various shops buying clothes for her niece.

When Bertha protested, she said, 'I'll not have a niece of mine wearing cast-off clothes which are several sizes too big and quite unsuitable. I shall speak to your father. Don't interfere, miss.'

So Bertha thanked her aunt and got joyfully into skirts and blouses and dresses which fitted her slender person and were made of fine material in soft colours. If only Oliver could see her now. She had talked to her aunt about what she should do and that lady had said, 'Do nothing, gel. Let your step-mother wonder, if she can be bothered to do so. You are not to write to her nor are you to telephone. You will stay here until this doctor finds you.'

'He won't,' said Bertha. 'He'll never find me...'

'Have you never heard of the proverb "Love finds a way"? I have great faith in proverbs,' said Aunt Agatha.

Oliver had presented himself at half past twelve exactly to collect Bertha, and had been shown into the drawing room. Mrs Soames had come to meet him.

'Oliver, thank heaven you have come. I tried to get you on the phone, but there was no answer.'

She'd found his calm unnerving.

'Bertha!' she'd exclaimed. 'She must be ill—that accident. She got me out of bed early this morning and insisted on being driven to Euston Station. I begged her to stay, to phone you, to wait at least until you came. She was quite unlike herself—so cold and determined.'

'You did as she asked?' His voice had been very quiet.

'What else could I do? She wouldn't listen to reason.'

'She had money? Did she say where she was going?'

'I gave her what I had. She told me that she was going to an aunt—a relation of her mother's, I believe, who lives somewhere in Yorkshire. I begged her to tell why she wanted to leave us and I reminded her that she was to visit your mother—she said she would write to you.' Mrs Soames managed to squeeze out a tear. 'I really don't know what to do, Oliver. Clare is terribly upset.'

Oliver sounded quite cheerful. 'Why, I suggest that we wait until one or other of us gets a letter. She is quite capable of looking after herself, is she not?'

'Yes, of course. Will you come this evening so that we three can put our heads together? Dinner, perhaps?'

'Not possible, I'm afraid, Mrs Soames.' He spoke pleasantly, longing to wring the woman's neck. There was something not right about the story she had told him. He would get to the bottom of it if it took him weeks, months...

'The whole thing is fishy,' he told Freddie as he drove away. Someone somewhere would know where Bertha had gone; he would send Cully round later with some excuse or other and he could talk to Crook—both he and Cook were obviously fond of Bertha, and in the meanwhile he would see if the nursery school knew anything.

'Gone?' asked Matron. 'Without a word to anyone? I find that hard to believe. Why, she telephoned not a day or two ago to say that she would be coming back after Christmas, when she had had a short holiday.'

Oliver thanked her. It hadn't been much help, but it was a start.

Cully's visit had no success, either. Crook was disturbed that Bertha had gone so unexpectedly, but he had no idea where she might be. Certainly there was an aunt of hers somewhere in the north of England, and the master had a sister living, but he had no idea where.

The doctor phoned his mother and sat down to think. Mrs Soames had been very glib, and he didn't believe a word of what she had said, but there was no way of getting her to tell the truth. To find this aunt in Yorkshire when he had no idea of her name or where she lived was going to be difficult. Her father's sister—unmarried, Crook had said—was a more likely possibility. He went to bed at last, knowing what he would do in the morning.

Mr Soames QC was well-known in his own profession. The doctor waited patiently until a suitable hour the next morning and then phoned his chambers.

'No,' he was told. 'Mr Soames is still in the States. Would you like to make an appointment at some future date?'

The doctor introduced himself. 'You are his chief clerk? So I can speak freely to you? I am a friend of the Soames family and there is a personal matter I should like to attend to—preferably with Mr Soames. Failing that, has he a relation to whom I could write? This is a family matter, and Mrs Soames is not concerned with it.'

'Dr Hay-Smythe? You have a practice in Harley Street. I remember that you were called to give evidence some time ago.'

'That is so. You would prefer me to come and see you?'

'No. No, that won't be necessary. Mr Soames has a sister living in Cornwall. I could give you her address.' The clerk sounded doubtful.

'I will come to your chambers to collect it, and if you wish to let Mr Soames know of my request, please do so.'

* * *

It was impossible to go down to Cornwall for at least two days; he had patients to see, a ward round at the hospital, an outpatients clinic, and then, hours before he intended to leave, an urgent case. So, very nearly a week had passed by the time he got into his car with Freddie and began the long drive down to Cornwall.

It was already later than he had intended; he had no hope of reaching Miss Soames's house at a reasonable hour. He drove steadily westward, Freddie alert beside him, and stopped for the night at Liskeard in an old friendly pub where he was given a hearty supper before going to his room, which was low-ceilinged and comfortable. Since Freddie had behaved in a very well-bred manner he accompanied his master, spreading his length across the foot of the bed.

'This is definitely not allowed,' Oliver told him. 'But just this once, since it is a special occasion. I only hope that Bertha's aunt likes dogs.'

Freddie yawned.

They were on their way again after breakfast— bacon, mushrooms freshly picked, fried bread, a sausage or two and egg garnished with a tomato. A meal to put heart into a faint-hearted man—something which the doctor was not. In an hour or so he would see his Bertha again, beyond that he didn't intend to think for the moment. He whistled as he drove and Freddie, no lover of whistling, curled his lip.

It was shortly after ten o'clock when Betsy carried the coffee tray into Miss Soames's sitting room, which was small and pleasant, overlooking the wide stretch of garden at the back of the house. Bertha was out there, walking slowly, her hair in a plait over one shoulder, and wearing one of the pretty winter dresses which Miss Soames had bought for her.

Her aunt, peering over her spectacles at her, observed, 'The girl's not pretty, but there's something about her... Takes after our side of the family, of course.' She poured her coffee. 'Leave the child for the moment, Betsy. She's happy.'

Betsy went away, but she was back again within a minute.

'There's an 'andsome motor car coming up to the door...'

Miss Soames sipped her coffee. 'Ah, yes, I was expecting that. Show the gentleman in here, Betsy, and say nothing to Bertha.'

The doctor came in quietly. 'Miss Soames? I apologise for calling upon you unexpectedly. I believe that Bertha is staying with you?' He held out a hand. 'Oliver Hay-Smythe.'

She took the hand. 'What kept you, young man?' she wanted to know tartly. 'Of course, I knew that you would come, although Bertha is sure that she will never see you again.'

He followed her gaze out of the window; Bertha looked very pretty, and his rather tired face broke into a smile.

'I told her that if a man was worth his salt he would find her even if he had to search the world for her.' She gave him a level gaze. 'Would you do that, Doctor?'

'Yes. I do not quite understand why she is here. I think that her stepmother wanted her out of the way. That doesn't matter for the moment, but it took me some time to discover where she was.'

'You have driven down from London? What have you done with your patients?'

He smiled. 'It took a good deal of organising, but I'd planned a holiday this week.'

'You'll stay here, of course.' She looked over his shoulder. 'What is it, Betsy?'

'There's a dog with his head out of the car window.'

'Freddie. Might I allow him out? He's well-mannered.'

'Get the beast, Betsy,' commanded Miss Soames, and when Freddie, on his best behaviour, came into the room, she offered him a biscuit.

'Well, go along, young man. There's a door into the garden at the back of the hall.'

Freddie, keeping close to his heels, gave a pleased bark as he saw Bertha, and she turned round as he bounded towards her. She knelt and put her arms round his neck and watched Oliver crossing the lawn to her. The smile on her face was like a burst of sunshine as she got slowly to her feet. He saw with delight that she had a pretty colour in her cheeks and a faint plumpness which a week's good food had brought about. Moreover, the dress she was wearing revealed the curves which Clare's misfits had so successfully hidden.

He didn't say anything, but took her in his arms and held her close. Presently he spoke. 'I came as soon as I could, my darling. I had to find you first...'

'How?' asked Bertha. 'Who...?'

'Later, my love.' He bent his head and kissed her.

Bertha, doing her best to be sensible, said, 'But I want to know why my stepmother sent me here—she'll be so angry when she finds out.'

'Leave everything to me, dear heart. You need never see her or Clare again if you don't want to. We'll marry as soon as it can be arranged. Would you like Christmas Eve for a wedding?'

He kissed her again, and eventually, when she had stopped feeling light-headed, she said, 'You haven't asked me—you haven't said—'

'That I love you?' He smiled down at her. 'I love you, darling Bertha. I fell in love with you the moment I clapped eyes on you in that hideous pink dress. Will you marry me and love me a little?'

She reached up to put her arms round his neck. 'Of course I'll marry you, dear Oliver, and I'll love you very much for always. Will you kiss me again? Because I rather like it when you do.'

Aunt Agatha, unashamedly watching them from her chair, took out her handkerchief and blew her nose, and to Betsy, who was peering over her shoulder, she said, 'I must need new glasses, for my eyes keep watering!'

She sounded cross, but she was smiling.

HEAVENLY ANGELS
Carole Mortimer

Peter,
miracles do happen

Dear Reader,

I believe in miracles!

At the age of thirty-eight, I finally experienced my own Harlequin romance. Love found me when I least expected it. After a year of typical "He-loves-me-he-loves-me-not, I-hate-him-no-I-don't," both of us decided to give in and admit we loved each other very much and wanted to spend the rest of our lives together.

That was the first miracle. The second one, against all odds, took nine months to appear. But when I was forty-one, I gave birth to our beautiful son, Peter Raoul.

Miracles do happen. They happened to me. So keep believing, and they might happen to you, too!

Lots of love

Carole Mortimer

CHAPTER ONE

'WHO the hell are you?'

Bethany's auburn brows rose over dark green eyes at the unexpected attack by the man who'd answered her knock on the door. Her second knock, she might have informed him, but didn't—her first knock having gone unanswered.

He hardly looked in the mood to be told such a thing. He was a tall, dark-haired man in his late thirties, with flinty grey eyes that at the moment, she was sure, had a look of desperation in them. The short dark hair seemed to be standing up on end too, and judging by the orderly look of the rest of his appearance—tailored dark suit and pristine white shirt, perfectly knotted tie at his throat—Bethany didn't think this was a usual occurrence.

In fact, she was sure that it wasn't; she wouldn't be here at all if anything about this situation were as it usually was!

She gave the man a smile, determined not to be put off by his aggressive attitude; after all, her last assignment had involved a man who'd had all the endearing qualities of Scrooge before the transformation, so anything had to be an improvement on that. Of course, she hadn't complained at the time—it wasn't for her to complain—but this Christmas, she had to admit, it would be nice—

'I asked who you are?' The dark-haired man impatiently interrupted her wandering thoughts. 'If you're collecting for something—'

'No.' She smiled dismissively, her smile widening as a tiny golden-haired bundle came into view behind him, doing cartwheels across the pale blue carpet, while two dark-haired boys wrestled quite happily together on the rug in front of the fire.

Christmas was such a joyous time for everyone, Bethany acknowledged happily, but especially for children. She was pleased, and a little excited herself, that children were involved in this assignment. She loved children. She had been a child herself once—and there were certain people who believed she still was, she accepted ruefully, a slight shadow darkening her creamy brow. She had tried so hard to show them how responsible she was, how adult she could be, but each time they gave her some responsibility something seemed to go slightly wrong.

'No, I'm not collecting for anything, Mr Rafferty,' she assured him smoothly. 'It is Mr Rafferty, isn't it?' She hadn't been told too much about him, but as he seemed to be at the right address, and in charge of three children, then she assumed he had to be Nick Rafferty.

Bethany gazed up at him as he turned to scowl at the three highly active children, her hair a long blaze of red down her back, her green eyes huge in her small heart-shaped face, her nose pert and snub, covered with a liberal sprinkling of freckles, and her mouth wide and generous. That mouth was smiling now, the green eyes aglow.

'Yes, I'm Nick Rafferty,' he finally acknowledged with a sigh, visibly wincing as the volume of noise in the room behind him seemed to rise to crescendo level. 'Shut up, you lot!' he turned briefly again to shout—an effort he might just as well have saved himself as, after one brief glance in his direction, the two boys carried on wrestling and the golden-haired little girl proceeded to cartwheel in the other direction across the room.

'Oh God!' The man in front of her seemed to pale visibly, displaying the reason for his hair standing on end as he ran agitated fingers through the darkness, making it stick up even more. 'Can I help you?' he prompted agitatedly.

Bethany calmly shook her head. 'No, but I hope I can help you.' She continued to smile at him—something that seemed to irritate him even more.

He shook his head. 'I wish you could,' he sighed. 'I'm sorry, who did you say you were?' He frowned darkly.

'Heavenly Angels,' Bethany informed him lightly as she walked past him into the apartment, unhurriedly separating the two boys as they came dangerously close to the artificially warm fire and standing the two of them up to dust them down and straighten their dishevelled appearance.

She smiled warmly at them and the golden-haired bundle, having ceased cartwheeling now, walked slowly over to join them as curiosity got the better of her concerning this newcomer in their midst. Bethany's smile became even warmer as she looked at the angelic child—her curls golden, her face pure innocence, her blue eyes candid and freckles dusting her snub nose.

'How the hell did you do that?' an amazed Nick Rafferty demanded to know, when all three children were standing calmly in a row, looking up at Bethany.

'You really shouldn't swear in front of the children, Mr Rafferty,' she advised him softly. 'It isn't good for innocent ears to—'

'*Children!*' he repeated scathingly. 'In my book children should be seen and not heard—and preferably not the former either, if it can be arranged. And these three are demons from he—'

'You're becoming agitated, Mr Rafferty,' Bethany calmly understated, ruffling the golden curls of the little girl as she smiled up at her so endearingly, with her two front teeth missing. The little girl was sure to have a lisp too, which must sound absolutely adorable coming from such a beautiful child. 'That isn't good for children. Children need firm, unflappable guidance, not—'

'I don't need a lecture from you on how to behave towards children!' he exploded furiously. 'Just how many children of your own do you have?'

'Well...none. But—'

'I didn't think so,' he said scornfully. 'You aren't much more than a child yourself!' he added disgustedly, with a scathing glance at her five-foot stature and childlike features which didn't make her look much older than the cherub standing at her side.

Bethany smiled at the knowledge of just how wrong he was. Looks could be deceptive. She might look young, but she was actually—

'I asked who you were,' he reminded her harshly. Her smile seemed to have infuriated him even more as he glared down at her from his superior height, dark brows meeting frowningly together across those steely grey eyes.

'And I answered you, Mr Rafferty,' she replied evenly, turning to smile at the little girl at her side as a tiny warm hand slid into hers. 'Heavenly Angels—'

'Which tells me precisely nothing,' Nick Rafferty interrupted impatiently. 'You look absolutely nothing like an angel to me!'

Her smile became wistfully sad at the correctness of that statement. He wasn't the first person to mention that fact. Angels were reputedly golden-haired and blue-eyed—ethereally beautiful creatures. Her green eyes and freckles certainly didn't lend themselves to beauty, and, though she had tried to rectify the colour of her hair once, it had turned out purple, which hadn't gone down too well with the powers that be.

'I like her, Daddy Nick,' the little girl next to her said, smiling up at Bethany with that toothless grin.

Nick's mouth twisted disgustedly. 'I'm sure that's a great recommendation, Lucy—' his tone implied that it was the opposite '—but—'

'It certainly is,' Bethany agreed happily, deciding to ignore his caustic tone as she bent down on one knee so that she was on the same level as the little girl. 'As it's you and your brothers I've been sent here to care for.'

'You have?' The cherubic face brightened as she turned to the tall man towering gloweringly over them. 'Daddy Nick, did you hear what the angel said? She's—'

'I heard, Lucy,' he rasped dismissively. 'And I would like an explanation of that remark.' He turned to Bethany. 'You don't look like a friend of their mother's,' he added scathingly. 'But if you are,' he continued, before Bethany could make any reply, 'I can assure you I don't need one of Samantha's cronies to— Lucy, will you stop pulling on the young lady's arm like that!' he thundered as the little girl did exactly that to Bethany's coatsleeve.

Lucy gave him a reproachful look from under lashes that were long and golden. 'I only wanted to know if the angel can make jam sandwiches,' she muttered petulantly, her bottom lip starting to tremble precariously.

Bethany, spotting the tell-tale tremble, picked the little girl up in her arms, cuddling her close. 'Of course I can, darling,' she crooned comfortingly. Couldn't Nick Rafferty see that he was upsetting Lucy with his aggressive attitude?

'Now?' Lucy prompted hopefully.

Bethany smoothed back the tumbling golden curls. 'Well, maybe not now—it will ruin your tea. But—'

'We haven't had any lunch yet,' put in the younger of the two boys hopefully.

'You haven't?' Bethany nodded understandingly. That explained a lot.

It was usually her experience—and, contrary to Nick Rafferty's belief, she did have quite a lot of experience with children!—that children either became bad-tempered or hyperactive when they were hungry. The latter she had never quite understood, when it was food for fuel that they were in need of, but she had always been told she asked too many questions anyway, and, to be honest, that particular one hadn't seemed as important as some of the others she had wanted answers to.

'No wonder you're all a little—over-excited. Could you point me in the direction of the kitchen, Mr Rafferty?' she enquired brightly.

'It's this way.' The younger of the two boys again took charge, taking hold of Bethany's hand to lead her in the direction of a doorway to the left of this main room.

'I— But— Josh! Jamie!' Nick Rafferty thundered at them again.

Neither boy took any notice of him, but he sounded rather desperate, so Bethany was the one to take pity on him and briefly halt their progress to the kitchen, turning to look at him enquiringly.

'We don't even know who this young lady is!' Again he directed his words to the two boys.

Bethany smiled in sympathy with his agitation. 'Children are like that, Mr Rafferty; they rarely bite the hand that chooses to feed them. They also,' she went on firmly as he seemed about to explode once again, 'instinctively know who they can trust. And who they can't,' she added pointedly, before entering the kitchen with two hungry boys trailing after her and an angel—if not quite a heavenly one!—in her arms.

CHAPTER TWO

NICK thought of following them, of demanding answers from the 'heavenly angel', but as peace descended over the room for the first time in the last chaotic twenty-four hours he thought better of it. After all, what harm could come to the children when they were only a few feet away from him in the kitchen? And they were finally quiet. And being fed...

Damn it, he had forgotten all about giving the children lunch. He so rarely ate that particular meal himself, he just hadn't thought—

Goddamn it, he didn't know how to look after children for any length of time! What the hell Robert had thought he was doing bringing them here, he had no idea. What had made it even more difficult was that it had been the first time he and Robert had spoken more than abrupt words of greeting and parting in over five years.

Robert, who had been his best friend, his business partner—and who had taken Nick's wife and children from him five years ago!

And now, through necessity, he had brought the children back. But Nick had never had any idea of how to look after the children—had always left that part of their marriage to Samantha. Oh God, Samantha... Was she going to be OK? Was she going to live? They had left so many things unsaid between them, so much bitterness, so much pain.

112

And now she had been seriously injured in a car accident, might die from her injuries. Why was it, Nick agonised, that people never felt remorse for past hurts until it was possibly too late? Why—?

'Mr Rafferty?'

He looked up blankly, blinking as he focused on the angel. A red-haired angel! Whoever had heard of such a thing? And yet, as he looked up at her, he could almost swear that he saw a glow about that red hair. A little like a halo...?

'Your lunch, Mr Rafferty.' She held out a plate, pushing it into his unresisting fingers before turning away to return to the children in the kitchen. Children now quietly eating the lunch she had prepared for them...

Nick shook his head in self-disgust. A halo! He was losing his mind. The woman had merely been standing with the light behind her, giving a glow to the deep red of her hair. Almost twenty-four hours of caring for the children had obviously started to affect his judgement.

The woman was no angel, was only flesh and blood—rather pretty flesh, he decided as he watched the gentle sway of her bottom as she returned to the kitchen. She was a little young for his tastes, probably only in her early twenties, but nevertheless the tiny body looked to be perfectly proportioned—the breasts small and pert, the hips narrow and shapely. And that hair, it was—

God, he was losing his mind! What the hell did the physical attributes of that young woman matter? His life was in chaos! He was supposed to be leaving for Aspen, Colorado, tomorrow, for a skiing holiday over the Christmas period, instead of which he had three children to care for until further notice. What the hell was he going to say to Lisa when he told her they couldn't go away, after all?

Lisa! Damn, he hadn't given her a thought since Robert had delivered the children to him here early yesterday evening. She was going to throw a tantrum at his lack of attentiveness. Oh, damn Lisa— a diamond bracelet would soon calm her ruffled feelings. Lisa was the least of his worries at the moment; it was what he was going to do with the three children over Christmas that should be uppermost in his thoughts. It *was* uppermost in his thoughts; he just didn't have an answer!

'You haven't touched your sandwich, Mr Rafferty.' The angel had returned, a cup of tea in her hand this time and her coat removed now, her hair falling softly onto a green jumper that exactly matched the colour of her eyes.

How did she do that? Just suddenly appear in front of him, almost as if— He shook his head, rousing himself enough to take the cup and saucer with his free hand, realising as he did so the impracticality of doing so; now he couldn't eat his sandwich even if he wanted to. Which he didn't. The children may have a partiality for jam sandwiches, but he certainly didn't!

'Everything will be all right, Mr Rafferty.' She reached out to touch his arm gently. 'Mrs Fairfax is very ill at the moment, but I'm positive she will recover.' She smiled, a smile as gentle as her touch. 'I would have been told if it were to be otherwise.'

Nick could never remember feeling at a loss for words, but somehow this young woman seemed to have that effect on him. What did she mean; she 'would have been told' if Samantha wasn't going to come through this? Perhaps he should be concerned about the children being alone in the kitchen with her after all; she was obviously slightly deranged. First claiming to be an angel and now assuring him that his ex-wife would recover from the accident that had left her with multiple injuries.

'The baby is going to be fine too,' the strange young woman continued smilingly. 'Now, please eat your lunch, Mr Rafferty. Everything will seem much brighter once you've eaten.'

Nick had the impression that she was talking to him as if he were another of the children, and he— Baby! What baby? Samantha wasn't pregnant; Robert would have told him if she was.

This young woman was the strangest person he had ever met in his life, and made the most outrageous remarks. Why, she— He turned helplessly in the direction of the telephone as it began to ring, looking down at the cup and saucer he held in one hand and the laden plate in the other.

'I'll get it for you, Mr Rafferty.' Once again there was that gentle pat on his arm. 'Perhaps it's Mr Fairfax, with news of your wife,' she added brightly.

Ex-wife. Samantha was Robert's wife now, had been for the last four years. And it was more likely to be Lisa making the call, furious with him for not calling her—and having another woman answer the telephone would not improve her temper!

Too late—the angel had already answered the call, was lifting the receiver to her ear. Hell, what was this young woman's name? He couldn't keep thinking of her as an angel!

'Mr Fairfax!' she greeted brightly, smiling re-assuringly at Nick. 'Yes, of course Mr Rafferty is here. Just a moment and I'll get him for you.' With the minimum of effort she put down the receiver and divested Nick of the cup of tea and the plate, putting them both down on the coffee-table before disappearing from the room.

Nick stood watching her for several dazed sec-onds, too bemused to move. And then he remem-bered that Robert was on the telephone. 'Robert.' He barked the greeting, wincing as he heard his own aggression. 'How is she, Robert?' He gentled his voice as he spoke of the woman who had once been his wife but belonged irrevocably to this man.

'Off the danger list,' the other man said thank-fully. 'But I can't leave her, Nick. I'm sure you understand.'

Yes, he understood. Robert loved Samantha more than anything else in the world—more than his own friendship with Nick, more than the wealth his busi-ness partnership had brought him. More than any-thing. It had come as a blow to Nick to realise that Samantha felt the same way about Robert.

Had Nick ever loved her that deeply? Had Samantha ever loved him in the same way? Maybe, in the beginning—before other things had become more important, before complacency had made him take for granted the one thing that had given every-thing else in his life meaning. But if he had loved Samantha enough surely that wouldn't have hap-pened? He—

Oh, God, not now; he had been over all of this so many times in the last five years, and in the end it changed nothing. Samantha was now Robert's wife, and the two of them loved each other—they had for a very long time.

'The children?' he prompted Robert abruptly, part of him envying the other man, another part of him knowing it had never been that way between himself and Samantha.

'Their presents are all at the house, Nick, hidden in the wardrobe. If you—'

'Robert, Christmas is still two days away,' he interrupted agitatedly. So Samantha still hid the presents in the wardrobe... 'Surely you'll be able to get away by then?'

There was silence for a moment at the other end of the telephone line, and then Robert drew in a ragged breath. 'Lord knows I love the children as if they were my own, Nick,' Robert finally rasped. 'I've had to; you've practically disowned them the last five years. But the truth of the matter is they are your children, Nick, and it isn't going to kill you to give up your usual skiing holiday with the latest bimbo to spend Christmas with them!'

How well this man knew him, Nick acknowledged self-derisively. Strange, he had forgotten how well Robert *did* know him, with the five-year gap in their friendship. But Robert was wrong about one thing. They weren't all his children. Jamie and Josh, yes—and he admitted he should have spent more time with them since Samantha had left him—but Samantha wouldn't hear of him taking Jamie and Josh without Lucy, and Lucy wasn't—

'I'm not leaving Samantha, Nick,' Robert told him determinedly. 'So you'll just have to cope. I'm sure the young lady who answered the telephone just now is more than capable of lending a hand;

she sounded rather sweet. It's quite easy; Jamie and Josh just want to watch television and fight with each other all the time, and Lucy will take to anyone who gives her jam sandwiches!'

'The "young lady" has already given her those,' Nick told him drily. And Jamie and Josh had done nothing but watch television and fight since they'd arrived yesterday!

'There you are, then,' Robert said with satisfaction. 'More than capable.'

Maybe she was—it certainly still seemed very quiet in the kitchen—but that wasn't the point. The point was what was he going to do with three children over Christmas? 'Robert—'

'I'm not leaving the hospital, Nick,' the other man cut in with vehement determination. 'I want to be here when Samantha wakes up. Her life is out of danger, but there are still complications.'

Nick felt his stomach contract; he and Samantha might be divorced, and Samantha with Robert now, but that didn't mean he didn't still care what happened to her. 'What sort of complications?' he asked warily.

'They're concerned about the baby,' the other man told him distractedly. 'Sam has wanted another baby for so long, I can hardly believe it's happened now,' he continued worriedly. 'It will break her heart if anything goes wrong.'

Nick had stopped listening, was barely aware of his own agreement to take care of the children until such time as Robert could leave Samantha, or of the other man terminating the telephone call, of replacing his own receiver.

He sat down heavily, staring at the closed kitchen

door. She had known about the baby, had told him, 'The baby is going to be fine too.' How had she known about the baby? How—?

Nick looked down at the sandwich in his hand, which he had begun to eat without being aware of it, staring at it uncomprehendingly. Not jam at all, but smoked salmon. His favourite...

CHAPTER THREE

BETHANY was sitting at the breakfast bar chatting to the children as they ate when Nick Rafferty came thundering through the doorway. Really, the man seemed to charge into everything at an aggressive rate. Into rooms, out of them again—and into conversations too, she quickly realised!

'I would like a private word with you, Miss— Miss— What the hell is your name?' He scowled across the width of the room at her.

The children took absolutely no notice of the aggression in his tone, continuing to munch quite happily on their sandwiches. Which didn't seem right to Bethany either; it couldn't be healthy for the children actually to be used to Nick Rafferty's constant abruptness.

'Her name is Beth, Daddy Nick,' Lucy was the one to inform him, with traces of strawberry jam about her rosebud mouth. 'Isn't that nice?' She grinned happily, obviously pleased that her lisp was totally irrelevant when she said 'the angel's' name.

Bethany was glad that her name pleased the little girl, but this wasn't the first time she had heard Lucy call Nick Rafferty Daddy Nick; it seemed rather a strange thing to call her father. Of course, the three children were growing up with a stepfather, which must be confusing for children so young if they were fond of him, but even so...

'Very nice.' Nick Rafferty agreed with the little

girl with a distinct lack of conviction. 'Would you come through to the sitting-room, Miss—Beth?' He sounded impatient with the lack of a surname. 'We need to talk,' he added grimly.

'Of course.' She nodded smoothly, smiling reassuringly at the children. 'When you've finished eating put your plates on the side and then go and wash your faces and hands, so that you don't get sticky fingers all over your daddy's furniture,' she advised ruefully, sure that that wouldn't go down too well at all. The apartment was beautifully furnished and decorated, and expensively so—not at all suitable for young and active children. 'As soon as I've finished talking to your father we'll all wrap up warm and go for a walk—'

'A walk?' Nick Rafferty interrupted incredulously. 'My dear Miss—young woman.' He scowled. 'I'm sure it can't have escaped your notice; it's been snowing for almost twenty-four hours!'

Of course it hadn't 'escaped her notice'. Silly man, that was the reason she was here. If it hadn't been snowing, Samantha Fairfax's car wouldn't have skidded on the ice and snow and then driven down the side of an embankment. If it hadn't been snowing so heavily then the accident wouldn't have happened that way. Besides, she loved the snow. Always had. At least, she presumed she had...

'Children love to be out in the snow, Mr Rafferty,' she explained over the excited shouts of Jamie, Josh and Lucy.

'Obviously.' He glowered darkly at the din her suggestion had created. 'The sitting-room,' he bit out harshly. 'Now.' He turned on his heel and marched from the room, obviously expecting Bethany to follow him.

She calmed the children and repeated her instructions before following him, frowning a little as she watched him pour himself half a tumblerful of whisky before throwing the fiery liquid to the back of his throat and swallowing it in one gulp. She had tried whisky once; it had made her eyes water, her nose run and her throat burn!

Nick Rafferty turned and saw her watching him, and those dark brows met fiercely again over icy grey eyes.

She moved further into the room, quietly closing the door behind her, noticing with pleasure the empty plate on the table; the whisky shouldn't have too much of an effect when he had eaten first. 'Tell me, Mr Rafferty—' she smiled at him '—do you have a dog?'

He looked taken aback by the question, as if it was the last thing he had expected her to say. Which it probably was... 'A dog?' he repeated blankly. 'No, of course I don't have a dog,' he snapped. 'What would I do with a dog up here?'

'A cat, then?' she suggested smoothly.

'A cat would be no more happy in a penthouse apartment than a dog would,' he dismissed impatiently. 'Why do you ask?' He looked at her warily.

Bethany gave a dismissive shrug, her expression bland. 'You seem to be in the habit of issuing orders without the customary "please" and "thank you". I could only assume that came from dealing with a pet,' she explained evenly, tidying his cup and saucer and plate into a neat pile.

Grey eyes narrowed to steely slits as he watched

her economy of movement. 'Point taken, Beth,' he finally rasped abruptly. 'I apologise for my lack of ''customary'' politeness,' his voice grated harshly, as if it weren't 'customary' for him to apologise for his behaviour too often either.

Probably not because it wasn't ever applicable, Bethany decided as she met his gaze unwaveringly, more likely a case of him just not being a man who usually felt the need to apologise for anything.

'But it must be apparent to you that this situation isn't ''customary'' either!' He ran an agitated hand through his already ruffled hair. 'Robert dumped the children on me last night, their mother is critically ill in hospital, Christmas is only two days away and then you turn up here claiming to be an angel!' He shook his head, staring down at the bottom of his empty whisky glass. 'Is it any wonder I felt the need of a drink?' he muttered, almost to himself. 'But to answer your initial question.' He straightened. 'No, I don't have a dog any longer. I did have. It died five years ago.'

Bethany watched him as he paced the carpeted floor. He was such a man alone. He had three children, was obviously rich, and yet he seemed such a solitary figure—as if part of him was missing. It must be through choice, Bethany decided. A man of his means, a man with his handsome good looks, could have had such a different sort of life. She wondered why he didn't...

'How sad,' she sympathised. The undemanding love of a pet might have softened him slightly, might have removed those lines of cynicism from the ruggedly handsome face.

'Very,' he acknowledged harshly. 'It was the day

my ex-wife decided she couldn't stand the sight of me!' he added self-disgustedly.

Bethany gasped at his vehemence. Samantha Fairfax was obviously a lovely woman; she had to be to have evoked such love in two such powerfully attractive men as Nick Rafferty and Robert Fairfax. And then there were the children—sweet, adorable children, with a well-balanced outlook towards life and their own family situation, which meant that Samantha Fairfax was a good mother too. And yet she now hated this man she must once have loved...

Nick's mouth twisted self-derisively as he saw Bethany's shocked expression. 'Someone else died that day five years ago, Beth.' He spoke aggressively, the words seeming to be dragged out of him, as if he didn't really want to talk about it even now.

And yet, Bethany could see, something compelled him to do so. Probably the shock of Samantha Fairfax's accident; tragedies of that kind tended to bring to the fore the past regrets of the people around them. And Nick Rafferty was obviously no exception; his strain was evident from the lines about his eyes and the grimly set mouth. He was a man in emotional torment. And not in the least happy about it!

Nick drew in a ragged breath. 'It was a young woman,' he stated abruptly. 'She was coming to the house to be nanny to the children. It was my fault,' he added, looking at her with hard challenge.

Bethany returned his gaze with dawning comprehension, at last beginning to understand exactly what she was doing here. She had believed she was here for the children, but, apart from being concerned about their mother, they were well-adjusted children obviously being brought up in a loving, caring family. And the marriage of Robert and Samantha Fairfax, judging by Robert's concerned behaviour towards his wife, was a deep and loving one.

No, it was becoming more and more apparent to her that Nick Rafferty was the real reason she was here.

Someone had slipped up very badly this time; if she had failed on her other assignments, how on earth did they expect her to succeed with a man as hardened to all human warmth—let alone a heavenly one!—as Nicholas Rafferty?

CHAPTER FOUR

NICK poured himself another drink, lost in the dark thoughts of a time long gone, only dragged back to the present when he sensed that Beth was quietly watching him. There was such a stillness about this young woman—almost unnerving.

He mentally shook himself. 'You see, I didn't want Samantha to have a nanny for the children,' he explained hardily. 'She had never felt the need before, when we just had the two boys. But she claimed she wouldn't be able to cope with everything that needed to be done once the new baby was born—'

'Lucy?' Beth put in softly.

'Lucy,' he acknowledged harshly, scowling darkly as he thought back to the time when Lucy had been born. 'The two boys were going to be palmed off on some stranger now that Samantha was to have the daughter she had always craved. At least, that's the way I saw it at the time.' He shook his head self-disgustedly. 'I've had plenty of time to reflect on my attitude the last five years.'

He grimaced. 'Even more so during the last twenty-four hours; if I'm finding it difficult to cope with an eleven, eight and a five-year-old, how the hell did I expect Samantha to cope with a new baby and two active boys of six and three? Samantha had a rough time of it when Lucy was born, and was told she could probably never have any more children.'

But Samantha was expecting another baby now, he realised, and this young woman had known about it! And here he was pouring his whole damn life story out to her, a complete stranger, who had just walked in off the street into their lives. He, who rarely told people even his name if he could avoid it—the name Rafferty was synonymous with the wealth and power he had built up over the years. And he was talking to this young woman, Beth, about things he had tried not even to think about the last five years, let alone talk about. He was losing his mind!

He straightened. 'Robert says that Samantha is off the danger list, but that there are still some fears for the baby.' He looked at the woman challengingly. 'So now I want to know who you are, where you came from—and how the hell you know so damn much about my family!'

Never mind the fact that he had been in the process himself of telling her totally private things about his own life; there was something not quite right about this situation. And he wanted to know exactly what it was. He certainly didn't buy the 'angel' story!

But she looked so damned angelic, he acknowledged impatiently, sitting there on the edge of the armchair, her hands neatly folded together, green eyes looking up at him so candidly.

'And don't give me that story about angels again,' he rasped impatiently. 'It may have impressed the children, but I'm way past believing in Father Christmas, the Tooth Fairy—and angels!'

'How sad,' she said again, looking as genuinely concerned as she had when he'd told her about the death of his dog. The reason for that was quickly explained! 'Did you know that an angel falls to earth every time someone makes that state-ment—?'

'I did,' Josh put in eagerly as the three children passed through the room on their way to get their coats. 'I saw this film once where—'

'I don't believe the remark was directed at you, Josh.' Nick spoke sternly to his youngest son.

'Sorry,' Josh returned brightly, completely un-deterred. 'Will we be going out soon, Beth?' His young face was alight with excitement. 'I haven't got my sledge here with me, but I suppose we could—'

'Josh!' Nick thundered impatiently. 'None of you are going anywhere, with or without a sledge, until Miss—Beth and I have finished our conversation. So the sooner the three of you leave the room, the sooner we can do exactly that,' he added as Josh looked ready to come back with yet another retort.

He watched with raised brows as the three chil-dren filed off, their expressions disappointed, into the bedrooms they had been allocated for their stay, knowing that he had once again made himself un-popular. Oh, well, it was far from the first time, he acknowledged ruefully.

He turned back to Beth as soon as they were alone again. 'And the first thing we have to get straight is that if you do stay on here to look after the children, I do not want you adding to this non-sense about angels. As far as I can tell, Jamie and Josh seem to have filled their heads with rubbish they've seen on one television programme or another, and an adult adding to that is unacceptable.'

He shook his head disgustedly, knowing that he was probably only impatient with the situation because he knew he should have played a more active role in the boys' lives these last few years than he had. 'So any further talk about angels and— What's this?' He frowned as Beth held out a card she seemed to have produced from one of the pockets in her denims—denims which clung to the shapely bottom he had taken such an interest in earlier.

He took the card from her hand, looking down at it uncomprehendingly. It read simply 'Heavenly Angels', with an accompanying telephone number underneath. What the hell—?

'Mr Fairfax was the one to ask for help, Mr Rafferty,' the young woman supplied. 'He was worried about his wife and the children, and obviously yourself, and he called Heavenly Angels for help—'

'You're an agency,' Nick suddenly realised with satisfaction, his expression lightening as he tapped the card in his hand. 'An agency sent you,' he added with some relief. Somehow, he realised, amongst all the other worries that had beset him the last twenty-four hours, Robert had found the time to contact an agency to get someone to come and help him with the children.

He wasn't losing his mind after all. He had known there had to be some sensible explanation for this situation. Good God—angels! Ridiculous!

CHAPTER FIVE

BETHANY watched him as the differing emotions flickered across his face. She had seen the self-doubt, the puzzlement, then the relief as he'd read the card she had given him. And then she saw the self-derision.

She couldn't in any way blame him for his disbelief. It was universal. Besides, she didn't think she was here to bring back his belief in Father Christmas or the Tooth Fairy—or to convince him of the existence of angels. She wasn't one hundred per cent sure why she was here yet, but she did know that it concerned this tall, cynical man before her.

'If you would care to call the telephone number on the card, Mr Rafferty,' she advised softly, 'Mrs Heavenly will be only too happy to confirm my presence here.' It was the usual practice, and seemed to satisfy most people.

Although Nick Rafferty, she acknowledged wryly, wasn't 'most people'... But he was distracted at the moment, had so many other things on his mind, and gave the impression that he just wanted to get some normality and order back into his life. And having someone to look after the children for him was sure to help with that.

'Mrs Heavenly...' he repeated with some relief. 'Hence the name Heavenly Angels?'

Not quite, but... 'Of course,' Bethany confirmed lightly.

He arched dark brows as he looked down at the card again. 'And Robert hired you, you say?' he murmured thoughtfully.

'Robert Fairfax is the name of the person who required our services, yes,' she answered with great care. After all, she wasn't in the business of telling outright lies, only prevaricating with the truth; there had been no formal call from Robert Fairfax, only a heartfelt plea for help. And that was something she was in the business of dealing with—not very successfully to date, she admitted, but maybe this time it would be different... 'If you would just like to make the call, Mr Rafferty?'

'Nick,' he put in abruptly, although he was obviously mellowing a little.

Probably because he could now see the possibility of lightening his own load as well as Robert's by accepting this unexpected offer of help with the children!

Bethany nodded acceptance of this concession. 'I'll just go and check on the children while you make the call.'

She had noticed they seemed to have gone very quiet since going to their bedrooms—and she quickly realised the reason for that as she approached the door, hearing a faint scuffling noise on the other side of it; the children had been listening to her conversation with their father.

It was naughty of them, but she could understand only too well their concern; they were wondering if the 'angel' was to stay or to be despatched back to where she had come from. But if that were to happen—and she sincerely hoped that it wouldn't—then she had no doubt that someone else would be sent in her place. This family needed help.

She hoped it wouldn't be the case; she wanted to stay herself—she liked the children, felt an affinity with Nick Rafferty that she couldn't altogether explain. Perhaps it was because she felt that his harsh cynicism hid pain he hadn't shared with anyone else. Or perhaps it was that she wanted to help him show his love for his children. Or perhaps it was just that she liked Nick Rafferty...

The children were looking very busy by the time Beth managed to locate their bedrooms, their expressions angelically innocent as they turned to look at her. Bethany laughed softly at her own thoughts. These three weren't angels—but they were innocents. Which was exactly as it should be.

'Ready?' she enquired brightly.

'Is it all settled? Are you staying?' Jamie, the oldest and more reserved of the three children, looked at her expectantly.

Bethany's heart went out to him. He was so much like his father to look at, and, being the eldest, the break-up of his parents' marriage must have affected him the most. 'I think your father may be sorting out the details with my—superior, right now,' she answered dismissively. 'We'll just wait and see, shall we?'

'Can we still go and play in the snow?' Josh frowned, this immediate matter of much more interest to him than any long-range 'details'.

'I should think so.' She ruffled the darkness of his hair playfully, sure that during his telephone call to the 'agency' Nick Rafferty would receive all the assurances he needed to allow her to stay on here. 'Are you all ready?' They certainly looked it, with their thick coats, bobble hats and gloves. 'Come on, let's go and see what your father has to say.'

She didn't feel she was being unfair to Nick Rafferty by having the children on her side in this way, and really was convinced that Mrs Heavenly would give him all the confidence in her ability that he required.

She only hoped she lived up to Mrs Heavenly's expectations!

Three identically angelic faces beneath differing coloured hats looked expectantly at their father once they were in the sitting-room, though Bethany's expression was much less anxious than the childrens'. She was needed here; she became more sure of it with each passing minute.

'Well, it seems Robert did indeed ask for you,' Nick Rafferty reported cheerfully, looking like a man who had just had a great weight lifted off his shoulders. 'Where did the four of you intend going to play in the snow?'

'One of the parks should do,' Bethany replied as she pulled on her own jacket, freeing the fiery length of her hair from her collar.

Nick Rafferty was watching her admiringly; now that the immediate responsibility for the children had been lifted his masculine instincts seemed to have returned to the situation—and from the expression on his face he was seeing her as a rather attractive female!

It wouldn't do, of course, Bethany ruefully acknowledged. It wasn't her that Nick Rafferty was supposed to take an interest in. She had a feeling that his interest was to be directed towards the children, and also to adding some purpose to his life. Financial success alone—of which, judging by these sumptuous surroundings, he appeared to have plenty—couldn't be enough. But she, personally, wouldn't be the one to enrich his life. That certainly couldn't be allowed. She was here only temporarily, would be moved on to another assignment once this one was completed satisfactorily.

Why did she suddenly feel so saddened at that prospect...?

'We can get public transport back, if you could just drop us off?' Her voice was sharper than normal, and she was inwardly annoyed with herself because of that. She was here to help these people, yes, but she couldn't become emotionally involved with them—or they with her. That would just make the situation worse, not better!

That brief recognition of her as an attractive woman had gone from Nick Rafferty's face now, and he began to scowl. 'What do you mean, drop you off? Can't you drive?' He sounded incredulous at the very idea.

She wasn't sure; she had never tried. But she certainly didn't have the necessary licence or the appropriate paperwork, that she did know; how could she, when she didn't exist?

'Come and play snowballs with us, Daddy Nick.' Lucy grasped his arm, pulling on it imploringly.

Bethany almost laughed at his dazed expression; obviously throwing snowballs wasn't on Nick's list of priorities at the moment. Perhaps it never had been. Maybe Lucy had had a good idea after all...

'I—' He broke off as the telephone began to ring,

looking relieved at the interruption. 'I have to get that, Lucy.' He extricated himself from her clinging fingers, picking up the receiver.

'Lisa!' He had instantly recognised his caller. 'Yes, I— No, I— But— Will you just shut up for a minute and listen, woman?' His initial placatory tone had quickly turned to anger; he was scowling darkly now. 'Just hang on a minute, Lisa,' he coldly instructed the woman on the telephone, putting down the receiver to reach into the pocket of his jacket and pull out a wad of notes.

'Take a taxi to wherever you want to go,' he told Bethany distractedly as he handed her several of the twenty-pound notes. 'And you had better take a key, just so that you can let yourself in if I'm not home when you get back.' He handed over the key too. 'Have a good time,' he added dismissively, returning to his telephone call without giving them a second glance.

Bethany didn't move, looking at him wordlessly for several seconds, frowning herself now.

Nick continued his conversation, coldly clipped now, until he suddenly became aware of Bethany's stare, and there was an irritated expression on his face as he put his hand over the receiver. 'Yes?'

She raised auburn brows at his terseness. 'Say goodbye to your father, children.' She took the opportunity to pocket the money and the key as the children took it in turns to kiss their surprised father briefly on the cheek—almost as if it weren't a regular occurrence, she realised. Maybe it wasn't?

She noticed that Nick looked even more uncomfortable when it came to Lucy's kiss, and the little girl threw her arms about his neck to hug him for good measure.

'Thank you for giving us the angel, Daddy Nick.' Lucy grinned up at him.

'You're welcome,' he answered shortly, moving abruptly away.

Thankfully the little girl looked completely unperturbed by her father's distant behaviour, but Bethany was still frowning as they left.

And not, she realised, just because of Nick's reaction to Lucy's show of affection. Who was Lisa? And why should she care...?

CHAPTER SIX

WHAT a day, Nick inwardly groaned as he made his way up to the apartment. The children. An angel. Lisa. Good God, Lisa! He had never realised, until an hour ago, what a temper the woman had.

Talking on the telephone earlier had been far from satisfactory, and so, with the children out, he had agreed to meet Lisa for an early dinner. Dinner? They hadn't got past the drinks stage! Lisa hadn't believed a word he'd had to say about Samantha and the accident, how he had the children to take care of over Christmas—and she certainly hadn't been interested in hearing about the 'angel of mercy', as Lisa had so scathingly called Beth. Maybe it hadn't helped the situation that he had smiled at that particular analogy, but in the circumstances he hadn't been able to help himself.

It was at about that time that Lisa had decided her drink would look much better over him than in her glass. About the same time as he lost all patience with her ridiculous accusations that he had obviously become involved with someone new and had decided to go skiing with this 'someone new' instead of her. About the same time as he had got up and left...

He doubted he would see the lovely Lisa again. Strange, but until today he had found her good company, very accomodating, both in and out of bed. He had even started to think along the lines of

137

a possible marriage. Lisa had suited his lifestyle, was beautiful to look at, an accomplished hostess, satisfied him in bed—what more could he ask for in a wife?

Love.

Where the hell had that come from? He scowled as he put the key in the lock of his apartment, as quickly dismissing the thought as he prepared himself to face the chaos that had existed in his previously ordered home since the children had invaded it.

Silence. Peace. No children fighting. No noise of the television. Just a soft murmur of voices as he approached the sitting-room.

'Hi, Dad,' Jamie greeted him as he entered the room, looking up from the game of Scrabble he and Josh were playing on the coffee-table. 'Beth is just putting Lucy to bed,' he added before going back to his game. 'Your turn, Josh,' he prompted evenly, once he had taken his own turn.

'Hi, Dad,' Josh greeted him, as calmly, before concentrating on the letters in front of him.

Nick walked over to join them, looking down at the two bent heads before slowly sitting down in the armchair nearest them, continuing to watch them for several minutes. They were miniature versions of himself, dark-haired, grey-eyed. It was only Lucy who—

'I called the hospital before I went out earlier,' he told his sons abruptly. 'Your mother is still doing very well.' He hadn't managed to talk to Robert, but the nurse in charge had assured him that 'Mrs Fairfax is making a miraculous recovery', and that she might even be able to see the children for a short time tomorrow, if her recovery continued as rapidly. Although Nick didn't intend telling them that just yet, thought it better to wait. There had been no mention of the baby either, and he hadn't liked to ask, was sure that Robert would get back to him personally on that once he had some news.

'We know,' Jamie informed him now. 'Beth rang the hospital when we got in. They said we might be able to go in and see Mum tomorrow,' he added excitedly.

'Beth rang the hospital when we got in...'

'Did you enjoy your snowballing earlier?' Nick lingered to ask.

'It was great!' Josh's face lit up. 'Beth showed us how to make snow angels. Do you know how to make snow angels, Dad? It's quite easy, you just lie down in the snow and—'

'Josh,' Jamie cut in warningly. 'Remember what Beth said about letting Dad relax when he came in.'

Josh looked sheepish. 'Sorry, Dad.'

Nick shook his head, standing up. Angels again—this time snow angels! 'I'll just go and change.' He ruffled Josh's hair, frowning as he realised it was damp. 'I think you should have dried off earlier when you got in from snowballing; your hair is still wet.' The last thing he needed was the lot of them coming down with a cold.

'Oh, that isn't from snowballing,' Josh told him dismissively. 'Beth gave us all a bath when we got in.'

'Before she gave us our tea,' Jamie added happily.

'Yours is being cooked in the oven,' Josh put in with satisfaction.

Beth had showed them how to make snow angels. Beth had rung the hospital. Beth had given them all a bath. Beth had cooked them tea. Beth was now putting Lucy to bed. Beth had obviously managed to achieve the impossible where Jamie and Josh were concerned—to stop them fighting each other. Beth had a meal warm in the oven... What the hell else had Beth done while he had been out?

And why was he so damned mad at her efficiency? Probably because it threw into sharp contrast his own efforts of yesterday, he acknowledged ruefully as he went through to his bedroom to change out of his suit and formal shirt.

He had to pass Lucy's bedroom on his way to his own room, and he couldn't resist glancing in at the open doorway as he walked by. Lucy lay in one of the single beds, listening with rapt attention to the story that Beth was relating to her. Not from a book, but obviously straight from her own imagination. About an angel on top of a Christmas tree...

Damned angels again—

'Daddy Nick!' Lucy cried happily as she spotted him in the doorway, holding out her arms for him to join them.

He had never been able to understand why Lucy showed such affection to him, in spite of all his efforts that she should do otherwise. Samantha hadn't even been living with him when Lucy was born, and Nick had had very little contact with any of the children during the next five years. And yet

Lucy persisted in showering him with innocent affection every time she did see him.

Beth stood up, and he thought again how beautiful she was. So tiny, and yet perfectly proportioned, those small breasts pert beneath the green of her jumper, her hair gloriously long and luxurious, making him want to entangle his fingers in it and—

'Have I usurped your place?' she asked pleasantly. 'I wasn't sure what time you would be returning, so I thought it best to put Lucy to bed and tell her a story,' she explained. 'But if you would—'

'No, no, you carry on,' Nick assured her quickly, his wandering thoughts on Beth's feminine attributes dying a sudden death as he took a step backwards; he had never read Lucy a bedtime story in her life. And he wasn't about to start now! 'I have to go and change,' he added hastily, before Lucy could add her pleas to the argument that he could see she was about to make.

'Your dinner—'

'Is in the oven,' he finished drily, smiling ruefully. 'The boys already told me.' He nodded.

She smiled. 'I hope you like lamb.'

It was one of his favourite meats. But he knew there hadn't been any in the refrigerator, so where the hell had she got lamb from in amongst all the other things she seemed to have managed to achieve this afternoon? Oh, God, he gave up where the enigma of this young lady was concerned; he would just have to accept that she was efficiency itself.

He certainly wasn't about to accept any other explanation!

CHAPTER SEVEN

BETHANY moved quickly about the kitchen; the vegetables were slowly cooking, the meat was ready for serving, the table was already laid. All she needed now was Nick Rafferty to come and eat.

She had spent a wonderful couple of hours playing with the children in the snow; their faces had been glowing by the time they had all returned home, and the good news about their mother had added to their happiness. All in all it had been a successful day. She hoped it continued that way.

'The boys appear to be clearing away in preparation for going to bed.' A puzzled Nick entered the kitchen.

She had been instantly aware of him when he'd returned to the apartment, had heard him talking to the boys before he'd joined her in Lucy's room on his way to change. But, even so, she hadn't been quite prepared for how handsome he now looked.

So far she had only seen him in business clothes, but he had changed into close-fitting black trousers and a pale blue shirt, the latter giving his eyes the appearance of being the same colour. He looked very attractive, totally male. And Bethany wasn't supposed to think of him as such!

'They need an early night.' She nodded abruptly, turning back to the food she was cooking. 'Apparently they were rather late last night—probably due to the unusual circumstances,' she excused lightly.

'And they've had an exciting afternoon too. Besides, tomorrow is going to be a busy day—'

'I wasn't criticising, Beth,' Nick cut in softly. 'Merely congratulating you on your ability to get them to go to bed without the usual arguments. I— What's happening tomorrow?' He frowned as he suddenly realised what she had said.

'Well, there are the presents to get, the tree to buy and put up, the food for Christmas to—'

'Hold it.' He held up a silencing hand. 'Robert told me where to collect the presents from his house, but as for the rest of it—I don't usually bother with a tree and things.' He frowned again.

Bethany nodded. 'The children explained that you're usually away at Christmas—'

'I've always thought it better for the children to spend Christmas in a family atmosphere, not to be torn between—'

'Now you've misunderstood, Nick; I wasn't criticising either.' It was the first time she had used his first name, and it sounded huskily intimate. Perhaps she should stick to Mr Rafferty, after all. But that wasn't how she thought of him. She didn't want to delve too deeply into how she *was* starting to think of him! 'But this year is different. And children expect a tree—and things,' she added dismissively.

'Do they?' He looked troubled.

She smiled. 'Didn't you have a Christmas tree when you were a child?'

'I suppose I did.' He sighed. 'I just didn't think... And food, you say?'

'A turkey and the trimmings.' She nodded. 'And a cake. All the usual Christmas fayre.' Although she had a feeling that this man hadn't been involved with 'the usual Christmas fayre' for some time now. Perhaps that was another one of her tasks—to help him see that Christmas wasn't about being on a ski-slope in some fashionable part of the world but about being with the people you loved, in this case his children. All three of them.

Nick still looked perturbed. 'Will you be able to get all those things at such short notice? Don't you have to order the turkey? And the trimmings?' He grimaced.

'We can get them,' Bethany assured him; somewhere in the depths of his memory he obviously remembered that his wife had dealt with these things. It was a start, at least. 'No doubt the children will enjoy being involved in the choosing of them,' she added—before he could suggest ordering Christmas just to be delivered from some exclusive store.

No doubt a man of his obvious means could afford to do that; she would just rather he didn't. It was too impersonal that way—rather like the way this man ran the rest of his life! 'And it will be great fun tomorrow evening, when we all decorate the tree together.' She almost laughed at the look of consternation on his face now. It must be years since Nick had been involved in such a mundane task—if he ever had.

'If you think so,' he finally conceded, with obvious reluctance. 'It's the kids' happiness we have to think about, I suppose.'

'Exactly,' Bethany agreed brightly. 'Now, if you would like to sit down—' she indicated the small table she had laid at one end of the large kitchen '—our dinner is ready now.'

He hesitated momentarily on his way to the table, looking across at her. 'I thought you had eaten earlier with the children...?'

She smiled. 'Fish fingers may be their favourite, but they aren't mine!'

His stern features relaxed into a smile—his first as far as Bethany could remember. And what a difference it made. His face came alive with humour, laughter lines appeared beside his eyes and mouth. 'Mine either,' he agreed ruefully, sitting down at one of the two placcs Bethany had laid at the table. 'Is there anything I can do to help?'

'No, I— Hello, you two,' she greeted Jamie and Josh as they came into the room dressed in their pyjamas. 'All ready?'

Jamie nodded. 'I checked on Lucy when we went through to get changed; she's fast asleep.'

'Good.' Bethany smiled her satisfaction. 'Would you like to take the boys through, or shall I?' She looked enquiringly at Nick.

'I'll take them.' He stood up abruptly. 'While you continue to deal with the meal.'

Bethany watched him leave with the boys, two carbon copies of himself. His relationship with Jamie and Josh, although a little awkward on occasion on Nick's part, she had noticed, seemed quite strong. It was only with Lucy that Nick's barriers came up. Of course, Lucy hadn't even been born when her parents had separated, and therefore the bond between father and daughter couldn't have been formed as strongly as it already had been between Nick and the boys. Although Lucy didn't seem to feel the same constraint where her father was concerned...

There was still so many questions about this family that remained unanswered. Hopefully, she would be here long enough to answer some of them...

'This is good,' Nick told her after several mouthfuls of the meal.

Bethany smiled her pleasure at his praise. 'I'm glad you like it.'

He relaxed back in his chair. 'God, this is peaceful!' He drew in a thankful breath. 'Would you join me in a glass of wine?'

'That would be nice,' Bethany accepted, sitting back to watch as he deftly opened the bottle of red wine before pouring a glass for each of them.

'Cheers!' Nick smiled at her warmly.

He was obviously a lot happier than he had been when she'd arrived here this afternoon, and as far as Bethany was concerned that could only be a good thing.

'*Salut!*' she returned. 'Mmm, lovely wine.' She could feel the heat in her veins after her initial sips of the wine.

'I'm glad you like it,' he said with genuine pleasure. 'It goes very well with this excellent meal you've prepared for us.'

Bethany laughed softly, her cheeks glowing. 'We sound like a mutual admiration society!'

Nick looked startled for a moment, and then he relaxed, grinning. 'So we do.' He leant his elbows on the table, sipping his wine. 'I was supposed to be out for dinner this evening,' he mused.

'I know.' She nodded.

'And then I would have missed this excellent—

What do you mean, you know?' He looked at her sharply.

She shrugged. 'It wasn't too difficult to guess; it was rather late for you to be working at the office.'

'It has been known,' he put in drily.

Bethany was sure it had—had a feeling that this man used work to fill a lot of his life. Besides, he was very successful, and he couldn't have become that way without putting a lot of effort into it.

'Not so close to Christmas,' she dismissed lightly.

'Straight through Christmas one year—but that's another story!' He frowned. 'I've forgotten what the initial question was now. I don't... I know!' His brow cleared. 'We were discussing—'

'Where I'm to sleep tonight,' Bethany put in easily, changing the subject from his interest in how she had known he would be home for dinner this evening, after all.

It had the desired effect; Nick looked totally stunned by the question. Obviously it hadn't even occurred to him, until this moment, to wonder where she was to spend the night.

CHAPTER EIGHT

NICK hadn't given a thought as to where Beth would be sleeping! He had been so relieved to have someone here to help him with the children that he just hadn't thought beyond that. He supposed if he had thought about it at all he had assumed Beth would be staying on here, with the children. But then that begged the question of where she was going to sleep; there were only three bedrooms. Of course, he had a big double bed in his room...

'I did think I could sleep in the second single bed in Lucy's room.' Beth questioningly interrupted his wandering thoughts.

It was an infinitely better idea than the one that had started to go through his own mind! From a practical point of view. Privately, he didn't think he would have any objection at all to this beautiful young woman sharing his bed. But it was probably a complication he didn't really need at the moment...

'If that suits you.' Nick nodded abruptly. 'Obviously I would prefer it if you could sleep here, and so be on hand for the children in the morning.' Breakfast this morning had been absolute chaos—which was probably the reason he had chosen to forget about lunch! 'That way you can make an early start on the other things you say need to be done.' The thought of all that shopping, and on Christmas Eve of all days, sent shivers down his spine! Luckily Beth seemed to have no such qualms...

'You don't have to convince me of the sensibility of my staying on here,' Beth assured him lightly. 'I'm quite happy to do so.'

He nodded abruptly, topping up their wine glasses. 'I'll collect the childrens' presents from the house.'

'And I'll do all the other shopping,' she agreed. 'We have to give the children Christmas, despite the circumstances.'

Nick agreed with her, although he admitted that it was going to be easier if he had someone— Beth!—to help him get through it. 'I've been giving some thought to taking the children to see Sam tomorrow,' he said slowly.

Beth looked at him interestedly. 'Yes?'

He grimaced. 'Sam and I— We haven't been very good friends in recent years—'

'Near tragedy has a way of nullifying things like that,' Beth cut in, touching his hand sympathetically. 'I'm sure it's the very last thing on Mrs Fairfax's mind,' she added ruefully.

'Exactly,' he agreed thankfully. 'And seeing me at the moment is only likely to bring back unhappy memories. Everyone agrees Sam is making a wonderful recovery.' God, it was years since he had called her Sam; he had lapsed into the more formal Samantha after their separation. 'I don't want to do anything—like turning up with the kids!—to upset that.' He looked at Beth searchingly. 'I wondered if you would take the children to see their mother?'

She returned his gaze unwaveringly. 'If you think

that would be the thing to do,' she finally said
slowly

Nick felt irritated—and he knew it was because
he suspected this young lady wasn't altogether convinced that his reason for not visiting Sam was a
valid one. But Beth would only have to see himself
and Sam in the same room together to realise that
their antagonism towards each other was only too
real! He and Sam hadn't exchanged more than half
a dozen polite words with each other in the last five
years!

Beth was still watching him with those calm
green eyes of hers. She really *didn't* believe that his
suggestion would be the best thing all round!

He stood up abruptly, picking up his wine glass
in preparation for leaving. 'Believe me, Beth,' he
rasped, 'I'm the last person Sam would want to see
just now.' It was too much like last time—Sam
pregnant, with a baby she desperately wanted to
keep.

'Nick...?'

Beth's soft query halted him at the kitchen doorway, and he turned slowly to look at her, his expression grim. 'Yes?' he bit out harshly.

A delicate frown marred her creamy forehead.
'Would you like to talk about the antagonism between yourself and Mrs Fairfax?' she prompted
gently.

His mouth twisted. 'Only if you have a couple
of hours to spare!'

Beth shrugged. 'I don't have anything else to do.'

That wasn't what he'd wanted to hear. The friction between himself and Sam had been going on
for so long now— But hadn't he decided, when

Sam's life had been in danger, that all that had to stop? Maybe Beth could give him a female point of view on exactly how he could approach doing that?

'I'll help you clear away first.' He finally nodded. 'Then you can sit and be bored for a while!' He grimaced.

'I won't be bored,' Beth assured him as she stood up to start clearing the table.

Nick looked at her wordlessly for several seconds. No, he had a feeling that this young woman, with her candid green eyes and gentle smile, wouldn't be bored at all. But he knew he wasn't going to find it an easy subject to talk about. It was something he had avoided doing for the last five years—a subject, he realised with bewildered surprise, that still caused him pain.

'A brandy?' he offered once they had gone through to the sitting-room. The rest of the apartment was quiet, all the children asleep now, Beth had assured him after checking on them. He wasn't quite sure how she had created calm out of chaos—he just hoped that it continued!

'I'll join you if you would like one,' Beth accepted, obviously realising that he was in need of one!

It wasn't easy finding the words to talk of that time five years ago, to tell of the pain of betrayal he had felt when Sam had told him she was in love with Robert, his best friend, and, even worse, that Robert loved her in return, and that they wanted to be together. And yet as he told Beth of that time he had a feeling she already knew about that, that she knew there was more. And there was. The last final blow that he had never quite recovered from. The final act of betrayal. And there was only one way to say that!

'Lucy isn't mine!' he finally blurted out.

Instead of the shocked sympathy he had been expecting, Beth continued to look at him with those calm green eyes.

'Did you hear what I said?' he rasped with bitterness, his jaw clenched, his hand gripping his brandy glass so tightly it was in danger of shattering.

'Yes,' she replied softly, her own brandy remaining untouched in the glass. 'But you're wrong. Of course Lucy is your daughter—'

'And what the hell do you know about it?' Nick cut in harshly. 'And don't give me that ''angel'' rubbish again; the kids may be intrigued by it, but I'm not! You don't know anything about what happened five years ago. You weren't there, so how could you?' he added accusingly.

'Nick—'

'Lucy isn't mine, Beth,' he repeated gratingly.

She shook her head. 'I realise she has a different colouring from the boys, but—'

'She has a different colouring because she has a different father!' Nick exploded. 'Oh, Sam tried to tell me otherwise, but it doesn't take too much intelligence to realise that Lucy is Robert's child!' He threw his brandy to the back of his throat, slamming the glass down on the coffee-table. This time it did break, the glass shattering all over the table and the carpeted floor.

'Leave it!' he instructed harshly as Beth made a move to pick up the ragged pieces. 'I said, leave it!' he repeated furiously as she stood up. 'Perhaps it's time we tested this "angel" theory,' he muttered coldly, even as he pulled her purposefully into his arms. 'Are angels allowed to kiss human beings?' he challenged scornfully.

Beth looked up at him unflinchingly. 'I've kissed Lucy,' she pointed out softly.

It was hardly the thing to say to appease his rapidly rising temper, and without further prevarication his mouth came down crushingly on hers.

CHAPTER NINE

BETHANY had had no idea, until that moment, whether angels were allowed to kiss human beings of Nick Rafferty's kind or whether she would disappear in a puff of smoke, never to see this man or his children again.

But nothing like that happened. Nick's mouth was savage against hers as he demanded a response from her, and she was unable to deny that there was one, melting into the hardness of his body, returning his kiss with a passion that matched his own, his mouth not crushing hers now, but sipping and tasting, drawing every last ounce of pleasure from the caress.

He finally raised his head to gasp, 'God almighty, Beth!' His eyes were dark with pain, his hair as dishevelled as the first time Bethany had seen him—but this time it was from her own restlessly caressing fingers! 'Who the hell are you?' he groaned, his arms like steel bands as he held the slim length of her against his hardness.

She couldn't think straight, was dazed by the power of the desire that had exploded so suddenly between the two of them.

Nick shook his head to clear his own desire-filled brain. 'I don't think you're an angel at all, more like a dev—' He broke off abruptly as the doorbell rang, frowning darkly. 'What the hell—!' He re-

leased Bethany abruptly. 'It's ten-thirty at night!'
He scowled.

She knew what time of night it was—it was
about the only thing she did know! She had never
before been kissed in the way Nick Rafferty had
just kissed her—at least, she didn't think she had...

It had been the most amazing feeling being in his
arms, as if, having been in the wrong place at the
wrong time all of her life, she had suddenly found
where she did belong—in Nick Rafferty's arms.
Which was ridiculous. She didn't belong anywhere
any more, was merely here to unravel a complicated
situation. She had a feeling she might just have
made things worse. As usual. Only this time she
really *had* made things worse. There was going to
be no forgiving or second chances on this one!

'I should answer that, if I were you,' she advised
Nick shakily as the doorbell rang a second time. 'It
may be Mr Fairfax with news—' He didn't need
any more telling, hurrying to answer the door.

The glamorous blonde standing on the doorstep
definitely wasn't Robert Fairfax!

'Lisa!' Nick greeted her, stepping back slightly
in surprise.

Definitely not Robert Fairfax!

However, it *was* the woman of the telephone call
earlier today. The woman Nick should have had
dinner with this evening. The woman currently in
his life. The woman he should have been kissing
just now instead of her...!

And Bethany being here wasn't going to help
whatever friction seemed to have arisen between
Nick and the lovely Lisa!

Bethany took the opportunity of Nick's back being towards her, and so effectively blocking her from the view of the other woman, to escape from the room and go to the bedroom she was to share with Lucy.

But long after she lay down in the bed her eyes remained open, staring up at the ceiling. Could angels fall in love? Because she was very much afraid she had really done it this time; she had fallen in love with the very man she had been sent here to help! Was this what was meant by a fallen angel? If it was, she was very much fallen—had fallen deeply in love with Nick Rafferty.

She couldn't stay here, of course, would have to leave—

'Beth?'

She turned to look at the little girl in the bed a short distance from her own; she had left a light on so that Lucy wouldn't be troubled by the darkness. 'Yes, darling?' she returned softly.

Lucy gave her a sleepy smile. 'I'm very glad you're here,' she murmured, before turning over and going back to sleep.

She had been being selfish a few minutes ago; of course she couldn't leave here. The children needed her. Her feelings for Nick Rafferty couldn't be lasting ones. As his attraction towards her couldn't be either.

The fact that he had already left for the office—or with the lovely Lisa the night before!—when she got up with the children the next morning seemed to indicate that he had already dismissed it. It would hurt for a while, Bethany was sure, but she would get over her latest folly. Angels couldn't be in love!

And she realised, later that day, that Nick couldn't love her either! If she had thought Lisa was beautiful the night before, then Samantha Fairfax was even more so, Bethany discovered that afternoon, when she took the children to the hospital to see their mother.

Samantha Fairfax, once Samantha Rafferty, had been moved from Intensive Care to a private room, and now lay propped up against the pillows, her long black hair cascading about her shoulders, her deep blue eyes lighting up with happiness at the sight of her children. Children it took all of Robert Fairfax's gentle persuasion to stop from throwing themselves at their mother with equal exuberance. With a broken arm and several cracked ribs, plus a recent case of concussion, that was the last thing Samantha Fairfax needed! Although there was no doubting her pleasure in seeing her children again.

They made such a happy family group, Bethany realised wistfully as she stood at the back of the room quietly observing them. Robert Fairfax was as darkly handsome as Nick, but with a much less cynical expression, and love glowing clearly in his eyes every time he looked at his wife—a love that was returned every time Samantha Fairfax gazed back at her husband. Poor Nick. He had been so hurt by the love these two felt towards each other, and yet, seeing Samantha and Robert together, it was obvious it could never have been any other way...

'And you must be the young lady Nick has to take care of the children for me?'

Bethany looked across at Samantha Fairfax as she realised the other woman was talking to her.

'Yes,' she confirmed, moving forward slightly so that she wasn't so much in the shadows at the back of the room. 'And to date they have been little angels.' She ruffled Lucy's hair affectionately as the little girl giggled at the in joke.

'Jamie and Josh too?' their mother questioned teasingly.

'Jamie and Josh too,' Bethany nodded—much to the chagrin of two squirmingly uncomfortable little boys. 'We've been shopping for food today, and a tree and the decorations to go with it, and Jamie and Josh have been most helpful.'

'I'm glad to hear it,' Robert Fairfax put in approvingly.

'That's very good,' Samantha Fairfax agreed distractedly, still looking at Bethany. 'I hope you don't think I'm being rude,' she added slowly, 'but don't I know you?'

'I don't think so,' Bethany said with certainty.

'But I'm sure I— Robert?' She looked up appealingly at her husband.

'We've never met Beth before, darling,' he dismissed easily. 'How could we? She's a friend of Nick's.' And the two families did not meet on a social basis, not any more.

Nick believed she had been sent by Robert, while Robert believed she was a friend of Nick's, just helping out in a difficult situation. It was the way it had to be, of course; neither of them could know the truth. Not that they would believe it anyway. In fact, Nick had already scorned such an idea as an angel!

'Hmm,' Samantha acknowledged frowningly. 'It's just that—you seem familiar, Beth.' She still looked puzzled, as if there was an answer to her confusion that was just beyond her reach.

'The nurse said the children could only stay for five minutes, darling,' her husband smoothly reminded her. 'Beth has to take them home soon.'

'Even the name sounds as if it should— Oh, never mind,' Samantha Fairfax impatiently dismissed the subject from her still slightly befuddled brain. 'I'm very grateful to you, whoever you are. And I'm sure Nick is too,' she added, with dry recognition of her ex-husband's inadequacies.

'Very,' Bethany acknowledged, and the two women shared a smile of understanding.

'We're *both* very grateful to you,' Robert Fairfax assured her as he walked her and the children outside to the waiting taxi. 'I only hope Nick realises what a lucky man he is!'

With the assumption both Robert and Samantha Fairfax had made concerning her relationship with Nick, it was easy to understand what he'd meant by that last remark. She had no idea how Nick thought of her after last night—but she doubted he considered himself a 'lucky man'!

CHAPTER TEN

ANOTHER bloody awful day!

Actually, it had started last night, when Lisa had arrived so unexpectedly at his apartment—only to walk out again minutes later when she saw Beth moving quietly out of the sitting-room to the bed-rooms, her calculating mind adding two and two together and coming up with an answer that had been crude to say the least!

Or had it started before that, when he had kissed Beth...?

God, what had he been doing? The woman was here to help with the kids, and he had repaid her by attempting to seduce her! Although he wasn't too sure the bunch of flowers he held in his hand as a peace offering was such a good idea either... What if she took the gesture the wrong way and thought he was trying another seductive ploy? What if—? Oh, damn it; he had brought the flowers as a peace offering, and she could damn well accept them as such!

She wasn't anywhere in sight to accept anything when he let himself into the apartment. In fact, there was no sign of anyone when he walked into the sitting-room. And after the last couple of days of noise and chaos it was very strange to be met with complete silence, to find himself completely alone. Was this what it was going to be like once the children had gone back to Samantha?

Nick sat down heavily in an armchair, looking about him at the home he had created for himself over the last five years. It was expensively decorated and furnished, unstintingly so, but as he looked at the beautiful objects that adorned his home he could see that that was all they were—objects, beautiful objects, but with no warmth, or caring, or—or laughter. There had been laughter, genuine laughter, in his home yesterday—a warmth that owed much to Beth's presence, he knew. And somehow his ordered existence—completely selfish, he now admitted—no longer had the appeal it had once had. Oh, it was disruptive and noisy having the children here, but at the same time it was real.

And he knew from last night that Beth was very real too...!

'Shall I put those in water for you?'

He turned sharply at the sound of Beth's voice, all his logical reasoning about his behaviour last night disappearing the moment he looked at her again. She was beautiful—the warmth of her hair glowing in those clear green eyes, her smile wide and endearing. Only for him? In a moment of blinding truth, Nick knew that he wanted it to be.

'Nick?' Her smile wavered slightly as she looked at him concernedly.

He didn't like her smile disappearing like that, realised he had been looking forward to seeing this particular smile all day. 'They're for you.' He thrust the red carnations at her, inwardly wincing at how ungracious he sounded, almost as if he half resented giving her the damned flowers. But then, it was a long time since he had actually given any woman flowers; he usually telephoned a florist and had them delivered to the latest woman in his life.

But Beth wasn't like those other women, and his feelings towards her weren't the coldly calculated ones of those other relationships either. He didn't know what they actually were yet, but—

'Thank you.' Beth accepted the flowers much more graciously than he had given them, breathing in their perfume. 'They're beautiful. And the colour is so appropriate to this time of the year. We've bought some lovely red and gold decorations for this room,' she explained at his blank look.

God, it was Christmas Eve! He had been so busy sitting here staring at Beth, like some love-sick teenager, that he had completely forgotten what day it was.

'I collected the childrens' presents,' he told her abruptly, not wanting to think about how it had been to go into the home Sam now shared with Robert, to have to go into their bedroom, to Sam's personal wardrobe, to find those presents. It had been a painful experience, not one he would like to repeat in a hurry. 'They're downstairs in my car; we can get them later, when the children have gone to bed. Talking of the children,' he added sharply, 'where are they?' He looked about pointedly.

Beth smiled. 'They're in their bedrooms, wrapping up your Christmas presents.'

He frowned. 'My Christmas presents?'

She nodded. 'Apparently their mother usually takes them out on Christmas Eve to shop for gifts for you.'

And this year, because Sam couldn't do it, Beth had taken them. With everything else she'd had to do today, she had thought of doing that. Was there no end to this woman's warmth and kindness towards others? He didn't think so—it radiated out of her. And last night he had kissed her, wanted to make love to her. And he wanted the same thing now...

'Beth—'

'Daddy Nick!' Lucy rushed excitedly into the room at that moment, throwing herself into his arms, pressing her flushed cheek against his.

Nick's arms moved about her instinctively as he gathered her close to him. She smelt clean and warm, slightly chocolatey, and looked absolutely adorable as he gazed down at her. Was it possible that he had been wrong all these years—that Lucy was his daughter after all? He had been so angry last night when Beth had insisted that she was, and yet as he looked down into Lucy's guilelessly innocent face, at that endearingly toothless grin and the glowing blue eyes, something shifted inside him, almost like the collapse of an iceberg. Or was it just the melting of ice around his heart...?

He looked at Beth over the top of Lucy's golden curls, feeling the unaccustomed sting of tears in his eyes at her barely perceptible nod at his silent questioning. Lucy was his. He somehow knew it so clearly and he ached with the pain of all the wasted years—years when he should have been Lucy's father, and not the stranger he had tried to make of himself.

'Just Daddy, darling,' he told his daughter gruffly as he gently stroked her silky hair.

'I love you, Daddy.' She snuggled trustingly

against him, instantly accepting this sudden change in him with all the childlike innocence she had.

Nick felt the emotion catch in his throat, knowing he didn't deserve this instant forgiveness for his past coldness but accepting it anyway, almost overwhelmed by the wave of love that swept over him as he held his daughter tightly to him. 'I love you too, Lucy,' he told her huskily.

But as he looked over his daughter's head at the woman who had, in such a short time, melted his heart, he saw that her smile was tinged with wistful sadness. As his sons came bouncing into the room too, he knew that he couldn't ask her why just yet. That it would have to wait until later. Much later. But he would ask her.

And he would try to tell her how he felt about her too.

CHAPTER ELEVEN

As BETHANY watched Nick with his young daughter she knew that her job here was almost over. And in amongst the joy of her knowing that she had at last succeeded in one of her tasks was a deep sadness. Because she would have to leave here now. Quite soon too.

Nick Rafferty was a man who had at last opened his heart to his daughter; he had only to reconcile the situation with his ex-wife and then he could open his heart to a loving relationship. Which meant she would have to leave. Because she loved him herself. And from the look in his eyes a few minutes ago as he had looked at her, she had a feeling he was half in love with her too. And he couldn't be. To love her would only cause him more pain.

But she made an effort to shake off the sadness as quickly as it had arisen, determined that all the family would have a happy Christmas Eve.

They certainly appeared to—the children falling about with hysterical laughter as their father endeavoured to put up the balloons they had spent part of the evening blowing up, also with much hilarity. It was even funnier when it came to putting up the tree, with everyone disagreeing as to whether it was standing level or not and the children eventually deciding that it didn't matter, putting the decorations on anyway.

'You have a piece of tinsel in your hair,' Nick told Bethany gruffly as he reached up to remove the offending glitter.

Bethany looked down at the tinsel in his hand, laughing softly. 'It would have to be red!'

'Your hair isn't red,' he murmured admiringly. 'It's Titian.'

'A more poetic name for red.' She laughed openly now.

He slowly shook his head, still gazing at her hair. 'In some lights it looks almost golden... Beth, I—'

'Time to put the angel on top of the tree,' Josh announced importantly.

'Beth's far too big to go on top of our tree!' Lucy giggled mischievously.

'But you may not be!' Nick warned, swinging his daughter threateningly towards the top of the over-decorated tree—to the sound of her squeals of delight.

Bethany watched with loving eyes as Nick tickled his daughter mercilessly.

'Beth should put the angel on top of the tree,' Jamie told them decisively. 'She's the one that did all the work.'

'Quite right, son.' Nick ruffled his eldest son's hair affectionately, looking over expectantly at Bethany. 'Would you do the honours?' he asked huskily.

Bethany looked away in confusion at what she could see shimmering in his eyes. 'Only if you'll turn the lights on at the same time; I think it will look more effective that way. All make a wish as the angel goes on the tree,' she encouraged the children, reaching up to the very top branch just as Nick clicked on the switch for the lights.

The effect was magical, and all of them stood in complete silence, gazing upon the beauty of the glittering lights and shimmering decorations.

'Daddy, I wished—'

'You mustn't tell your wish, Lucy,' Bethany told the little girl gently. 'If you do, it won't come true.'

'Lucy probably wished for the same thing as me,' Nick told her huskily as, later, the two of them prepared a light supper for them all before the children went to bed.

Bethany looked across at him with troubled eyes. From the way he had looked at her earlier, all his emotions laid bare in grey expressive eyes, it wasn't too difficult to guess what that wish might be. But she couldn't stay—was surprised that she hadn't already been summoned away.

The children were so excited when it came time to go to bed that it took all of Bethany and Nick's persuasion to calm them down. Even so, it was obvious that it was going to be some time before they settled down for the night and fell asleep. Some time before 'Father Christmas' could put their presents out under the tree.

'I'll go and get the things up from the car,' Nick told Bethany smilingly when at last he could hear that the excited chatter of the children from their bedrooms had stopped. 'I have something for each of them in my room too.' He gave a troubled frown. 'The only person I don't have a present for is you. I didn't think—'

'I really don't want anything,' Bethany assured him softly. 'You've already given me the only present I could want.' Or accept! 'Lucy,' she explained as he looked puzzled.

'I've been so damned stupid!' Nick shook his head in self-disgust. 'Sam never lied to me during our marriage, not even when it came to her feelings for Robert. Once she realised they were too strong for her to continue in our marriage, even though she was pregnant with Lucy, she had to tell me. My pride made me grasp onto the fact that Lucy couldn't be mine. I've been such a fool!' He groaned.

'Lucy has forgiven you,' Bethany told him gently.

'But will Sam?' He shook his head. 'I wouldn't, if the positions were reversed.'

'Samantha will,' she said with certainty.

'And the accident five years ago?' Nick frowned. 'Will she forgive me for that too? If I hadn't left the house in such a temper that day, because she had told me she was engaging a nanny for the boys, then the dog wouldn't have run out after me and that young lady wouldn't have tried to stop him from being run over by a car driving by!' He shook his head. 'I didn't even know any of it had happened, had already left, and by the time I got back from the business trip I'd decided to take myself off on the girl and the dog were both dead—and Sam hated me.'

Bethany lightly grasped his arm. 'I'm sure that if you talk about all this to Samantha she will understand.'

He looked at her with tortured eyes. 'Would you? Would that young girl who died so senselessly?'

'The past can't be changed, Nick,' Bethany told

him with feeling. 'It can only be lived with. And Samantha is expecting another child now—would like, I'm sure, all of you to be reconciled before its birth. It will be all right, Nick,' she assured him firmly.

'God, I hope so!' he said fervently. 'It's suddenly very important to me that all the bitterness and pain stops.' The look in his eyes told her that she was the main reason for his change of heart.

'I should go and get the childrens' presents from the car now,' she advised softly, avoiding his gaze. 'It's getting late.'

After only the briefest hesitation he turned and left the apartment, leaving Bethany to breathe a sigh of resignation. Nick was on the brink of making a declaration that she couldn't bear to hear. What would she do, what would she say, if he should tell her that he loved her?

Arranging the childrens' presents under the tree with him was something so emotionally intimate that Bethany felt as if she were about to cry; it felt as if the two of them had done this a dozen times before. But they had never done it before, and they would never do it again...

'This is the best Christmas I've ever had.' Nick sat back with satisfaction to view their handiwork once they had finished putting the presents out; the tree was really looking beautiful now.

Bethany smiled. 'Children have a way of—'

'It's not just the children, Beth,' Nick cut in forcefully, moving to stand directly in front of her. 'You're the one that's made this Christmas perfect for me. And it's not over yet.' He smiled down at her, looking nothing like the stern-faced man who had opened the door to her only a day ago. 'I love you, Beth—'

'No!' Now she had her answer to how she would react if he should say those words; she panicked! 'You can't—'

'Oh, but I do.' He laughed softly, taking her gently into his arms. 'Somewhere in between the tales of angels, Father Christmas and the Tooth Fairy, I fell in love with you.' His laugh was exultant now. 'I love you, Beth.'

She knew that she should stop him as he began to kiss her, knew that she couldn't allow this to happen. But as his lips gently claimed hers, as passion flared so hotly between them, she knew she couldn't stop it. She loved him in return—deeply, irrevocably—and probably would for all time. For all eternity.

CHAPTER TWELVE

NICK stirred sleepily, smiling happily as the memories of last night came flooding back. Beth in his arms. Beth kissing him. Beth touching him. Beth lying naked beside him. Beth crying out as they reached their pleasure together. Beth lying cradled in his arms, both of them satiated. Beth falling asleep, their bodies entangled, their arms about each other even as they slept.

He loved that woman. Loved her more than he had ever believed it possible to love anyone.

And, as he felt his body stir with the warm, scented memory of her, he knew he wanted to make love to her again.

But when he turned in his bed to reach for her it was to find the space next to him empty—still warm from the imprint of Beth's body, but empty none the less.

Of course, it was Christmas morning; Beth would have gone to see to the children. He hoped he hadn't missed the present-opening by lazing in bed like this. He had just been so tired—satiated tired—from hours of making love with Beth.

He slid out of bed to pull on his robe, a piece of white paper fluttering to the floor as he did so. He looked at it curiously after bending down to pick it up, the first thing he noticed being the signature 'Bethany' at the bottom of the brief note. He had wondered what Beth was short for, had thought it must be Elizabeth. Bethany... It suited her, gentle and beautiful.

He read the note quickly, his face pale as he reached the end. She had gone... Had had to go, she said. And she wished him well. She wished him well! How the hell could he be 'well' without her?

It was still quite early, he discovered as he rushed frantically about the apartment, checking to make sure that Bethany had actually gone, that it wasn't all a dream, some terrible joke.

It wasn't. Every last thing she had brought with her was gone too. Just as if she had never existed...

But she had existed! And she was very firmly in his heart. A heart that felt heavy as he sat on the floor with the children a short time later as they opened their presents. He had explained that Bethany had had to go to her own family this morning, that he wasn't quite sure when she would be back. None of the children had looked too happy about this explanation, especially Lucy, but the lure of their presents under the tree had soon diverted their attention. For the moment.

The trouble was, Nick didn't even know if Bethany had any family—had no idea where she lived. And there was only an answering machine taking the calls at Heavenly Angels at the moment. Not surprising really; it was Christmas Day. As soon as the holiday period was over he was going down to the office to demand some answers where Bethany was concerned. If she hadn't come back before then... It was the one thing he hoped for.

In the meantime, he had a responsibility to help the children enjoy Christmas, and, once they had opened their presents and eaten breakfast, the four of them prepared and put the turkey in the oven before he drove them all to the hospital so that the children could see their mother. He needed to see Sam himself now—and what better day than Christmas Day to try to heal the rift between them?

'Robert.' He held his hand out warmly to the man who had once been his friend. Who he sincerely hoped would become so once again.

'Nick.' The other man greeted him more reservedly, although he returned the handshake.

'Merry Christmas,' Nick added, with a rueful smile towards the impatiently waiting children. 'If they don't soon give their mother her presents they are going to burst with excitement!' he said indulgently. 'Although I would like to speak to Sam alone once things have calmed down a little; is that all right with you?' He spoke softly, so that the children shouldn't hear.

Robert looked at him coldly. 'As long as you aren't going to upset her.'

Nick knew he more than deserved the other man's suspicion, knew he must have hurt Sam time and time again over the last five years. 'The opposite, I hope.' He gently grasped the other man's shoulder. 'It isn't easy—especially when you're an arrogant bastard like me,' he added ruefully, 'to admit when you've been wrong and say you're sorry. Humble pie was never my favourite food.' He grimaced. 'But I do owe you and Sam my deepest—'

'Daddy, please can we see Mummy now?' Lucy grabbed his arm, jumping up and down in her agitation at the delay.

'Of course you can, love.' Nick touched her curls affectionately. 'If Robert says you may?' He looked at the other man, knowing from the slightly shocked expression in Robert's eyes that he had recognised the shift in the situation concerning Lucy and Nick. But, while Nick had come to terms with his daughter, he also knew that he owed a debt of gratitude to Robert that could never be repaid, in as much as Robert had become her father because her own father had simply refused to recognise her. He would never forget that.

'Of course,' Robert agreed dazedly. 'Mummy has been looking forward to seeing you all.'

'Robert...?' Nick held the other man back momentarily from joining the children in their mother's room. 'I really am sorry. For everything,' he added gruffly.

Robert hesitated only briefly before thumping him lightly on the shoulder. 'Good to have you back, Nick.' He grinned. 'And I really mean that!'

Nick wasn't completely sure that he deserved the other man's magnanimity, but he was grateful for it none the less. He could see that Sam was surprised to see him there too, and even more so to see Lucy's obvious closeness to him and his own warm reaction to his daughter. His daughter. And for five years he had denied her existence. He didn't deserve to be forgiven——by either of them.

'The children seem——happy,' Sam said awkwardly once they were alone, Robert having taken the children to buy a chocolate bar each from the machine down the corridor.

'It's time we all were,' Nick acknowledged grimly. 'I've been such a fool, Sam. So damned selfish. And it's taken loving someone myself to make me see that love is the most important thing you can have in your life. Without it, you don't have anything.'

Sam relaxed slightly, eyeing him teasingly. 'Would this have something to do with the young lady I met with the children yesterday? Beth, I believe her name is?'

'Everything to do with her!' he admitted forcefully. 'I love her so much. So completely. She—' He broke off, looking uncomfortably at the woman who had once been his wife. 'I loved you too once, Sam.'

'Not in this way. And not in the way I love Robert, otherwise the two of us would still be together.' She squeezed his hand understandingly.

'Yes,' he accepted huskily. 'I understand that now. Now that I know love like that myself. And even though she seems to have disappeared off the face of the earth for the moment,' he added fiercely, 'I'll always be grateful to Robert for hiring her to—'

'Robert didn't hire her,' Sam cut in frowningly. 'We assumed she was a friend of yours who had kindly taken over the care of the children. Robert didn't even know of her existence until you told him she was at the apartment looking after them for us.'

Now it was Nick's turn to frown. 'But—Heavenly Angels.' He shook his head dazedly. 'Bethany said the agency sent her—'

'What did you say?' Sam was looking at him with startled eyes.

'I know it's a damned stupid name for an agency,' he dismissed impatiently. 'I was just as sceptical myself when Bethany first told me, but somehow it seems to fit. And Bethany told me—'

'Bethany,' Sam repeated breathlessly. 'I *knew* she reminded me of someone yesterday. My God...' Sam lay back weakly against the pillows, her face almost as white as they were now.

'What is it?' Nick sat forward worriedly. 'Sam, what is it?' he demanded. 'Do you need a doctor? Speak to me, damn it!' He rasped his concern.

She drew in a ragged breath. 'I don't know where to start. What to say. I just— It's incredible. I don't understand why or how—definitely not how!—but I—' She looked at him with wonder in her eyes. 'Nick, I think we've all met an angel!'

CHAPTER THIRTEEN

'You see, Bethany, sometimes mistakes are made. Not very often and completely unintentionally, of course,' Mrs Heavenly quickly added, her kindly face creased into lines of concern. 'But occasionally they are made—'

'I know I shouldn't have left Nick that note,' Bethany accepted miserably, sitting opposite the elderly grey-haired lady in her 'office', 'that we have to bring everything away with us. But I just couldn't leave Nick in that cold way, without any sort of word,' she explained brokenly. 'Like—like some sort of thief in the night!' She sniffed emotionally, the tears still flowing two hours after she had arrived.

'I wasn't referring to the note, dear.' Sympathy beamed from the rounded cherubic face. 'No, no, occasionally—very occasionally, I must stress,' she fluttered nervously, 'a little mistake is made, and we—well... Sometimes we can rectify it. And sometimes we can't. Of course, once the deed is done we usually try to make the best of the situation, but in this case it obviously didn't work out. *You* didn't work out,' she added kindly.

'I've succeeded this time,' Bethany protested huskily. 'Nick is reconciled with his daughter, his ex-wife and his ex-friend. And—'

'I wasn't talking about that, dear.' Mrs Heavenly handed her another tissue. 'I don't think you've really been listening to what I've been trying to tell you.' She shook her head in gentle reproof.

'But Nick's life is fine now.' Bethany frowned. 'He—'

'I'm afraid it isn't.' The older woman shook her head.

'But I... He'll be all right, won't he?' The distress on Bethany's face deepened at the thought of him not being all right.

'He's in love with you, my dear.' Mrs Heavenly gave an understanding sigh. 'He's telephoned the agency at least half a dozen times today, each time leaving a message on the answering machine—the last one pleading with me to tell him where you are.'

Bethany couldn't stand the thought of Nick being in that much pain. She should have left as soon as she knew he was starting to love her. She should have—

'Of course, we always knew there was a danger of this happening,' Mrs Heavenly continued more briskly. 'As soon as we realised Nicholas was about to make a totally unsuitable marriage to this woman Lisa, we knew that we had to do something about it.' She shook her head. 'The poor man—his life has been such a mess the last five years.'

Bethany nodded. 'Since he and Samantha separated.'

'Oh, no, dear.' Mrs Heavenly looked surprised at this assumption. 'It had nothing to do with his separation from his wife. Well... Only indirectly,' she conceded thoughtfully. 'Nicholas didn't love Samantha in the way that he should have, and Samantha is to be admired for realising that, for making the decision to be with the man she did love—and more importantly who loved her!—at that difficult time in her life. No, no, dear.' Mrs Heavenly shook her head dismissively. 'Nicholas's life hasn't been a mess because of that; that has been because the woman he was going to love was denied him.'

Bethany swallowed hard. 'Nick is in love with someone else?' It would be better for everyone if he were, but it would also break her own heart. But she mustn't be selfish; she wanted Nick to be happy!

'I don't know whether it's me, dear—' the normally unruffled Mrs Heavenly was certainly becoming so '—or whether your own distress is just making you not listen to what I'm saying. Of course Nicholas isn't in love with someone else; what sort of fickle man do you think he is?' the elderly woman admonished her.

'The truth of the matter is, Bethany, that someone slipped up five years ago. At the time it was decided just to leave things alone, let them develop—but recent events in Nicholas's life have shown us that they haven't developed at all, that without the life that should have been his Nicholas Rafferty has just drifted along, becoming more and more cynical—bitter, even. He was even in the process of embarking on a second marriage that would have been even more disastrous for everyone than the first one was!

'Well, of course, it was our mistake in the first place.' Mrs Heavenly frowned. 'Over-impetuosity on the part of a relative novice. So it was decided that we should see what would happen if Nicholas met the woman he should have fallen in love with five years ago,' she said with satisfaction.

Bethany shook her head dazedly. 'And just how did you do that?' She had no idea what the other woman was talking about.

The elderly lady gave her an impatient look. 'Why, we sent you back, of course,' she said dismissively. 'I'm sure you'll understand, Bethany, when I say you haven't worked out too well in your new capacity either—that something always seems to go wrong when we send you on an assignment. The powers that be decided that perhaps it was for the same reason that Nicholas's life has been such a dismal failure. So we sent you back to him and he fell in love with you, just as he should have done five years ago. So it's been decided—'

'Sent me back?' Bethany burst in incredulously. 'Sent me back where?'

'To Nicholas, dear.' The elderly lady patted her hand soothingly. 'You see, you were a nanny five years ago, and Samantha was going to employ you to look after her two sons, Jamie and Josh. And—'

And instead she had died, in a totally senseless accident, her own path and Nick's never crossing after all. God, no wonder Samantha Fairfax had thought she looked familiar that day at the hospital; the other woman had half recognised her as the nanny she had been going to employ five years earlier. But instead Bethany had died.

But if she had lived she and Nick had been going to fall in love, would have married, probably had children of their own. Oh, God, what had gone wrong? How had it happened that they hadn't even met after all? And what was going to happen now—now that they had met and fallen in love with each other, in spite of all the odds? Surely that couldn't be snatched away from them a second time? They couldn't be that cruel!

'Mrs Heavenly!' She looked desperately across at the other woman. 'We're in love now. You can't do this to Nick a second time.' Tears darkened the green of her eyes.

The other woman's face softened as she looked at her compassionately. 'You're such a kind young lady, Bethany,' she said warmly. 'You aren't thinking of yourself at all in this, but of Nicholas. It's that warmth in you that he loves so much, of course. He—'

'Please, Mrs Heavenly,' Bethany cut in emotionally, 'tell me that Nick isn't going to be left alone, as he has been the last five years.'

'Well, of course he isn't, my dear.' The elderly woman looked wounded that she should even suggest such a fate for him. 'How insensitive do you think we are?' she chided gently. 'You were never meant to die at that time, Bethany, it was the mistake of a relative newcomer that you were taken in the way that you were. Now you're to go back, my dear, to the beginning.

'Of course, the two of you won't know each other to start with, because you've never met each other before, but it won't take long for the two of you to get to know each other.' She gave her a conspiratorial wink. 'And it won't take long, under your loving influence, for Nicholas to be reconciled to his daughter's existence and to the relationship between his ex-wife and best friend.' She sat back with satisfaction. 'Altogether a much better arrangement all round for everyone.' She nodded her approval.

'But where will we meet?' Bethany said desperately. 'How will we—?' She broke off as everything around her seemed to be falling away, rapidly spiralling out of focus.

'Have a good life with your Nicholas, Bethany.' Mrs Heavenly's voice seemed to come from a great distance. 'You were never meant to be an angel. Not for a long time yet, anyway...'

CHAPTER FOURTEEN

BETHANY sat on the carpeted floor and watched as Nick swung the angelic little girl in his arms round and round. She giggled and giggled, her blonde curls bouncing, her blue eyes aglow, father and daughter hugging each other as Bethany turned to look at the two boys putting the decorations on the Christmas tree. There were far too many decorations, of course, and the hanging of them was haphazard to say the least, but to her the tree looked beautiful.

'Will Aunty Sam and Uncle Robert be here soon?' the eldest of the two boys bounded over to demand.

He had been asking the same thing at five-minute intervals for the last half an hour! 'Very soon now, darling,' Bethany answered smilingly, smoothing the dark hair back from his brow, gazing up lovingly at her eldest son. Tall for his age, at only four Richard was a small replica of his father.

'And Jamie, and Josh, and Lucy!' Three-year-old Peter cried excitedly as he joined them.

'What a houseful we're going to have this year!' Nick shook his head ruefully as he strolled over, still carrying two-year-old Beth; the little girl was in her favourite place of all. Her father's arms.

'No more hectic than usual.' Bethany smiled as she stood up, still sometimes having to pinch herself at how happy she was. Whoever would have believed, when she'd gone to start her job with Samantha Fairfax five years ago, as nanny to her two children—soon to be three—that she would meet someone as wonderful as Nick? And it had all happened so dramatically too—Nick snatching her, literally, from the jaws of death when she'd run out into the road to stop the family dog from being run over.

The last five years had been good to her, and she was sure that she fell more in love with her husband every day they were together. Their home in the English countryside was always full of love and laughter, and children, and happiness.

'Time for the angel, Mummy.' Richard jumped up and down with excitement as he handed her the angel to place on top of the tree.

Bethany was never quite sure how this family tradition had begun, but every year it was the same, Nick and the children always insisting that she be the one to place the golden angel on top of their Christmas tree.

'I think perhaps we should just wait a while for the other children to arrive.' She gently tried to delay the moment.

The two families—Nick's ex-wife and his three children, and Sam's second husband and Nick's business partner, Robert—always spent the holiday period together, and this year it was Nick and Bethany's turn to play host and hostess.

'Oh, but—' Peter broke off his disappointed protest as the doorbell rang. 'Here they are. Here they are!'

Nick put the baby down on the floor, he and Bethany watching as their three children rushed from the room to greet their uncle and aunty and their three half-siblings.

Nick moved to Bethany's side, putting his arm about her shoulders to gaze down at her with adoring eyes. 'Have I told you yet today that I love you, Mrs Rafferty?' His mouth trailed a path of passion down her throat.

'I believe so.' Bethany smiled as she remembered the completely satisfactory way he had told her earlier in bed this morning that he loved her. 'But I don't mind in the least if you tell me again.' She snuggled closer in his arms.

'I love you so much, Bethany Anne Rafferty,' he murmured huskily, looking deeply into her eyes as he cradled her face in his hands.

'I love you too, Nick,' she told him warmly.

He smiled. 'I have a feeling this is going to be our best Christmas yet!'

She laughed throatily. 'You say that every year!'

He pretended indignation at her humour at his expense. 'And am I not always right?'

'Invariably.' She nodded solemnly, containing her humour with effort. 'Actually, this year is going to be rather special.' She looked up at him. 'Sam and Robert have an important announcement to make.'

Nick frowned his puzzlement. 'What sort of an announcement? It can't be business, because Robert and I are still in the middle of this—'

'Sam is pregnant, Nick,' Bethany put in quietly, watching him closely.

He had been very angry and hurt when Sam had first fallen in love with his friend and business partner Robert Fairfax, but over the years, and with their own happiness so tangible, he had come to accept the situation, and he and Robert had even gone back into business together four years ago. Bethany and Sam had become very good friends—both of them being extremely happy with their respective husbands—which had made it all so much easier for the children. But, even so, Bethany wasn't quite sure about Nick's reaction to Sam's pregnancy...

'That's great!' Nick enthused instantly.

Much to Bethany's relief. She had promised Sam she would break the news to Nick before the announcement was made, just so that he wouldn't be too surprised. It was all right; she had thought it would be.

'I know the two of them have wanted a child of their own for years.' Nick nodded. 'My only concern is Sam's age...' he added frowningly. 'She's thirty-nine now, and—'

'Both Sam and the baby will be fine,' Bethany assured him with certainty—instantly feeling a wave of *déjà vu* as she made the claim.

This happened to her occasionally. Her foreknowledge was always unexplainable, and she was never quite sure where her certainty came from, but it usually turned out to be correct. She certainly hoped it was where Sam and her baby were concerned; the other couple deserved the happiness of their own child.

'My little know-all.' Nick tapped her affectionately on the nose.

Not really, she just seemed to know some things with certainty. As she did with her love for Nick, and his love for her. It was for ever.

'The angel now, Mummy!' Peter demanded excitedly, once they were all standing around the tree a few minutes later, greetings kept to the minimum by the childrens' overflowing excitement.

Bethany reached up to the very top, placing the golden-winged, golden-haired angel carefully on the highest branch, then moving back to Nick's side as awed silence fell over them all.

'I don't know whether it's my imagination,' Nick finally murmured softly, 'but our angel seems to glow a little brighter this year. And for a moment—' he sounded slightly awed '—just a fleeting moment, I could have sworn her hair was as red as yours!' He looked at Bethany dazedly.

She had thought the same thing herself. Only fleetingly. But, just for the briefest moment, the angel *had* looked a little like her.

But it looked perfectly normal again now—the same angel she and Nick had purchased from a shop together four years ago. Their feelings of it being otherwise were probably due to an over-indulgence in the wine they had been sipping as they'd put up the tree and decorations!

'I hope you all made a wish!' she said brightly.

Her wish had been that her happiness as Nick's wife and mother of his children would never change. And as she glanced up at the angel on top of the tree she could have sworn it smiled conspiratorially at her...

A DADDY FOR CHRISTMAS
Rebecca Winters

Dear Reader,

Christmas has always been my favorite holiday of the year. In my family the youngest child always went downstairs first on Christmas morning to see if Santa Claus had come. Of course, Santa always had, leaving our home looking like fairyland—everywhere covered in presents!

So you can imagine how we felt when, one year, our folks asked us what we thought of giving money to help build a new church, instead of spending it on Christmas. We all agreed it would be fine with us. We spent the day together singing carols and reading the Scriptures. It turned out to be the best Christmas ever!

For once we understood that it is better to give than to receive. I'll always be thankful to my wonderful, unselfish parents for teaching us the real meaning of Christmas.

With love

Rebecca Winters

CHAPTER ONE

'JILLY? Where's my daddy?'

As the seaplane taxied to the lonely-looking pier Jill Barton would have liked the answer to that question herself.

'I don't know, but we'll find him,' she assured the little five-year-old boy strapped in next to the pilot.

She'd never met Kip's father, nor had she ever been to Kaslit Bay. The smattering of buildings and trailer houses grouped around the shoreline looked barren of human life or activity. A thin layer of snow had fallen during the night and gave the added impression that the area had gone into hibernation for the rest of the winter.

However, on closer inspection she could see the movement of a truck on the gouged out road leading into the camp from the forest. By the time they drew alongside the pier she could see a man in a red plaid coat and black baseball cap, who was waving his hands over his head in greeting.

He was probably the ticket agent and store-owner Kip's mother, Marianne, had told Jill about. In the distance, she spotted another man emerging from the truck. Her heart pounded hard. Hopefully it was Kip's father.

With a feeling akin to relief flooding her system, she unfastened her seat belt and helped Kip out of his, making sure his hood and parka were fastened up tight, that the neck-warmer was pulled over his nose and cheeks to protect his face from the wind.

While the pilot started unloading cargo from the belly of the plane the older man with the weathered face helped Jill and Kip onto the dock, his smiling eyes welcoming them.

'Hi. I'm R.J. Ross, owner of the store over there. I was told to expect two passengers. I don't mean to sound unfriendly, or anything, but I can't rightly figure out why you've come. Most everybody's gone till spring.'

Though used to the rainy cold of Ketchikan, Alaska at this time of year, Jill had noticed a distinct drop in the temperature since they'd landed—probably because the wind had started up. She tightened the hood of her parka, which hid most of her short white-gold hair, then reached out a gloved hand to squeeze Kip's.

'I've brought this little guy to stay with his father for the holidays,' she confided, looking beyond R.J.'s shoulder to the other man, possibly in his mid to late thirties, who was fast approaching.

The second she spied his dark blond hair and rugged features, which were appealing in a hard, male way, the promise of the man in the boy she was clinging to came to breathtaking life.

Hatless and beardless, Kip's father stood over six feet tall and was powerfully built beneath the faded jeans and parka he was wearing. He looked more than fit enough to handle the heavy equipment of a logger, and his eyes mirrored the deep blue of the bay.

When Jill had told her class the tale of Paul Bunyan it had captured their imagination—Kip's especially. He had maintained that his lumberjack daddy looked just like the legendary American folk hero. In fact there was only one difference Jill could see between Kip's daddy and Paul Bunyan. He didn't have black hair.

For a brief moment he made a masculine assessment of her face and parka-clad figure, causing an emotional stir deep inside of her that she'd never experienced before. Then his glance fell on Kip, before he acknowledged R.J. with a nod and moved toward the pilot.

Jill blinked in total confusion, because neither father or son was acting as if they recognized each other. Instead of Kip crying out to his father, or his father sweeping the boy in his arms, as Jill would have expected, they were behaving like total strangers.

A few yards away now, Kip's father had engaged their driver in conversation while the two of them worked quickly to unload the last of the supplies from the truck.

Jill didn't know what to think. Had it been so long since Kip had seen his father that he mistakenly thought he had black hair?

She blinked again. Surely Zane Doyle could spot his own boy, even if Kip had on unfamiliar clothes and a face-warmer.

Feeling the hairs stand up on the back of her neck, she walked Kip a little way away from everyone, then got down on her haunches and turned him around so he was facing her.

'Sweetheart—it's very, very important you tell me the truth right now. Have you ever seen your daddy?'

Kip didn't have to say anything. A shadow lurked in his eyes and he finally gave a negative shake of his hooded head.

Dear God. Kip had never met his father—and she had the strongest suspicion Zane Doyle had never met his son!

Was it possible he didn't know of Kip's existence? From her dealings with Marianne Mongrief, Jill supposed that Kip's negligent mother was capable of anything...

Pain clutched at her heart like a giant hand. She had to get Kip out of here before any damage was done. But it was too late. R.J. had already said something to the attractive stranger. In a state of absolute panic, she watched him approach her, his narrowed blue gaze lacking its earlier sensuality.

'I understand you're looking for that boy's father.' He spoke in a low, vibrant voice. 'I'm Zane Doyle, but my wife and I were happily married until ten years ago when she was killed in a plane crash. We had no children. I'm sorry you've come all the way from Ketchikan to find the wrong man.'

Jill believed him.

Even though he was a perfect stranger, she knew to the marrow of her bones that he was telling the truth.

But she knew something else equally well, and she pulled the lapels of her parka up around her face.

He wasn't the wrong Zane Doyle. Not with his little replica standing just a few yards away, asking questions of the men while they worked.

At some point in the past Marianne had known this devastatingly attractive man—perhaps during the period when he had been trying to assuage his grief over losing his wife.

Suddenly all the things Marianne hadn't said, hadn't explained, became crystal-clear. So did Kip's obsession with Paul Bunyan, the make-believe daddy of his dreams.

Jill felt so ill she must have moaned, because the man standing in front of her reached out with his strong hands to steady her. At five feet five, she felt tiny next to him, and tried to back away.

'You've gone pale. What's wrong?' The concern in his voice was real enough.

'It's nothing,' she lied. Imploring him with her velvety brown eyes, she whispered, 'I just feel bad for Kip. He's been looking forward to seeing his father. I'll have to tell him there's been a mistake. The agent at the other end probably sent us to the wrong island.' She moistened her lips nervously. 'There are s-so many of them with names that sound alike.' Even before the words had left her mouth, she knew she was making everything worse.

He searched her eyes intently. 'Are you a relative of the boy's?'

'No.' She shook her head, wishing she were any-where but here—wishing he would let go of her before he saw too much. 'I'm his kindergarten teacher—Jill Barton.'

His hands remained on her upper arms. She could feel their heat through the padded material. 'Why are *you* delivering him? Where's his mother?'

Her eyes slid away from his. 'It doesn't really matter.'

'Jilly? I'm cold.' Kip called to her in a plaintive voice. 'When's Daddy going to come?'

'Just a minute, Kip,' she answered over her shoulder. Facing Zane Doyle once more, she said, 'I have to go. The pilot is waiting.'

'Not yet,' he murmured with a trace of authority, his hands remaining in place. 'For your information, the wind is picking up and it'll be a wild ride back to Ketchikan. Neither the pilot nor I would advise taking the boy up.'

'But I don't have a choice. There's no place to stay here.'

'My home is available until the storm passes over. You can fly out on the next plane.'

She shook her head in fear. The last thing she wanted to do was to be stranded with Kip's father—a man who didn't know he *was* a father.

'We'll be all right.' But even as she said the words she could see whitecaps forming on the bay.

'That's what my wife said before she climbed in the cockpit and disappeared in a whiteout.'

He sounded as if he were still in mourning. His eyes had turned a haunting inky blue, producing another stabbing pain inside of her.

'If you've been living in Ketchikan, then you know every Alaskan's home is open to travelers—especially during a blizzard. Are you—a schoolteacher, no less—really willing to risk the life of someone else's child because you're too frightened to accept the hospitality of a stranger?'

A wave of heat engulfed her body, and tears unexpectedly spilled over her lashes. 'I would *never* put my own fears ahead of Kip's welfare!'

Mortified that he'd seen her break down like that, she frantically dashed the moisture away with her glove.

'Then what's the problem?' he demanded in a silky tone.

Marianne Mongrief is the problem, Mr Doyle. Jill's heart cried. You're Kip's biological father, but Marianne will have to be the one to tell you the truth. Not I.

'Ma'am? Are you coming? If we're going to leave, it has to be now.'

The pilot's voice galvanized Jill into action, thankfully preventing her from having to fabricate an answer to Mr Doyle's question. She pulled away from her captor's grip and hurried over to Kip, drawing him close.

'Your daddy's not here, but the storm's growing worse. This nice man here, Mr Doyle, says we can stay with him till the weather clears. Would you like that?'

'If *you* would.'

Disappointment at not finding his father had robbed him of his earlier excitement. Right now Jill could have strangled Marianne for putting all three of them in such a precarious situation. How dared she play God with innocent lives?

Jill finally lifted troubled eyes to the pilot, who was conversing with the others. 'I think Kip and I will wait out the storm here.'

'That's the best idea.' The pilot smiled down at Kip. 'See you, partner.' After giving Kip's shoulder a pat he got into the plane, and within seconds was taxiing away from the dock.

R.J. turned to Jill. 'If you need anything, just come on over to the store. The missus will give you what you want. Be good, young fellar.' He shook their hands and headed out.

'Kip? You look strong enough to carry this carton to my truck.' Mr Doyle took immediate command of the situation. 'The sooner we clear off the dock, the sooner we can get your teacher home and out of the cold.'

'I can carry more!' Kip rose valiantly to the masterful challenge, his former lassitude forgotten.

Surprised at Kip's reaction, because normally he shied away from adults, she wondered if Mr Doyle's tactic was accidental or instinctive. Reaching for their suitcases, she followed behind him and his son, who walked the length of the pier with their hands and arms full. Now she knew where Kip got his kind of loping gait. His father moved exactly the same way. How incredible!

By the time they'd put everything in the back of the half-ton vintage Chevy pickup, the plane had long since soared out of sight. The drone of the engine became lost in the whooshing, mournful sounds of the wind.

Again, Jill felt a surge of anger over Marianne's treachery. With no thought for anyone's feelings, especially not Kip's, she'd deliberately placed Jill in the middle of a delicate situation which was distinctly private and should have remained undisturbed.

To her shock, she realized that a pair of disturbingly inquisitive blue eyes had been studying her mutinous expression.

'Relax, Ms Barton. You haven't been abandoned to an igloo.'

Relieved that he'd misread her mood, she retorted, 'Actually I've been in several igloos, and I can think of worse places to take shelter during a storm.'

The hard line of his mouth unexpectedly curved into a smile which under any other circumstances would have lighted her world. With careless grace he opened the passenger door.

'Kip, why don't you climb in next to me? While you keep a lookout for reindeer we'll see if your teacher can spot a family of Queen Charlotte goshawks.'

'Jilly says they're enjanedered.' Though the word didn't come out right, he made his point with absolute confidence and climbed in the cab, scooting over to make room for Jill. His neck-warmer had slipped down, revealing his pink cheeks. Surely when Mr Doyle took a good hard look at Kip, he would see the amazing resemblance to himself.

Before their host closed the door, a low chuckle ensued—one she felt invade her body. 'Your teacher's right. That's why my company has set aside forty thousand acres of no-logging buffers for nesting sites.'

Secretly pleased by his admission, Jill tried not to stare at him as he walked around the front of the truck and got in behind the wheel.

'You have a *company*?'

Again Jill marveled that Kip didn't act at all shy around this man. Judging from the wonder in Kip's voice, this was only the first of a thousand questions. Mr Doyle had no idea what he was in for. Poetic justice for a man who probably got his own way all of the time, Jill mused, then chastised herself for having *any* personal thoughts about him.

'I do.'

Though he had just answered Kip's question, it sounded as if he'd gotten inside Jill's head.

After starting up the engine he elaborated a little more. 'It's called Bellingham-Wales Pulp and Lumber.'

'Jilly? Have you ever heard of that company?'

Not in the least surprised to learn that Zane Doyle had suddenly gone from logger to owner of a major thriving timber concern spanning two states, she once again found her gaze trapped by his.

'Since you're the oracle, I'm waiting with bated breath, Ms Barton.'

'What's an orkle?'

Deep masculine laughter reverberated inside the cab of the truck as they drove away from the dock. It infected Jill, whose gentle laughter soon joined his in spite of the tension. She pulled Kip onto her lap, needing the comfort of his warm body because hers was shaking.

In a voice filled with quiet irony Zane Doyle said, 'It means your teacher is infallible.'

Kip turned so he was facing Jill, who was trying to suppress a grin. 'What's infowlable, Jilly?'

'Go on,' her host prodded mercilessly. 'I'm anxious to hear your answer.'

Jill felt her cheeks catch fire. 'Mr Doyle is enjoying teasing me. All he means is that because I'm your teacher you think I know all the answers.'

'You *do*! Robbie says you're smarter than his dad.'

'That's high praise, Ms Barton,' came the mocking comment from the other side of the cab. 'I wonder what *Mr* Barton has to say about that?' he added in a quiet voice, but Kip heard him.

'Jilly's not married! Mommy says lots and lots of men want to carry her off, but she's waiting for a prince charming.'

'*Kip…*' Jill groaned out loud.

'I'm afraid there aren't too many of those living in Alaska,' her host growled.

'What's a prince charming?'

'That's a good question, son. If we men knew the answer, your Jilly would be married by now.'

'Are *you* married?'

'I *was*, once upon a time.'

'What happened?'

'She died.'

'That's sad. Where are your kids?'

'I don't have any.'

'How come?'

There was a slight pause. 'We didn't get around to it soon enough.'

'I'm glad my dad had me. Do you know him?'

'What's your last name?'

'Mongrief.'

CHAPTER TWO

A LONG, unbroken silence filled the cab before he answered, 'I can't say that I do.'

Jill broke out in a cold sweat, because she knew that the name Mongrief had meant something significant to Mr Doyle. Otherwise his voice wouldn't have sounded as if it had come from a dark cavern. The very subject she'd prayed to avoid could no longer be ignored or wished away.

According to Marianne, the Mongrief side of her family was Scottish. After her father had died, her mother had emigrated to Northern Idaho to be with her relatives. In time they had become U.S. citizens, but financially life had been difficult.

Needing money fast, Marianne had moved to Alaska looking for work, which had probably been about the time she'd met up with Zane Doyle. Jill assumed that Marianne was the only Mongrief in the state of Alaska.

'Look, Kip!' In panic she turned in her seat, forcing him away from their host. 'Watch that grove of trees. Can you see movement?'

'Where?'

'Right there.' Jill pointed a trembling finger to a dense stand of pines being buffeted by high winds, where a buck and two doe had taken cover.

'*Reindeer*! See, Mr Doyle?' he blurted to their driver, who was somehow managing to keep the truck from veering off course in the fierce wind.

'Call me Zane. How many are there?'

'Three.'

'You have good eyes.'

'But Jilly saw them first,' he confessed honestly. 'Robbie's father says she has eyes in the back of her head.'

'Is that so, Ms Barton?'

'I don't know. I can't see that far.'

'You're silly, Jilly.' Kip giggled and moved closer to their host. 'Zane, do you live in a trailer?'

'As a matter of fact, I don't. Wait a few moments and you'll see my place.'

Jill hated to admit that she was as curious as Kip. Now that they'd left the camp, she strained to see any sign of civilization in this world of snow-dusted trees bordering the bay.

Another minute and he had followed the turn in the road which wound its way up the side of the mountain. After a lot of jostling they came to a clearing.

'Oh—' Both she and Kip cried out at the same time when they saw the modern two-story home built of glass and weathered timber. Power and telephone lines were already in place.

It stood alone in a meadow, with an unobstructed view of the bay full of forested islands she'd seen from the plane. She could imagine that in summer wildflowers would turn the mountainside into a riot of color.

Right now light snow flurries eddied around the truck as the strong gusts of wind picked up in intensity. Yet every so often the wind changed course, blowing the flakes in another direction, allowing her a glimpse of glacier-topped mountains in the distance.

'How beautiful!' Her voice throbbed with emotion.

'My exact words the first time I stood on this spot.'

'How long ago was that?' She sounded like Kip, wanting to know everything about him.

'Twenty years ago, when this part of Prince of Wales Island was virgin territory.'

'Do you live here all alone?' Kip piped up.

'Nope. I have a friend named Beastlie.'

'Is he *really* a beast?'

Zane chuckled. 'Why don't we find out?'

'Jilly—' Kip rounded on her in a mixture of fright and excitement. 'Do you think it's a beast?'

'Well, I don't know for certain, but I rather imagine Beastlie is a mongrel.'

'What's a mongrill?'

'A combination of several breeds of dog.'

'Oh, yeah. Like Mr Ling's. He calls him Mutt.'

'Exactly.'

At that remark Zane's head swung around, and he leveled a penetrating gaze at her. After mumbling something about Robbie's dad being right after all, he drove them the rest of the way to the house.

When they pulled in around the back, she was surprised to see piles of lumber and sheet-rock covered by plastic standing in the semi-protection of the oil tank. Major construction was still going on.

'The outside was finished two years ago. Now I'm attempting to get the inside done.' He read her mind with astonishing ease. 'Why don't you go on in and get acquainted with my—' he hesitated a moment '—mutt, while Kip and I unload the truck?'

His odd question combined with the indecipherable glimmer in his eyes brought out the prickles on the back of her neck.

With her heart starting to race, she said, 'I believe that since I'm an unexpected house-guest the polite thing to do would be to get the work done first. Then you can introduce Beastlie to Kip and me at the same time.'

His mouth quirked before he gave an aside to Kip. 'I'm kind of glad I didn't have her for a teacher. She's so smart it's scary.'

'I *told* you,' Kip responded with great solemnity.

Once more Zane's glance darted to her, but this time there was no lingering mirth in his eyes. In fact, she couldn't read his enigmatic expression. After a suspiciously long moment she heard him say, 'I'll consider myself warned.'

Something in the strange timbre of his voice let her know that beneath the affable, friendly façade put on for Kip's benefit, Zane Doyle had a hidden agenda.

She felt pure revelation flow through her. Under normal circumstances this man, whom she instinctively felt was a very private person, would never have made his home available to her.

Surely if the pilot had deemed it safe enough to fly back to Ketchikan then it would have been equally safe for her and Kip? Too late, their host's comment that the pilot hadn't advised taking Kip back up didn't ring true, sending an icy shiver through her body.

Zane Doyle wasn't the head of a big corporation for nothing. Long before he'd heard the name Mongrief, he'd sensed a mystery here. Determined to get to the bottom of it, he'd not only used the excuse of his wife's death as leverage, but he'd also allowed Jill and Kip to invade his inner sanctum for an unknown period.

Maybe he'd already figured everything out before they'd left the dock, and assumed that Jill was playing a willing and active role in Marianne's unconscionable scheme.

How careless, how cruel of Kip's mother to have involved Jill in this way—to have thought up this particular method to inform her former lover that he had a son.

But maybe cruel was the wrong word. Maybe Marianne wasn't capable of being intentionally cruel.

Perhaps there was something lacking in her make-up that kept her from being a whole human being. Whatever the explanation, three people were about to pay the price. But it was Kip whom Jill would fight to protect, with every fiber of her being.

'What's that?'

Jill wondered the same thing. They'd just gotten out of the truck when she heard a terrifying howl that reverberated up and down the mountain, much like the sound of a wolf. She bent over and put a protective arm around Kip's shoulders.

Zane Doyle had already started unloading things from the back of his truck. 'That's Beastlie. You'll get used to him. He's greeting us.'

'Where is he?' Kip was jumping up and down in anticipation.

'Right behind you.'

Both Jill and Kip wheeled around in time to see a grey and white dog come bounding toward them. He looked mostly like an Alaskan husky, but Jill could tell there was part wolf in him too.

'He's *huge*,' Kip marveled as the dog headed straight for his master and rubbed up against his legs.

If Jill wasn't missing her guess, she was sure Beastlie was a vast improvement over Prince and King—the names he'd given to the imaginary dogs of his imaginary father.

'Take off your glove and put your hand out gently, so he can smell you.'

Without blinking an eye, Kip did his father's bidding, automatically giving Jill the glove. Already his trust in his parent was absolute. Zane Doyle had the uncanny ability to instill confidence in everyone he met.

'That's it. Now rub the top of his head right here, and he'll be your friend for life.'

With his tongue protruding over his bottom lip, Kip made a concentrated effort to tickle the dog in the exact spot necessary to produce such a miracle. But it was a rather difficult feat, because Beastlie on all fours stood taller than Kip himself.

The dog seemed almost human in the way he sensed Kip's problem and lowered his head with a low moan to allow the boy freer access. Kip's joy translated to delighted giggles as the dog inched his way closer, wanting the ecstasy to continue.

Jill's vision grew misty as she saw a tender expression break out on Zane Doyle's hard-boned features. She had an idea that most people rarely saw that look. It thrilled her that Kip was the reason for the sudden transformation.

Right now Zane Doyle seemed more relaxed and carefree—the way a younger father would be. With the fierce wind disheveling his short-cropped hair, flattening the material of his parka and jeans so they molded to his powerful physique, she thought him the most beautiful man she'd ever seen.

Apparently Marianne had thought the same thing. A curious ache in the region of her heart forced Jill to move away, but not before the flash of blue eyes almost blinded her with its intensity. He'd caught her staring and she felt shame—because her attraction to him was complicating an already untenable situation.

'Where do you think you're going, Ms Barton? It's *your* turn to make Beastlie's acquaintance.'

'He won't hurt you, Jilly. See?'

Kip grabbed her right hand, pulled off the glove and held onto her fingers for the dog to sniff. 'Now rub his head.' The student was teaching the teacher.

She plunged her hand into the dog's fur and scratched him, her lips curved in a smile. 'How do you do, Mr Beastlie?'

Kip giggled again. 'His name's not *Mr* Beastlie. You're silly, Jilly.'

'Since I'd rather have him for a friend, I thought I'd better be polite.'

'Wise woman,' her host murmured. Unfortunately the sound of the wind prevented her from detecting whether it had been jokingly said, or whether he'd meant it as a warning. In any event he stood too close to her, and she was unbearably aware of him.

To counteract her emotions she began roughing the dog with both hands. 'You're a beauty, even if you are a beast, aren't you?' He started making sounds that resembled the purrings of a cat rather than a dog.

'Keep that up and he'll forget all about me,' a deep voice mocked. 'Before I lose complete power over him, I suggest we go in the house. You lead the way, Kip. Right through that back door over there.'

'Can Beastlie come too?' asked Kip, after they'd crossed over the threshold onto a glassed-in back porch of sorts, which felt divinely warm after the freezing cold outside.

While Jill took off her coat their host removed his own parka and started to help Kip by unfastening the ties of his hood. 'He likes to be in the outdoors—especially in this kind of weather. But tonight he'll sleep at the foot of your bed.'

Kip turned his curly head, revealing a smile that lit up his beaming countenance. 'Did you hear that, Jilly?'

'*Lord*—'

Jill's eyes closed tightly for a moment. His father had just come face to face with his mirror image in pint-sized form. He needed no birth certificate to prove the boy's paternity.

All the Doyle traits were there: the curve of the well-shaped eyebrows, the set of the perfect ears, the way the identical dark-blond hair sprang from the same parting on the same side of their heads, the firm, square jaw and chin, the broad smile, the unique bone structure of their compact bodies...

Talk about the acorn falling close to the tree...

CHAPTER THREE

THIS was a private moment—one Jill would have given anything on earth not to have been witness to. Their first meeting shouldn't have happened like this. She wanted to shout that it wasn't fair.

The urge to wrap her arms around both of them and beg them to forgive her was almost overpowering. She should have seen through Marianne's ploy in time to prevent this from occurring.

'Let's go in the kitchen and rustle us up some lunch,' Zane suggested. 'I don't know about you, but I've just discovered I'm starving.'

Their host was behaving as if nothing earthshaking had happened, but Jill wasn't deceived. She'd heard the thickness, the huskiness in his voice. Those were the sounds of a person in the deepest throes of human emotion.

Kip made an assenting noise and followed him into a hallway, imitating his parent's walk to perfection without realizing it.

'Are we going to have tuna fish?'

'Nope. Hamburgers. I hate tuna fish.'

'So do I, but Jilly says I have to eat it for my brain.'

'My mom said the same thing. So you know what I used to do? When I got to school, I traded sandwiches with my friend, who hated peanut butter.'

'That's what I'm going to do next year, when I go to first grade and we have to stay there all day.'

'Good idea. The bathroom's down this hall—first door on the left—kitchen's on the right. Do you know which side is which?'

''Course. Jilly taught me.'

'Then I bet she also told you to wash your hands and face really well before eating.'

'Yeah. And I have to floss my teeth after I eat 'cause she says she doesn't want anything to happen to my beautiful pearlies.'

'*Pearlies?*' He chuckled.

'Yup. Jilly has funny names for everything.'

'Like what?'

'She says I have to cut the nails on my 'pendages and shampoo my mop. Stuff like that. She makes all the kids laugh.'

'I still say she's scary.'

Kip put his fists on his hips. 'She's not scary. I love her more than anyone in the whole wide world.'

'*Kip—*' Jill was overjoyed, yet stunned by his spontaneous declaration of affection.

'That's high praise coming from a kindergartner. I wonder if she's a good cook.'

'She makes the best cookies and the best chilli and the best Mickey Mouse pancakes in Ketchikan.'

'Is that so? In that case I'll put her to work fixing the rest of the meals around here while we men go out and saw wood.'

'With a real saw?'

'You can't saw with anything else.'

'Can we go after lunch?'

'It's storming out.'

'I don't care.'

'Then I don't either.'

'See ya in a minute, Zane. Don't go away.'

'I'll be in the kitchen with your teacher.'

'Promise *you* won't go away, Jilly?'

'I promise.'

The clopping noises he made on his way to the bathroom barely permeated the tension surrounding them. Jill's body stiffened as their host turned in her direction, impaling her with eyes that were mere slits darkened to black ice.

Gone was the charming, tender parent of a moment ago. Like quicksilver, he'd become someone else. Jill could feel everything from unutterable pain to rage emanating from him. She was helpless to do anything about it.

'I only want to know one thing.' His voice grated. 'Where's Marianne?'

Jill couldn't swallow. 'I—I don't honestly know.'

'What is *that* supposed to mean?' His voice sounded like ripping silk. 'With an act that beats Mary Poppins all to hell you spring my unknown son on me, and you have the gall to tell me you know *nothing* about his mother?' The cords stood out in his neck.

Jill was afraid to say another word. His mouth had thinned to a white line of anger.

'Sh-she went away to get married. But I don't know any details.'

A hand snaked out and caught her chin so she couldn't turn from him. 'That's not an acceptable answer, Ms Barton.' He was livid. Who could blame him?

'I agree, and I'm so sorry,' she whispered, with tears in her voice, her eyes beseeching him to believe her. 'Here.' She reached in her purse and pulled out the letter Marianne had left her. Jill had found it on the kitchen sink when she and Kip had come home from school the day before. 'Read this and it will tell you as much as I know.'

He stared mercilessly at her, his revulsion apparent as he studied each feminine feature before his gaze shifted to the envelope. Jill's heart was breaking for him.

It had to be the worst moment of her life. She couldn't bear to see him torn apart like this, to watch the way his chest rose and fell from the force of overwhelming emotion. Marianne—how could you have done this to him?

'Jilly? Are you and Zane kissing?' a young, curious voice wanted to know. Kip was back.

'Not exactly, sport.' Their host answered for her, because she wasn't capable of a response just then. Slowly, almost reluctantly, he relinquished his hold on her and plucked the envelope from her fingers.

She thought she would always remember the feel of his hand on her soft skin. If touch could convey emotion, then the man's turmoil was acute. If Kip hadn't intervened just then, Jill had an idea she would have learned the full extent of Zane Doyle's fury.

He had put Jill in the same category as Kip's mother, and she feared that not even Marianne's letter would exonerate her.

For the first time in her life, Jill knew real fear. She had an idea that until she could prove otherwise he would treat her as an accessory to the crime, deserving the same punishment.

What an irony. Especially now she had realized that Zane Doyle had already become more important to her than Harris Walker—or any other man in her life. And she hadn't even known him two whole hours...

'I was just thinking that your teacher probably wants to freshen up before we eat.'

Kip had no idea what was going on, but Jill knew that Zane's seemingly innocent suggestion had been meant as a command because he couldn't stand the sight of her. Moreover, he wanted to be alone with his son, to try to come to grips with this new reality.

Sensitive to his need and his pain, she stayed in the bathroom until Kip eventually came running down the hall to tell her lunch was ready.

CHAPTER FOUR

'WHY don't you help Jilly with the dishes while I go upstairs and change into some old clothes? Then we'll go outside and make a difference to that short little wood pile around the side of the house.'

'Okay, Zane. But hurry!'

Jill had already offered to clean up after their delicious lunch of green salad, hamburgers and ice cream.

Kip had devoured everything. Normally he didn't like salad, but today he was a different child and seemed to want to do everything his new male role model did.

Thankfully Kip had dominated the conversation, which otherwise would have been non-existent. Since entering the kitchen, Jill had avoided their host's arctic gaze, because she was painfully aware of Marianne's letter still sitting in his back pocket, waiting to be read. Five minutes upstairs would give him time to scan it and attempt to understand the way Marianne's mind worked.

Since he'd gone down to the dock to meet the plane, his life had been turned upside down. In the flick of an eyelid he'd become the father of a vulnerable, engaging five-year-old boy whom she could tell had already wound his way into his daddy's heart.

By some mysterious process the two of them had

already bonded in much the same manner Jill had done with Kip upon their first meeting at school.

Instinctively she knew that Zane Doyle was the kind of man who wouldn't shirk his responsibilities—not even if he had another woman in his life.

No matter how difficult the situation was for him on a personal level, no matter how ugly the talk this unexpected news might create among the people who worked for him or did business with him, he would act in Kip's best interests. Of that she had no doubt, and it relieved her of her greatest fear.

Those closest to him would rally around. As for anyone else, he was an individual strong enough to handle acquaintances who, not being privy to the true facts, might say unkind things.

Judging from his interaction with Kip, which came too naturally to him to be anything but genuine, Jill knew he was a wonderful man. Why on earth hadn't Marianne held onto him? Done everything in her power to keep such a man in her life? In Kip's?

Jill couldn't fathom it, and she decided she'd better keep busy so she wouldn't go crazy thinking and worrying about a situation which had now gone beyond her grasp.

Normally she would have found sheer pleasure in working in his large modern kitchen with its pecan-toned finished cabinets and lemon accents. Everything about the house had been designed to make it sunny and airy.

At times, the long, dark winter months could be depressing, even to seasoned Alaskans, and he'd created an interior that gave the illusion of light and made the most of it. She was curious to explore the other rooms.

Apparently there was still some sheet-rocking and electrical work to be finished in the upstairs bedrooms, but the workmen helping Zane had gone home for Christmas and everything had been put on hold until the holidays were over.

From his conversation with Kip at the table, she'd learned that he lived in a condo in Bellingham, Washington, where the headquarters of his company were located. His other plant was at Thorne Bay, thirty miles south of Kaslit Bay, where they'd landed earlier to pick up some freight for him.

Thanks to Kip's inquisitive nature, she'd discovered that when the house was finished their host planned to make it his permanent residence. He'd commute to Thorne Bay or Bellingham by company plane.

Jill had no way of knowing if he had planned to stay here over Christmas, which was two days away, or if they'd only managed to catch up with him before he closed the place and went back to Bellingham for the holidays. At this point, however, the weather would be a factor in determining where they would be come Christmas morning.

He'd mentioned his mother, but Jill didn't know if his parents were still alive or if he had brothers and sisters, with children who would be Kip's cousins. So many unasked questions—gone unanswered because she knew better than to approach him while he was attempting to cope with a situation that would have tried the mettle of a saint.

'Jilly? We're ready to go outside.'

She swung around from the cupboard where she'd been putting the glasses away and almost dropped one when she saw that their host had entered the kitchen dressed in full winter gear. He was too attractive by far.

From beneath his ski cap his veiled gaze swept over her white-gold hair and the full curves and slender legs of her body clothed in a long-sleeved navy pullover and jeans. But his face was wiped free of animation, making it impossible for her to decipher what he thought about Marianne's letter—let alone her part in the scheme of things.

With her heart sinking once more, she called to Kip. 'Come here, sweetheart. Let me make sure you're bundled up good and tight.' With trembling hands she retied the cords of his hood.

'What are you going to do while we're outside?'

She kissed the end of his nose before pulling his neck-warmer over it. 'It's a secret.' She smiled, but it faded when she flashed an anxious glance at their host. 'That is, if it's all right with you,' she added softly.

He put a hand on Kip's shoulder as if he'd been doing it all his life. She could tell that with every gesture he made Kip feel special and important. What a crime that they'd lost the first five years when they looked so *right* together. It made her want to cry, but she remained dry-eyed.

On his way out of the room, he said, 'As I told you earlier, the kitchen is your domain for as long as you're here.'

'For as long as you're here…' His words held an ominous ring.

Jill had been so preoccupied over uniting Kip

with his father that she hadn't given any thought to the possibility that he might not be in her kindergarten class much longer.

If Marianne got her wish and Zane Doyle decided to tell Kip that he was his father, that he wanted his son to live with him in Washington until the house was completed, it was conceivable that Jill might never see her favorite little boy again.

Since September, she and Marianne had been roommates, and over the last four months Jill had become like a mother to Kip, because Marianne had relinquished virtually all responsibility in that regard. To Jill, the thought of not living with Kip anymore, of not having him in her class anymore, was too painful to contemplate.

On her last visit home her parents had said, 'Harris isn't going to wait forever for an answer. You could be married by now and expecting his baby instead of doting on Kip.'

But something was missing in her relationship with Harris. As attractive and intelligent and devoted as he was, she still couldn't see herself married to him, bearing his children. No man had ever made her want it all. Not until today...

Dear God, what was wrong with her—fantasizing about the man Marianne had had an affair with? A man who might already be involved with another woman.

At lunch, Kip had asked him if he had a new wife now, and he'd said no. But that didn't mean he wasn't seeing someone outside of his work on a regular basis. A man as exciting and intriguing as Zane Doyle would never want for female company.

In fact, she imagined that no woman would be immune to him. Herself most of all...

Needing an outlet for her nervous energy, she made a tour of the main floor, and was delighted to find a step-down living room with enormous picture windows overlooking the bay. A study, which had shelves built from floor to ceiling along the inner wall, adjoined the living room and shared the same fireplace. Window-seats added a charming feature. A person would be able to observe nature at close range and enjoy the view of the nearby forest.

Both rooms contained only the bare essentials: a couple of couches, a few chairs, a desk. She had no idea if Zane intended to leave the hardwood floors exposed or put in carpeting. In her opinion the light wood's patina gave the rooms warmth and needed no other adornment.

Further exploration revealed the full bathroom she'd hidden out in earlier, and a pantry for food storage. The back porch contained a large freezer, plus washer and dryer facilities. As far as Jill was concerned, he'd created a dream house in paradise.

Being an only child, Jill had traveled everywhere with her parents during their summers. Europe, South America, the Orient. But it had been on their cruise to Alaska a few years earlier that her eyes had been opened to the wonders of nature unspoiled by civilization.

She could still find no words to describe the miles of sheer breathtaking beauty that went on and on in every direction. Brilliant blue skies free of pollution, lofty mountain peaks, glistening white glaciers, cascading waterfalls, impossibly green forests and sparkling brooks teeming with fish. In her opinion, Alaska was the world's best kept secret.

On that cruise she had determined to go back and live there for a while. And, when a temporary teaching opportunity had finally opened up while a teacher took a year's sabbatical, Jill had jumped at the chance to fill it. But it had been a mistake. She could see that now and was tortured by the knowledge.

Deep down inside, of course, she wasn't sorry that Kip and his father were getting this chance to know each other. It should have happened a long time ago. Marianne should have made sure it happened.

But from a personal point of view Jill wished she'd never come to Kaslit Bay, never met Zane Doyle, never set one foot on his glorious territory.

With an ache that was growing more acute, she admitted to herself that everything she'd ever wanted out of life was right here... A man to match the splendor of a country which had a stranglehold on her heart and a little boy she loved so much she might have been the one who'd given him birth.

She was in terrible danger, and she could only pray that the weather would clear by morning so she could go home to her family and try to get a perspective on matters which were already out of control.

Just the thought of leaving produced such a wrench that she couldn't imagine how she'd survive the holidays, let alone the rest of her life.

Terrified by the strength of her feelings, she fled to the kitchen to plan out their dinner.

While she searched for various ingredients to

make Kip's favorite cookies she heard the sounds of a chainsaw over the noise made by the wind. The exuberant child outside would be in heaven.

Several weeks earlier Jill had bought him a toy ax and saw to complete his Paul Bunyan gear. But today he was experiencing the real thing, under the guidance of a man who would teach him the proper way to handle equipment and give him some hands-on experience.

More than anything, she wanted to go outside and join them. Instead, she plunged into her work with greater vigor than usual, enjoying what she could of the view from the kitchen window. Though it wasn't snowing heavily, the wind seemed to be getting worse.

The unexpected ringing of the telephone shouldn't have surprised her, but for a little while she'd felt they were beyond the reach of civilization. Should she answer it? Would Zane want her to?

The ringing persisted. Whoever was on the other end seemed determined to make contact. Maybe it was Marianne. Maybe at the last second she'd had an attack of conscience and decided she'd better call to find out if her son had arrived safely, if he was all right.

It would be a first for her, but Jill was ready to give her the benefit of the doubt—because Jill loved Kip and refused to believe that his mother could abandon him like this.

Without wasting another second, she dashed to the study to answer it. A female voice spoke right up, minus any Scottish brogue.

'Have I reached Zane Doyle's residence?'

Jill's hand tightened on the receiver. 'Y-Yes.'

After a brief pause, the voice demanded, 'Who are you?'

Anxious to be sure she didn't give the other woman the wrong idea, Jill said, 'I'm a temporary guest—stranded by a storm that was blown in. I'm waiting for it to subside so I can fly out again. Mr Doyle is outside cutting wood. Do you want me to get him for you?'

'No.' The woman sounded terribly disappointed. 'Don't bother him right now. I told him he should have left for Bellingham yesterday. Who knows when he'll get home now? Tell him to call Brenda when he gets in, will you?'

'Of course.' Jill replaced the receiver.

For a moment she'd been tempted to ask if he had her phone number, then had realized her mistake in time. If this woman had talked to him as late as yesterday and sounded so dejected because he hadn't left yet, then it meant that the two of them had a close relationship.

A shaft of pain pierced Jill's heart. Her first taste of jealousy in twenty-six years.

The phone rang two more times before she left the study. Both were business calls, but neither was an emergency. However, from the sound of their voices, neither man was thrilled that Zane wasn't immediately available. She put the messages on his desk and hurried through the house, afraid the cookies would have burned by now.

To her surprise, her flight to the kitchen coincided with Kip and his father's entry into the house. She could hear the boy's excited chatter and the stomping of feet.

As she pulled the pan out of the oven they walked into the kitchen. She couldn't help but notice how the wind had ruddied Zane's complexion, highlighting his incredible blue eyes. As for Kip, his cheeks were like roses, making the green of his hazel orbs more pronounced.

'Oh, boy—chocolate chip fudgies!' He darted a worshipful glance at his father. 'Wait till you taste them.'

'I hope you won't be disappointed,' Jill hastened to interject.

'Why would I be?' inquired a deep voice that thrilled her in every particle of her body without her permission.

She rubbed the back of her neck—a nervous gesture he seemed to find fascinating. 'There were three phone calls for you, and I'm afraid the cookies were in the oven too long.'

His searching eyes left hers to focus on his son. 'Shall we test them, sport?'

Kip nodded happily as his father reached for a couple of fudgies—which were devoured by both of them in no time. While she waited for the verdict their host gobbled two more, giving her the answer she craved.

He walked over to the refrigerator for milk, then poured two glasses and told Kip to sit down at the table so he wouldn't spill it or get crumbs on the floor.

After draining his own glass, Zane moved closer to Jill and murmured, 'You should have ignored the phone.'

If her ears didn't deceive her, he wasn't as angry-sounding, and she saw no censure in the eyes which were now leveled on her. 'I've been on holiday since Monday, so I put on the answering machine and have no intention of returning anyone's calls.'

Holding her breath, she ventured, 'Not even Brenda's?'

CHAPTER FIVE

An ODD gleam entered his eyes before he put the empty glass in the sink. 'My well-meaning sister wants the family together for Christmas. I'm afraid certain events have made that an impossibility now.'

For a multitude of reasons which Jill couldn't explore at the moment, she was so relieved to hear his answer that she blurted, 'I—I thought it might be Marianne, calling to check on Kip.'

In an instant, a black grimace stole over his arresting features. 'You don't honestly believe she's capable of giving a damn about anyone but herself or you wouldn't be here. So let's not pretend about something that's never going to happen,' he ground out.

There was a wealth of anger behind his words. They hinted at a history with Marianne which Jill knew nothing about—and frankly she preferred *not* to know.

'Can I have another cookie, Jilly?'

Her head jerked around. 'M-Maybe you'd better wait. We'll be eating dinner pretty soon.'

'Why don't you go to the back door and tell Beastlie he can come in now?' Thank heaven his father had had the presence of mind to suggest that.

'Yippee!'

The second he disappeared Zane said, 'You and I are going to have a long, serious talk—but not before Kip's in bed for the night. Which brings me to my next point. I have an idea he won't go to sleep unless he's in the same room with you. Since there's only a cot upstairs, and nothing else, the two of you will have to sleep in the living room.'

'That's fine.' She hurried to comply. 'Kip will be ecstatic.'

'As long as you're with him, there's no doubt of it,' he muttered in a dry undertone, but she heard him and felt the blood rush to her face.

'One of the couches makes up into a hide-a-bed. The other you can sleep on. I'm going to run down to the store and pick up some bedding.'

To her joy, it didn't appear that anyone else had ever stayed here with him. She shouldn't have been so excited that the three of them were going to spend the night together, but there was no way to tell her heart to stop hammering against her ribs.

'Is it all right if Kip takes a bath while you're gone?'

'Of course. Since the one upstairs still needs some plumbing done, we'll all have to use the one off the main hall. Which reminds me—I'd better pick up some more towels while I'm at it. Do you want anything?'

She shook her head. 'No. I'm afraid I brought everything Kip might need and then some, because—because—' She struggled to find the right words.

'Save the explanation.' He cut in on her harshly. 'You had no way of knowing if the father was as criminally irresponsible as the mother.'

So the letter had damned Marianne in his eyes after all...

'My question had to do with *your* needs,' he said forcefully.

Jill averted her eyes. If the truth were known, she had none. All that she would ever require from life was right here under this roof.

'Well, there is one thing... I had planned to finish up some last-minute shopping for Kip before Christmas. But finding Marianne's letter yesterday changed everything, and—'

'Tell me about it,' he bit out abruptly. 'What did you have in mind?'

'Some lumberjack boots and a hard hat—in orange, if possible.' She lifted her eyes to meet the disturbing intensity of his gaze. 'He wants to be just like you.'

She felt his body go taut with emotion. 'I'm afraid it will have to be yellow. As for the boots, R.J. can arrange to have some sent with the next shipment of supplies.'

'In this storm?' She was incredulous. 'I thought storms like this could last a few days.'

His gaze was vaguely speculative, and it sent a thrill of excitement through her body. 'That's true. However, special orders come by truck rather than boat. There's a logging road from here to Thorne Bay.'

Jill felt foolish. 'I didn't realize.'

'How could you when you didn't know of Kaslit Bay's existence until yesterday?' he countered in bleak tones, reminding her of how difficult this had to be for him. 'You still haven't answered my question.'

'I don't need anything.'

His brows met in a frown. 'What kind of woman

wants for nothing and would sacrifice her life for another woman's child?'

His question stung, probably because he'd detected from the beginning that her attachment to Kip had gone far beyond the bounds of friendship. Like her parents, he was cautioning her against becoming too possessive of his son.

No doubt he saw her as an old maid schoolteacher. Jill was mortified to realize that he'd probably sensed her attraction to him. Things couldn't be worse!

Battling her emotions, she retorted a little sharply, 'You don't have to worry, Mr Doyle. Believe it or not, I *do* have another life. Now that I know Kip is safe with his other parent, I'll be on the first plane out of here.'

'Which might not be for a while.'

The mocking reminder followed her out of the kitchen door. A burst of adrenalin sent her racing down the hall to the living room, where she could hear Kip trying to teach Beastlie some tricks.

By the time she'd coaxed him into leaving the dog alone long enough for a bath, his father had gone and she could breathe a little more easily.

While she put a meatloaf and potatoes in the oven Kip entertained himself in the tub. Apparently he found bathing at Zane's house a lot more fun than at home, because there was men's stuff around and all new kinds of soap and shampoo.

But as far as Jill was concerned the wine-red terry cloth bathrobe hanging on the back of the door, the hairbrush and razor only served as potent reminders of a man she had no business thinking about. A man who'd made it abundantly clear that he had no interest in her beyond a grudging pity.

For that reason, when she took her own bath right after Kip, she made no effort to fix herself up so their host would notice. Instead, while Kip got into his pajamas and robe, she pulled on her old red granny nightgown with the tattered collar, then slipped into her well-worn quilted blue robe, which buttoned from neck to hem.

Since she might as well look the part of an old maid, she didn't bother with make-up, and suggested that the two of them wear their matching rabbit slippers, whose giant ears flopped every time they took a step.

When their host finally made an appearance they were laughing and teasing Beastlie, who kept trying to catch a rabbit ear as they plopped around the living room.

'Zane!' Kip's burst of joy came out on a hiccup the second he saw him. 'Beastlie's trying to eat my slippers.'

'I can't say I blame him. If I were Beastlie, I'd want a good bite out of those myself.'

He stood tall and undeniably male, watching Kip with fatherly pride. And if Jill wasn't mistaken, she thought she saw his mouth twitch.

'Do you think the three of you could break this up long enough to feed a hungry man? It's seven-thirty and long past my eating time.'

Kip ran over to his father, his game forgotten in lieu of something—someone—far more important. 'Jilly has it *all* fixed, and I set the table.'

For an instant he took inventory of Jill in her robe and slippers, but he must have found the picture wanting. With no recognizable reaction one way or the other, his gaze swerved back to Kip, whom he caught up in his arms.

'Then I guess *I'll* have to do the dishes.' He chatted easily with his son as he headed for the kitchen. Evidently the desire to hold the child denied him from birth needed expression.

'I'll help.'

Jill heard Kip's spontaneous offer.

He could be so dear, and she envied his father the right to that closeness. The truth was that she envied them both, and she wished that she could become a permanent part of their lives. That was how far she'd lost her objectivity.

While putting dinner on the table she kept thinking that if she'd taught any grade but kindergarten—or if she'd been hired by any other school—none of this would have happened. But all the ifs in the world weren't going to change the situation at this late date.

Throughout the meal, Jill resisted the urge to stare at their host, and held back from contributing to the conversation to give he and Kip a chance to draw closer. When they reached the dessert stage she pushed herself away from the table. 'While you two finish off the cookies, I'll get busy in the living room.'

Zane knew exactly what she meant and seemed perfectly agreeable. In a bland tone of voice, he offered, 'You'll find new bedding out on the porch.'

During the next half-hour the men appeared to have a wonderful time doing the dishes. She, on the other hand, had to make do with Beastlie, who prowled around the couches she made up with new sheets, blankets and pillows.

Though the wind continued to howl ferociously, she felt cozy and safe in this little corner of heaven.

While their host locked up the house and flicked off lights she and Kip took turns brushing their teeth, and without her having to prompt him, he said his prayers.

Jill gave him the choice and he dived for the hide-a-bed, because it had room for Beastlie. He was supposed to stay at the bottom, but inch by inch he nosed forward until his chin rested on Kip's chest. Jill didn't have the heart to tell him to move, and neither did his father, who could see that both boy and dog were blissfully content.

Everything seemed so intimate in the dark.

'Goodnight, Zane.'

'Goodnight, Kip.'

'Zane? Do you think the plane will come soon?' Kip's little voice sounded anxious.

'I don't know, but let's not worry about that tonight.'

'I hope it never comes and we have to stay here for ever!'

'You think you'd like that?'

'Yes. I already told Heavenly Father.'

Jill hid her wet face in the pillow.

'Well, I guess that's that,' came the husky reply.

'Zane—what are we going to do tomorrow?'

'I thought we'd better look for that Christmas tree.'

'You have to come too, Jilly.'

'I—I think—'

'We'll all go.' He overrode her objection before she could express it.

'Zane? Will you stay in here till I fall asleep?'

'That was the plan.'

'Do you know any stories?'

'You mean like *Kabloona*?'

'What's that?'

'Kabloona's a strong, brave little Inuit boy like you, who got lost from his family when the ice broke up. He was carried far away to the north, where he made friends with a polar bear.'

'Was the bear *huge*?'

A low chuckle rumbled out of his father, infecting Jill. 'He was so big that at first Kabloona thought he was an iceberg.'

'Jilly's seen a real iceberg—haven't you, Jilly? What happened then?'

As their host spun his fascinating tale Jill found herself totally captivated. Like Kip, she wanted to stay here for ever.

Their host's voice had a hypnotic effect, especially on his son, who'd had a *huge* day and finally succumbed to sleep. Jill, on the other hand, was wide awake, and so entranced that it took the greatest self-restraint not to ask him to tell another story.

But the spell was soon broken.

'I think there've been enough fairy tales for one night. Shall we adjourn to the kitchen, Ms Barton?'

CHAPTER SIX

THE part Jill had been dreading couldn't be put off any longer. With her heart thudding sickeningly, she got to her feet, slipped on her robe and slippers and followed him out of the room.

When they reached their destination, he flicked on the overhead light and stood facing her with his hands on his hips, much like an adversary. Marianne's letter lay open on the kitchen table.

Jill understood his pain and commiserated with him. But anything she said would put Marianne in a worse light. Except that Jill didn't know how anything could be worse than Marianne's letter. She'd never forget it, not in a millenium.

Dear Jill

There's no easy way to say this, but last night Lyle asked me to marry him and I accepted. I know it happened fast, but honestly he's the one I've been waiting for. The problem is, he thinks Kip lives with his father.

I couldn't tell Lyle the truth because he's not ready for kids yet. After the holidays are over, and we get back from our honeymoon to settle down in Texas, I'll work on him to let Kip visit the ranch and we'll slowly ease into things.

I know I've never discussed Kip's father with you. The truth is, he's been begging me to let Kip come for visits ever since he was born. But

234

I've said over and over again that a logging camp is no place for a child, so he's had to fly to Ketchikan whenever he wanted to see his son.

Luckily Christmas vacation has coincided with our marriage plans. Kip's finally old enough to handle being away from home and will be ecstatic when he finds out he's going to live with his father for a while.

Unfortunately, Zane hasn't called me back yet to verify an exact time when he'll get there, but it should be around six. If he doesn't come to the apartment by then, that means bad weather has held him up. Should he not be able to make it in tonight, go in my top dresser drawer and you'll find an envelope with two round-trip tickets for you and Kip to fly to Kaslit Bay first thing in the morning.

Tell Kip I had to go into work early and that Santa is granting him his wish to see his dad. You can drop him off at the Kaslit Bay dock, where Zane will meet him. If there's a problem and you don't see him right away, tell the ticket agent who runs the general store to phone Zane Doyle. He'll make sure he gets the message. Then you can fly right back tr egon.

It'll be better if I'm not around when his father comes for him. I've packed his things with his Christmas presents, and they're in the two big suitcases in the closet, ready to go.

I've decided I'm going to call Kip Christmas morning and tell him I got married. Being with his dad will make it easier for him to hear the news, don't you think?

his dad will make it easier for him to hear the news, don't you think?

Don't worry about the rent, or utilities or food. Lyle has taken care of everything for the next three months, to give you time to find a new roommate. Naturally I'll be seeing you again to get everything moved. Probably around the end of January. I'll phone first.

Thanks, Jill. You've been a lifesaver in more ways than one, and you have such a great way with kids that Kip won't even notice that I've gone.

Have a Merry Christmas in Salem. Maybe you'll decide that Harris is your prince charming after all. I hope so.

Love, Marianne.

Every time she thought about it, Jill grew more appalled. She beseeched her host for understanding. 'Zane—I'm so sorry you had to find out about Kip the way you did. I would have given anything to have spared you.'

'You think I don't know that?' He bit out an epithet. 'It's obvious that when you realized Marianne had set you up you were ready to face the elements and put two lives in danger today in order to avoid placing me in a compromising position. But your eyes gave you away. That coupled with the fact that I don't know of another Zane Doyle living in this part of the country made me realize I couldn't let you two leave Kaslit Bay until I'd satisfied my curiosity.'

She shook her head. 'No matter what, this has to have come as such a shock.'

'I won't lie about that.' His voice sounded thick. 'But, strangely enough, I'm glad it happened the way it did.'

'How can you say that?'

'Being anonymous has enabled me to get to know my son without any awkward moments. *Lord*—if I had to choose one little boy out of the whole world...' He didn't need to say the rest. She knew what was in his heart, could see it in his eyes.

'Whatever else Marianne may be,' he murmured, 'she gave me a perfect son.'

'He *is* adorable,' Jill whispered.

'He asks a lot of questions.'

'You haven't heard anything yet,' she quipped, flashing him a quick smile. But it disappeared when she heard his next anguished comment.

'What am I to make of a five-year-old boy who has only mentioned his mother once in passing? He didn't even cry for her tonight! Hell,' he bit out emotionally, 'I have two nieces who'd be on the phone with Brenda right now if they were stuck here without her. But apparently so much damage has been done to my son, he'd cling to any male who looked twice at him.' Harsh lines had darkened his features until she wanted to weep.

'No.' Jill tried to clear the lump in her throat. 'That's not true. Normally he's very shy around people—especially men. In fact, on the first day of school it was obvious he had no friends and didn't know how to interact with anyone.

'Out of want for anything else, I enlisted the help

of our school custodian, Mr Ling, to befriend Kip.
He keeps his little dog in his office. I had him bring
Mutt to class on show-and-tell day, then pick Kip
out of the group to be the one to help feed and water
him every morning.

'It worked!' Jill enthused. 'Kip loved his new job
and soon the other kids crowded around him, wanting to help take care of the dog too. That's how he
became friends with Robbie, whom I encouraged to
come over to the apartment after school and play.

'Little by little, Kip started opening up. In the
beginning he avoided Robbie's father, and clung to
me every time they invited him to do something
with them. Not until this last month has Kip been
willing to leave me long enough to go with them
to the Saxman Native American Village to see the
totem poles. Even then Robbie's father arranged for
Kip to phone me a couple of times, to make sure I
was still at the apartment.'

His jaw hardened. 'Where was Marianne through
all of this?'

'At work.'

He raked both hands through his hair in a gesture
of abject frustration. She thought her heart would
break.

'Zane—there's something important you need to
know. I've found no evidence that anyone has ever
been unkind to Kip. Marianne has never been physically or verbally abusive with him. What I honestly
think is that she didn't know what to do with a
child. She just let anyone at hand raise him.'

His eyes blazed like blue fire. 'Thank God *you*
were there for him.'

The moment was so fraught with emotion that she had to look away. In a trembling voice she found herself saying, 'I thanked Him the second I saw you at the dock.'

'What would you have done if I hadn't been at Kaslit Bay?' The bleakness was back in his eyes.

'I'd already planned that we'd fly back to Ketchikan, where I'd take care of Kip indefinitely if I had to.'

He shook his head, as if in disbelief. 'I should have flown to Bellingham yesterday.'

'That's what your sister said.'

'At the last minute I decided to stay over another night, to do some chores around here.'

'I think it was meant to be,' she theorized. 'You know, Kip has always fantasized about the lumberjack daddy he's never seen. When he thought he was going to meet him, you've never seen such an excited little boy. Then today, at the height of his disappointment, *you* were there,' she cried.

'That's when something magical happened. I can't explain it. All I know is, I watched Kip bond with you. It didn't matter that you were a stranger. He instinctively chose *you*, as if he knew somewhere deep in his psyche that you were his father. I've never seen anything like it in my life.'

'It *was* pretty amazing,' came the husky admission. 'Particularly when I felt the same way about him. Damn Marianne to hell. I've missed his first five years!'

She bit her lower lip. 'I know. But you've got the rest of your lives to be together now.'

He'd been pacing the floor, but her comment

caused him to wheel around. 'You're right. However, there's just one problem. Kip needs to stay in school. If I take him to live at the condo in Bellingham he'll have to enroll in a kindergarten there and be separated from you. I've been asking myself if the boy I saw today would have responded to me in the same way if *you* hadn't been around.'

Though she could feel it slowly slipping away from her, Jill stood her ground. 'What happened between the two of you has absolutely nothing to do with me.'

A remote expression crept over his face. 'I'm not so sure of that. You've been the glue holding his world together. He worships you.'

'But you're his father!' she reminded him in a firm tone. 'When he hears the truth from you, he'll know real security for the first time in his life. I'm only his schoolteacher.' She said the words aloud, trying to convince herself of their veracity and failing.

'You're a hell of a lot more than that!' he fired back. 'If I didn't know differently, I'd assume you were Kip's mother.'

'But I'm *not*.' She felt hollow inside. 'Have you decided what you're going to say when Marianne calls?'

His expression was like thunder. '*If* she phones, and wants to speak to Kip, that's one thing. But I have no intention of talking to her. I'll let my attorney get in touch with her. He can tell her I'm asking for full custody of Kip. She'll be granted liberal visitation rights whenever—if ever—the mood strikes her.'

Jill trembled, never wanting to know what it would feel like to be on the receiving end of his anger. Suddenly he shot her a lancing glance.

'Since you're intimately involved in this situation, it's time you knew the truth about Marianne and me.'

Jill shook her head. 'You don't owe me an explanation.'

He folded his arms and leaned against the counter. 'I think I do. I wouldn't characterize our relationship as an affair. We became acquainted when some logger friends and their wives went salmon fishing with me for a couple of weeks. The crew had hired her as the cook.

'In the evenings, when we got tired of cards, she'd come and find me. I listened to her talk about her past—the struggles and hardships. She was the first woman after my wife died who appealed to me at all. Maybe it was her Scottish brogue.'

Jill could relate to that. She loved Marianne's brogue.

'However, being on a boat didn't allow anything but a superficial relationship to develop. Against my better judgement, I slept with her *once* before the holiday came to an end. We took precautions, but Kip's living proof that they don't always work,' he murmured in self-deprecation.

'She lived in Craig then. I made plans to fly to see her the following weekend, because I wanted to explore my feelings and get to know her when there wasn't a party going on all the time.'

From experience, Jill knew that if there was a party Marianne liked to be in on it.

'To my surprise, she'd moved from her apartment and had gone away without leaving a forwarding address. I made inquiries, so did my friends. For whatever reason, she'd disappeared without a trace.'

'That's exactly what she did yesterday,' Jill muttered, aghast. 'Zane? Were you the head of your own company back then?'

He shook his head. 'I was in the negotiation stage—drawing on every asset to make it go through. With hindsight, I can see that she was looking for a man with enough money to help her forget that she was ever dirt-poor. I wasn't that man. Not then.'

Marianne Mongrief, what a fool you were to let a man like Zane Doyle out of your sight, Jill thought.

'Because she'd gone off like that, without warning or explanation, I'm afraid that any budding feelings I had for her were killed on the spot. I considered myself lucky to have escaped before I became emotionally involved.

'Needless to say, I never saw or heard from her again. It's been six years—a faded memory until Kip told me his last name was Mongrief.'

So he hadn't been in love with Marianne. Jill's relief was exquisite. She finally found the courage to ask, 'When are you going to tell Kip you're his father?'

But she wasn't destined to know his answer, because they both heard the floor creak. Jill's head swung around in time to see a disheveled Kip wander unexpectedly into the kitchen with Beastlie at his heels.

He walked over to Jill and a small hand crept into hers. His solemn eyes stared up at her. 'Is Zane *really* my daddy?'

CHAPTER SEVEN

JILL'S gaze immediately sought his father's help. Zane gave an almost imperceptible nod. It told her to handle Kip the way she thought best.

Humbled by the trust both the man and the boy had placed in her, she got down on her haunches and put her hands on Kip's arms.

'How long have you been standing there listening?'

'I don't know. The wind woke me up. Is Zane my daddy?'

'He is.' Her voice trembled. 'How do you feel about that?'

His silence sounded ominous with the wind howling around the corners of the house. Zane's complexion had an odd pallor.

'Jilly, I don't think he likes me,' Kip whispered.

She smoothed the curls off his forehead, quite sure that Zane had heard his son. 'Why do you think that, sweetheart?'

''Cause yesterday he said he didn't have any kids.'

'Do you remember him telling you that his wife died before they could have children?'

'Yes.'

'Well, a long time after that, he met your mommy.' Praying for inspiration, she said, 'Do you remember the story about Kabloona? How he got swept away on the ice floe before his family knew about it?'

Kip nodded.

'That's what happened to you. Your parents only knew each other for a little while before your mommy moved away. She didn't know that you were going to be born until a long time after.

'Your daddy looked for her, but he couldn't find her—just like Kabloona's daddy couldn't find him. She was gone for almost six years and your daddy never knew where she was. When you and your mom moved to Ketchikan your father had no idea that your mom was in Alaska, or that you had been born.

'But, as soon as she could, your mommy asked questions and finally found out where your daddy lived so she could send you to him for Christmas.' Hopefully Jill could be forgiven for that one lie. 'The problem is, your daddy only found out that you were his son *today*. He was afraid to tell you that he was your daddy because he's never been a father before, and he feared *you* might not like *him*.'

'I *love* him!' Kip cried out spontaneously, his voice ringing with all the sincerity in his soul.

'Then come and show me, son.'

Zane held out his arms and Kip ran into them. When his father picked him up, Kip threw his arms around his neck and they clung.

'I've always dreamed of having a terrific boy like you. I love you, Kip, and we're never going to be separated again,' Jill heard Zane murmur as she slipped out of the kitchen, taking Beastlie with her. This was their time and they deserved to be alone.

Jill refused to allow her own pain of loss to super-cede the happiness of this night.

She went to bed on the couch with the realization that a miracle had been wrought, uniting father and son. Kip's future was secure. Marianne could do her worst, but Zane would be there—steady as a rock—eager to rear his son and give him the guidance he needed.

She could just imagine the plans they were making. Perhaps that accounted for the reason why Kip didn't come back to bed. After prowling around the the entry to the hall for a while, making low moaning sounds, Beastlie, too, must have decided it was no use. He finally gave up the vigil and lay down at the bottom of the hide-a-bed to wait for his new little master.

Despite the roaring of the wind, Jill's eyelids eventually grew heavy. She turned on her stomach and let out a deep sigh, her thoughts brooding over Kip's mother.

I hope and pray you realize what you've done, Marianne, because there's no going back. If history repeats itself and you wake up tomorrow morning deciding that you don't want Lyle anymore either, you can't expect to return to Ketchikan and pick up where you left off. Your son isn't the same insecure child you walked out on, and I'm no longer the heart-whole woman you left in charge of your most precious possession...

'Jilly? Jilly? Are you awake?'

'Good morning, sweetheart,' she murmured dazedly, and looked through bleary eyes at her watch. It was only seven-thirty and the wind outside was as fierce as ever, but Kip was too ecstatic to be aware of anything except his own happiness.

Apparently his father had finally brought him to bed last night, because the covers on the other couch were askew. Heavens! She hoped she hadn't snored or talked in her sleep or any such thing.

'Where's Beastlie?' She sat up and smoothed the white-gold hair out of her eyes.

'Daddy says now that we're a family, Beastlie is *my* department. I have to let him out every morning for his constitooshnel.'

Daddy. How easily the name came to Kip's lips. How wonderful that this morning he was able to wake up in his daddy's house and know he belonged here. For ever.

Jill realized that until now she'd always taken her own wonderful father's constant presence for granted. Kip could have no idea of how much his world was going to change, having a daddy like Zane Doyle to love and imitate.

One day, when he was a little older, he'd come to realize that his father was one in a million. A breed apart from other men. If all the children in the world could have such a parent...

'Will you fix breakfast, Jilly? Daddy says pancakes are his favorite too.'

She got to her feet on a groan, the old cliché about a woman's work never being done sounding loudly in her ears.

Five minutes later, freshened up and dressed in another pair of jeans and a hunter-green sweater, she told Kip to put on some warm clothes, then they headed for the kitchen.

'Breakfast is ready,' she announced shortly to her

little helper, who set the table and poured the orange juice with unprecedented enthusiasm.

'I'll get Daddy!' he squealed in delight, and dashed out of the room. Zane must have already been awake because it wasn't long before he emerged from the hallway, freshly shaven, his son in his arms.

Compelled by an urgency she couldn't suppress, Jill's gaze took in his rugged features, the intensity of his eyes, which looked impossibly blue against his cream-colored cable sweater. Well-worn dark tan cords molded to his powerful extremities, stretching taut over hard-muscled thighs...

To her shock, he was busy with an equally intimate scrutiny of her female attributes. The effect could be likened to a bolt of lightning striking her body.

Time stood still as his gaze played over her flushed face and gilt hair, which was overdue for another cut to retain its flattering wind-blown style. The slight tendency for it to curl at the jaw defined her classic features and brought out the rich brown of her darkly fringed eyes.

'I'm so hungry I could eat a dozen pancakes. How about you, sport?'

She had no idea what Kip said in response. Though Zane had been speaking to his son, his gaze had never left hers, forcing her to be the one who couldn't sustain the intensity of that searching regard.

Jill spun away from them, hearing the scrape of chairs as she started removing bacon and pancakes from the griddle. Once everything was served, and both father and son had started wolfing down their food, Zane commented, 'These pancakes are yummy, but they look like amoebas. Where's Mickey Mouse?'

Kip giggled. 'These look funny, Jilly.'

She couldn't help smiling. 'They're supposed to resemble Beastlie. I'm afraid I've got a way to go before they're perfected.'

'We're glad you said that—aren't we, son?'

'Yeah.'

'Why is that?' By this time, she had joined them at the table.

'You go ahead and tell her,' Zane urged his little look-alike.

She stopped eating, intrigued. 'Tell me what?'

'Daddy and I want you to stay with us.'

'I'm here right now.'

'We want you to live with us *for ever*!'

It was only natural that Kip should say something like that. Jill had been expecting it—just not this soon, and not in front of his father, who shouldn't be encouraging Kip in something that could never be. But when she darted a quick glance at him he was sitting there with a bland, unreadable expression on his handsome face.

She put down her fork. 'That would be wonderful, Kip, but it isn't possible.'

'Yes, it is. Daddy's going to marry you as soon as you can get a license. Tell her, Daddy.'

Marry...

Jill felt the blood leave her face, and she clung to the edge of the table for support.

Zane lounged back in the chair, his movements indolent as he put a hand on Kip's shoulder, yet she'd never seen those blue eyes more alive. 'We worked it all out last night. We need a woman to take care of both of us. I realize I'm not a prince charming, but I can learn.'

'Daddy's going to live with us in Ketchikan till school's out,' Kip elaborated. 'Then you won't have to work anymore and we can all live here.'

'Unless you want to keep teaching school,' came the voice of his father. 'If that's the case, I'll see about finding you an opening in Thorne.'

'Daddy said I can come on your honeymoon. We're going to see icebergs and w-walruses and polar bears—and in March we're going to watch the start of the I-dide-rod dog race. Where did you say it was, Daddy?'

'Wasilla.'

'Yeah. Wasilla.'

'So you see, Ms Barton...' One brow quirked. 'Everything has been arranged. All you have to do is say yes.'

CHAPTER EIGHT

JILL'S heart pounded so outrageously she thought she might be on the brink of cardiac arrest.

No man in his right mind proposed marriage to a woman within less than twenty-four hours of meeting her.

Since Zane Doyle was probably the most stable, altogether human being she'd ever met in her life, then it meant that he loved his son with such ferocity that he was willing to place Kip's happiness above every other need.

He'd already known love with his first wife, and obviously had no other expectations in that regard. What he had just proposed to Jill was a marriage of convenience. How perfect! Legitimize the housekeeper by giving her a ring and his last name. A married Zane Doyle would look good to the judge who had the legal power to determine Kip's future and declare which parent retained full custody.

Zane knew how much Jill loved his son, and in his eyes she had already drifted into spinsterhood. He figured that she'd never receive another marriage proposal, never have a child of her own, and had decided to do her a favor which, he assumed, would be mutually beneficial to the three of them.

Her blood froze in her veins. *He was wrong.*

Though she understood what motivated him, his marriage proposal was probably *the* most unkind act anyone had ever perpetrated against her in her life. It was probably the only unkind act he'd ever commited against another human being in *his* entire life.

Much as she loved Kip, the answer had to be a final and irrevocable no. She needed to tell him now, and she had to be totally convincing.

'Sweetheart, I wish things could have been different, but I can't marry your daddy. You see, I love another man.'

Kip stared soulfully at her. 'You mean the man who's a dentist?'

'Yes. He's waiting for me back in Salem.'

'You said he was a friend.'

'He is.' And I do love him in my own way, she thought. Just not the right way. Which is no one else's business but mine.

After meeting Zane Doyle, Jill knew for a certainty that she could never marry any man unless he attracted her the way Kip's father did.

How ironic that the one man who could make her heart beat as no other was the last man she'd ever consider marrying.

'Kip, sweetheart—you and I will always be friends, and I'll be in Ketchikan until June, so whatever you and your father work out about where you're going to live, where you're going to go to school, you can always call me and come for visits when it's convenient.'

'But we want you to *live* with us—don't we, Daddy?' Kip persisted.

'We do.' His voice grated. 'Maybe if your teacher spends enough time with us, she'll learn to love us more than the dentist. Dentists are kind of boring.'

'Why?'

'Well, they sit around all day listening to elevator music while they look at people's teeth.'

It didn't help that Jill had thought the same thing on more than one occasion, though she'd rather do anything else than admit it.

'Yeah. And they're scary too.'

'They're as important as loggers.' She felt compelled to defend Harris, who wasn't here to stand up for himself.

'That may be true,' Zane murmured, 'but they'll never know the excitement of getting out in nature every day of the year, where glaciers beckon and icy rivers flow, where the wind howls like a creature and the greenest green forest is your home along with the bear and the moose and the spotted owl. Now, *that's* the opposite of boring.'

'Yeah.'

Jill closed her eyes tightly. With one sweeping remark, Zane had not only influenced his son's whole attitude toward life and living, his words had also conjured up the same overpowering feelings and emotions which had captivated Jill on her first visit to Alaska and had brought her back a second time.

With their heads together like conspirators, she heard Zane whisper to Kip, 'Did you know that women are known to change their minds more often than men?'

'Change her mind, Daddy.'

'I intend to.' His deep response sounded like an avowal and it sent a stab of fear through her quaking frame, because Jill recognized that she was far more vulnerable to the Doyle charm than she'd thought.

Not able to take any more of this, she started clearing the table to avoid her host's unnerving gaze. 'Wh-Why don't you two go hunting for that Christmas tree while I clean up?'

'We're not going anywhere without you,' he declared in a no-nonsense tone. 'So we'll all help with the dishes first.'

In no time the kitchen looked spotless, coats and boots were put on and Jill had no choice but to join father and son outside in the truck. With one amazing spring, Beastlie leaped into the back and they were off.

More snow flurries buffeted by fierce gusts of wind made visibility difficult, but Jill had no worries because Zane knew exactly where to go and she felt perfectly safe. So did Kip, who bounced up and down between them, watching Beastlie through the rearview window while he commented on every subject which came into his mind.

They'd been traveling for about ten minutes along a logging road which cut a swath through the forest, when Zane pulled to a stop and pointed to the right. 'I've spotted our tree. Let's get out and walk over there.'

'Where, Daddy?' Kip strained to see.

'It's kind of hidden, but it's been waiting for you.'

Kip's eyes rounded in astonishment. 'It has?'

'That's right. Every tree has a job to do. This one was meant to be a Christmas tree. I knew it when I first came out here years ago. It was just a tiny baby sapling then, and probably looked like you right after you were born.'

While Kip giggled at the comparison Jill's heart turned over.

'Since then I've been checking on it, watching it grow taller and rounder and bluer.'

'*Bluer?* Christmas trees are supposed to be *green*!'

It was Zane's turn to laugh, and Jill chuckled right along with him. She couldn't help it. Kip was so adorable.

'Not the real ones,' his father asserted.

Since Kip regarded his father as perfection itself, she could sense his confusion.

'Jilly?' he whispered. 'Have you ever seen a blue Christmas tree?'

Above the hood covering Kip's dark-blond head, she caught the laughter in Zane's eyes, and it filled her with a warmth that radiated throughout her being. *I love him. I love this man.* How was it possible that anything so important could have happened this fast?

'A-Actually I have.' She stammered her answer as an afterthought. 'Your father is right. A blue spruce is the true Christmas tree, but there have been years when my family couldn't find one anywhere and we had to make do with something else.'

'Mommy and I never used to have a tree 'cause they're expensif. But Jilly got us a little one, didn't you, Jilly?'

This time Zane's gaze trapped hers, but a shadow of pain had replaced the laughter.

Feigning brightness, she said, 'Think how lucky you are that your father knows exactly where yours is growing. And because it's still alive, it's going to fill the house with a divine scent.'

'Can I call Robbie and tell him about it?' he cried out, oblivious to the undercurrents.

'Sure you can—as soon as we get home.' Miraculously the dark moment had passed, and once more there was a broad smile on his father's attractive face. He opened the driver's door. 'You help Jilly while I get the chainsaw out of the back.'

From the moment their feet made fresh tracks in the light snow covering the ground, Jill felt as if they'd entered a magical world. Once inside the protection of the lush stand of mature pines, the wind didn't bother them as much. It was like being in a cathedral, and a reverent feeling prevailed. Even Beastlie made no noise as they trod through the dense forest. Suddenly their treasure appeared.

A perfectly shaped ten-foot blue spruce with adorning pine cones stood among the cedars and hemlocks. It was like something out of a Disney cartoon, and Jill half expected Bambi and Thumper to emerge.

'But it's not blue!'

Jill had been anticipating that remark. So had his father, who was ready for him. 'It is, compared to all the other trees.' He hunkered down beside his son. 'Take a look at the evergreens surrounding us. See the difference?'

Avid hazel eyes studied one tree after another with a concentration that reminded Jill of Zane. Then Kip's little head nodded and he put an affectionate arm around his father's neck. 'It's the beautifullest one, Daddy.'

'I agree,' came the husky rejoinder.

'It'll die if we cut it?'

'That's right.'

'Jilly?' He lifted troubled eyes to her. 'Do you think we should kill it?'

She sucked in her breath. 'I think that's up to you.'

'If we cut it, then it won't be here next Christmas?' His voice wobbled.

After a brief silence his father nodded.

'It's going to get bigger and bigger every year, huh?'

'That's right.'

'Do we have to cut it?'

She heard Zane clear his throat before he shook his head.

'Goody. Then it will still be here when I'm as big as you.'

'That's right. One day you can show it to your children.'

'Yeah. And it will be *hu-u-ge*.'

Unconsciously, Jill's gaze strayed to Zane's. He's your son through and through, her heart whispered to him.

On a subliminal level, she felt that he understood what she'd been thinking. Streams of unspoken communication flowed between them, forging silent bonds. Jill had never felt this kind of oneness with a man before, and it shook her to the depths of her being.

'I saw a fallen tree a couple of miles back,' he finally said aloud. Jill had seen it too, and had been on the verge of mentioning it. Their psyches seemed to be functioning on an identical plane. 'We'll cut off the top and use it for the house.'

While Kip and Beastlie ran on ahead she slowly retraced her footsteps, more aware than ever of the exceptional man at her side. Just now she'd felt the essence of him, which transcended the physical. As surely as she knew anything, the knowledge came to her that she'd met the man she wanted for her husband. Just the thought of creating a child with him...

She stifled a sob in her throat, wishing she could have met him under different circumstances. As it was now, he'd never be able to see her without including Kip in that same picture.

Maybe Zane was attracted to her after all. There were certain signs she couldn't ignore. But she would never know for sure how much of it was due to chemistry, and how much to the fact that he needed her to help smooth the way with Kip.

Marianne would never know how blessed she had been to have met Zane when they were simply a man and a woman drawn together by attraction and circumstance.

If Jill had met him the same way, would he have looked her up when the fishing trip had been over? Would he have come after her because he couldn't help himself? Couldn't imagine life without her?

That was how she felt about him. It was killing her that she'd never have the satisfaction of being pursued for herself and no other reason...

Jill didn't know how to deal with this kind of pain, but she tried to enter into the morning's activities with her usual enthusiasm. After all, Kip had barely met his father. Every experience was a first for him and she refused to let anything mar his new-found joy—especially not this Christmas Eve.

By lunchtime, an eight-foot evergreen, complete with a wooden stand fashioned by Zane in minutes, graced the living room.

Over a meal of hot soup and sandwiches, they planned how they would decorate it. Zane hadn't known he'd be spending Christmas at Kaslit Bay, so there were no lights or ornaments. Undaunted, Jill suggested that they make a trip to the store to see what they could find.

At her urging, Zane agreed to let them take care of the shopping. That way he could get on with priming the walls of one of the upstairs bedrooms—a job which had been interrupted by their unexpected arrival.

After lunch was cleaned up, Zane walked them out to the truck. The relentless wind howled as strongly as ever and Jill had to strain to hear his directions for finding the small house-converted store situated halfway between the dock and the trailers.

As they were about to pull away he tapped on the truck window. She spied a couple of twenty-dollar bills in his hand. When she rolled down the glass he said, 'You're going to need money.'

Jill heard the words, but his compelling mouth was too close to hers to concentrate on anything else. A longing to kiss him was fast growing into an obsession.

'This is my treat.' Her words came out breathy, because his eyes had narrowed on *her* mouth and she wondered for the first time if he might be having the same struggle.

Kip chose that moment to squeeze between her and the steering wheel. 'We'll hurry, Daddy.'

Thankfully his intervention broke the tension holding them in thrall. 'Will you be here when we get back?'

Zane flashed her another nonverbal message. Like Jill, he realized that Kip's fear of being left alone went layers deep and would take years of constancy to eradicate.

In a surprise move, he strode around the back of the truck and levered himself into the passenger side next to his son. 'You know what, sport?'

'What?' Kip scrambled onto his lap in delight.

'I've decided the walls can wait.'

'How come?'

The same question had been on Jill's tongue, but she didn't have the temerity to ask.

'Because the house will be lonely without you two in it.'

His low-pitched voice vibrated with emotion, drawing Jill's attention against her will. What she saw coming from the depths of his eyes set her body trembling.

CHAPTER NINE

WHEN Jill nodded, Kip ran out of the living room and up the stairs. 'Okay, Daddy!' she heard him cry out. 'You can come down now.'

The second he disappeared, she put all the Christmas gifts she'd brought with her under the tree. She knew Zane would be adding more after Kip went to bed, because she'd seen a few packages change hands at the store when Kip hadn't been looking.

While she waited with pounding heart for his father to make an appearance she stood back to survey the finished product. It had taken them all afternoon and evening to fashion the decorations and get them hung. Kip had worked nonstop making chains out of old Christmas wrapping paper which Mrs Ross had had on hand for years.

Supplies at the store ran low this time of year, and Jill had been forced to make do with whatever she could find. A sack of baby tangerines and a box of cloves had been turned into ornaments with faces. An odd can of metallic silver spray paint used to touch up the fishing boats had transformed the freshly gathered pine cones. They gleamed like tinsel under the living room light.

An aluminum foil Christmas tree skirt dotted with cutouts from the wrapping paper had worked well around the base of the tree. And as a final touch Kip had ingeniously provided a star made out of a piece of glittery sandpaper he'd found upstairs. All in all, Jill felt more than satisfied with their efforts.

Beastlie, wearing a paper chain Kip had put around his neck, seemed to like the clove-scented tangerines and kept pacing back and forth sniffing them.

She stood back to survey their masterpiece. Her profession demanded that she be innovative and normally she was used to the cut-and-paste projects of her job and never thought anything about it. But this tree was different. She held her breath as Zane entered the living room, carrying his son.

She'd promised herself that she wouldn't look at her host, wouldn't allow him to dominate her thoughts and dreams. But all her good intentions vanished in the electric blue of his eyes as they zeroed in on her.

'It's beautiful, huh, Daddy?'

When his father finally answered he said, 'Everything is so beautiful, I'm in awe.'

Her heart leaped in her breast, because he was still looking at her.

'What's in ah mean?'

When Zane didn't answer his son, Jill felt compelled to say something. 'I-It means he can't find the words to describe how pretty you've made the tree with those chains, sweetheart.'

'Jilly made the faces on the orn-ments.'

'I can tell, sport,' came the thick-toned response as his father examined everything to Kip's satisfaction. 'No wonder all the kids love her.'

'Yeah. But I love her the most.'

'Has she told you that she's going to live with us, yet?'

Zane's question was the last thing she'd been expecting, and she barely heard Kip's negative response. Her pulse raced frantically because his father didn't play fair. She'd thought he didn't have a cruel streak, but his persistence on the subject of her living with them was forcing her to reassess her thinking.

She had to get out of there. Maybe Beastlie was intuitive because he followed her.

'Where are you going, Jilly?' Kip might only be five, but he had his father's eagle eye.

'I thought I'd take the dog outside for a few minutes before we all go to bed,' she said on a sudden burst of inspiration. Ignoring his father's probing gaze, she hurried down the hall to the back porch where she reached for her parka.

The wind was so strong she had to hang onto the door so it wouldn't slam shut. Oddly enough, she welcomed the fury of the elements as she and Beastlie slipped out into the howling maelstrom.

Her thoughts and emotions were so chaotic that she started through the shallow covering of snow having no particular destination in mind. Beastlie dashed here and there, obviously in heaven, but her mind wasn't on him.

To her horror, she found that she was actually entertaining the idea of Zane's unorthodox marriage proposal. The bald truth was that she wanted him in every way a woman could want a man.

Because Jill had never truly been in love before, she'd assumed that she didn't have a passionate side to her nature. But judging from the primitive feelings just thinking about him evoked she realized she hadn't known herself at all. The knowledge that she was as vulnerable as the next woman came as a shocking revelation.

So deep was her turmoil that she started walking faster, then cried out in surprise when a strong pair of hands suddenly took hold of her upper arms from behind.

Zane muttered something harsh and unintelligible, then pulled her around with such force that she was crushed against him.

'Why didn't you answer me when I called?' he demanded, his chest heaving. In the dark, his face and body were a mere silhouette.

'I—I didn't hear you.' Her breathing was as shallow as his.

'Why did you run out like that?' His hold tightened, making her unbearably aware of his hard, warm body practically molded to hers.

'I needed a little time to myself.'

'Then why in the hell didn't you go upstairs instead of running around out here where anything could happen?'

Beneath the anger, she could feel his anxiety. His reaction wasn't something he'd feign at a time like this, and it made her heart pound without mercy.

'Beastlie's with me.' Her voice sounded weak, even to her own ears.

'If a pack of wolves had started to attack, not even he could have protected you all of the time.'

At the mention of wolves Jill shivered and tried to pull away, but he held her in a vise-like grip.

'Did you stop to consider what your disappearance would do to Kip?'

'Zane—I'm sorry. I didn't mean—'

But she didn't get the chance to finish explaining because his mouth unexpectedly descended on hers, driving every thought from her head.

She was caught unaware, and her mouth opened to the hungry, compelling pressure of his. To her everlasting shame, she responded with all the newly awakened passion running riot inside her. She'd needed, wanted to discover this ecstasy since yesterday, when he'd walked the length of the pier right into her heart.

The violence of the elements paled in comparison to the tumult assailing her body. She should have tried to stop him, but right or wrong had no meaning to her, not when every kiss fueled the fire of her desire.

They couldn't seem to get enough of each other. Only when she felt herself being lifted more fully into his arms and heard him groan as he devoured her mouth over and over again did she have any cognizance of what she was doing.

Humiliated at having let go this way, because it proved what a pathetic, love-hungry woman she really was, Jill finally found the strength to tear her lips away. He made a moaning sound of protest as she wiggled out of his arms and started running up the road.

He obviously wasn't ready for this little interlude to end—not after the way she'd responded. Any normal, healthy male would have taken advantage of the opportunity so generously offered. Naturally he would have gone on enjoying it to the fullest, just as Zane had done.

Red-faced with embarrassment, furious at herself

for losing complete control, she dashed toward the house, praying that she'd reach it before Zane.

Once she gained the back porch, she kept on going into the house and down the hall to the bathroom, where she shut and locked the door.

'Jilly?' Kip cried her name on cue. 'Are you okay?'

Guilt struck her down. 'I'm fine, sweetheart.' She barely got the words out because she was struggling for breath. 'I'll be out in a minute.'

'Daddy? Is Jilly sick?' she heard him call out to his father, who must have just entered the hall.

'Nope. But she got cold out there and needs to warm up. I'll tell you a story while we give her some time in the shower.'

Jill rested against the closed door, her energy spent. If she got any warmer she'd burn up! What she needed was a *cold* shower—the normal remedy for men who were out of control. How mortifying that Zane knew exactly what was wrong with her.

After staying in hiding for forty-five minutes, during which time she took a shower and changed into her nightgown and robe, Jill decided she'd better make an appearance. Something told her that her host would eventually come to investigate. She wouldn't put it past Zane to find a way to unlock the door if he thought it necessary.

To her relief, all was quiet when she padded into the living room. Kip had fallen asleep with Beastlie's head on his chest and thank heavens there was no sign of Zane. He was probably upstairs working on the walls, their rapturous moment in the snow already a fading memory.

She turned off the light and climbed under the

covers. Women were so different from men, she thought angrily to herself, and kept pounding the pillow.

That poem about a man's love being a thing apart, but for a woman being her whole existence occupied her thoughts until she thought she'd go mad.

'Jill?'

She gasped at the sound of Zane's voice.

'I'm not about to attack you, if that's what you're worried about,' he murmured in a hushed voice so that he wouldn't waken his son. 'I need to put a few things under the tree.'

'I wasn't worried.'

'The hell you weren't!'

'Look, Zane—I thi—'

'I'm not going to apologize for what happened out there,' he interrupted savagely. 'We've both been wanting it. The fact is, you wouldn't have left Salem if you'd been in love with Harris. After your response outside, I can safely say you'll never end up with him, so that excuse won't wash for not marrying *me*.'

One thing about Zane Doyle—he was brutally honest. And if *she* were honest that was one of the reasons she'd fallen in love with him. It was the reason why nothing but the truth would do now.

Choosing her words carefully, she admitted, 'You're right. I don't love Harris enough to marry him. But that doesn't mean I'm going to marry a man I've only known two days—no matter how strong the attraction might be, no matter that Kip needs a full-time mother.'

'Attraction is a funny thing,' he murmured solemnly, as if she hadn't spoken. 'It's hard to trust, yet without the rare kind of chemistry you and I share, a man and woman would never come together in the first place.

'You can fight it all you want, but a fire has been lit, Ms Barton. I'm afraid it's one that neither of us is going to be able to ignore—Kip or no Kip. Goodnight.'

His warning frightened her so much that she couldn't form words. Long after his footsteps had faded she lay there wide awake, haunted by all she was giving up.

The night seemed to go on and on as she listened to the wind and heard the occasional sounds made by Kip and Beastlie while they slept.

Tears trickled down her face, moistening the pillow. This could be her life. The boy and the dog. The man...

CHAPTER TEN

'MERRY CHRISTMAS, Daddy.'

A joyous Kip, dressed in new clothes from Jill, a hard hat and boots from his daddy, and a play watch from Marianne, ran over to his father with the present he and the other children in her kindergarten class had made for their parents several weeks earlier.

Through her lowered lashes, Jill spied the telltale moisture in Zane's eyes as he took out the plaster of paris wall plaque containing the mold of Kip's right hand.

'I made one for you and one for Jilly.'

She saw his throat working before he reached for his son and hugged him hard.

'You couldn't have given me anything I wanted more,' he finally said in a choked-up voice. His gaze sought Jill's, silently thanking her for giving him this little portion of Kip's past.

A smile lifted the corners of her mouth in acknowledgement. Then she got to her feet, wearing the gorgeous blue and white hand-knit Scandinavian sweater he'd given her. Picking up a present from under the tree, she walked over to Zane. 'This is from me.'

He looked stunned.

'I'll open it for you, Daddy.'

'Go ahead, sport,' His voice still sounded thick. Having gained his father's permission, Kip tore the wrapping and undid the lid. 'This is a picture of me,' he said proudly. 'Mommy has the other side of my face.'

Without saying a word, Zane lifted it from the box. It was an eight and a half by eleven black silhouette of Kip's adorable profile, framed in silver with non-glare glass. Beneath it was a folder containing all Kip's artwork and little projects which she'd kept at the apartment for him.

While he proceeded to spread everything out on the floor for his daddy to see Zane's eyes lifted to Jill's once more. They'd gone dark with emotion.

Compelled to explain, she said, 'My mother collected everything I ever made in school. I thought you'd like to see how artistic and creative your son is.'

Suddenly he reached out and grasped her hand, conveying feelings he couldn't express in front of his son. Jill knew he was grateful, could sense it, feel it in the pressure of his fingers.

'Daddy?' Kip tugged on his father's khakis. 'Look! These are all of you!'

At this point Jill was fighting tears and had to look away. There were at least a dozen Paul Bunyan originals. Some had been drawn in crayon, others had been fashioned in chalk or poster paint. Every picture had him doing a different task: hauling logs, chopping wood, driving a truck.

'See the dogs? That's Prince and that's King. Now I've got to draw Beastlie in all the pictures. Jilly, do you have a crayon?'

He was utterly precious, and for a moment she had difficulty talking. She knew Zane was suffering the same affliction. 'I'm afraid I don't, sweetheart.'

His father cleared his throat. 'I have a yellow highlighter in my desk. Will that do?'

'Yeah.'

'I'll find it.'

'Let me,' Jill urged. She needed to get out of the room. Her feelings were too tender, too raw.

Without obtaining his permission, she hurried into his study and started rummaging blindly in his top drawer till she found it.

'Jill…'

Zane had followed her.

She whirled around, but only glimpsed a slash of blue before he pulled her into his arms with a speed that robbed her of breath.

'*Dear God*—how do I thank you?'

His arms tightened, but he couldn't have been aware of his great strength.

'You've already repaid me by claiming your son and showing him he has a place in your heart. He's a very blessed little boy to have you.'

His hands slid up her arms to her face. He stared down at her, his eyes flaming with the intensity of his feelings. 'Jill—' He was on the verge of saying something vital when the telephone rang.

Its discordant note shattered the moment, bringing a black grimace to Zane's features. He hadn't forgotten that Marianne might be calling. Neither had Jill, who had no desire to be privy to their conversation.

Her duty was over. Kip and his father were now united. The sooner she left Kaslit Bay, the sooner she could start picking up the pieces of her life.

But Zane was still holding her fast around the waist when he lifted the receiver and rapped out a brusque hello. Jill was so nervous that the blood pounded in her ears.

'Merry Christmas to you too, Marianne.' His voice resounded with chilling irony. 'Thank you for the present.'

Jill couldn't bear to listen to any more and pulled away from Zane, who had no choice but to let her go. Avoiding his eyes, she left the room and shut the doors to give him the privacy he needed.

Kip looked up from his drawings. 'Is it Mommy?'

'Yes.' She got down on her stomach next to him and handed him the highlighter. 'When your father has finished talking to her, it'll be your turn. Now, I want to see where you're going to put Beastlie in this picture.'

'He's going to ride in the back of the truck with Prince.'

Fifteen minutes must have passed before a sober-looking Zane appeared at the door and called Kip to the phone.

Taking advantage of the time alone, Jill hurried into the kitchen to finish making the cinnamon rolls. They'd been invited to Christmas dinner at the Rosses' at three, and she didn't want to show up at their home empty-handed.

The older couple were lonely for their own children and grandchildren, who couldn't make it this year. They'd doted on Kip at the store, and when they'd learned that he was Zane's son they'd insisted on a celebration.

Jill had been able to tell that their warm acceptance of the situation had pleased Zane. She was also very thankful that he'd said yes to their invitation.

For one thing, she wanted to take R.J. aside and arrange for an early-morning drive into Thorne. Even if the weather was still bad, there'd be a flight to Ketchikan. By tomorrow afternoon she could be in Salem. That was what she needed. To get far away from Zane.

As for the rest of Christmas Day, the Rosses would provide the laughter and voices of other people to break the tension between the two of them. There'd been way too much togetherness. The longer she spent in Zane's company, let alone Kip's, the more she could feel her resolve to say a permanent goodbye slipping.

While she was putting the last roll in the pan to rise she had the feeling she was no longer alone. Looking over her shoulder, she saw Zane propped against the doorjamb, watching her with a brooding expression. Something was wrong. She felt her heart drop to her feet.

'Marianne won't fight me for custody,' he began, 'and Kip didn't appear to be fazed by the news of her marriage. He thinks it will be real cool to visit her at the ranch once in a while.'

She leaned against the counter, puzzled. 'I—I thought you'd be pleased with that kind of news. What's wrong?'

'I'm trying to figure out how two human beings of the same sex could be the absolute antithesis of each other. Marianne went through childbirth but doesn't have the instincts of—' He broke off. 'Then there's *you*.'

She shook her head. 'Don't put me on a pedestal,

Zane. Billions of women, whether they've had a baby themselves or not, make wonderful mothers. Those who don't probably haven't had the proper role models or environment. Let's just be thankful that Marianne finally did the right thing and sent Kip to you. Deep down, she had to know the kind of man you are.'

As far as Jill was concerned, Marianne had let the most wonderful man who ever lived get away. 'A-Are your parents alive? Does Kip have a grandma and a granpa?'

He nodded. 'The news about my son will make them young all over again.'

'How wonderful for Kip. I'd like to meet them,' she blurted without thinking, then could have cut her tongue out.

A satisfied smile broke the corner of his mouth. 'I'm planning on it.' After that assertion, he straightened. 'Don't take too long in here. Kip and I are waiting for you to come and play Fish in front of the fire.'

'I'll be there soon.'

But it was a lie. The second Zane left the kitchen, she reached for her purse and drew out a notepad and pen. This was as good a time as any to write the letter she intended leaving for Kip and his father to find in the morning.

School was only eight days away. Kip might miss her, but a week wasn't that long and Zane would keep his son fully occupied until class started up again.

Hopefully the time apart would give Jill the perspective she needed to treat Kip and his father as she would any other family whose child was in her class.

She couldn't fathom the possibility that Kip wouldn't be back, so she didn't even try to deal with it.

CHAPTER ELEVEN

'WHAT'S going on, Jill? You've changed beyond recognition since you were here at Thanksgiving.'

'I'm sorry if I've ruined your New Year's Eve, Harris. I warned you I'd be terrible company.'

'Who is he?'

'I'd rather not talk about it.'

He pounded his fist against the steering wheel of his car. 'Are you going to marry him?'

If he'd asked her that question the day after Christmas, she would have said no. But the most hellish, agonising, empty week had gone by since she'd left Kaslit Bay. She had an idea that if she saw Zane again she'd follow him anywhere, do anything he asked—because life without him and Kip wasn't worth living.

As it was, there'd been no word from Kip or his father. And something told her Kip wouldn't be coming back to Ketchikan. It had all turned into an ugly nightmare.

She wished she'd never talked R.J. into driving her to Thorne the morning after Christmas. He wasn't the kind of man to interfere, but she knew he hadn't approved of her leaving like a thief in the night.

So many times she'd gone to the phone, needing to talk to them. But at the last moment she'd lose her courage. Zane was making a new life for himself with his son. She had no right to upset their routine at this late date. Children thrived on it, and the very fact that Kip hadn't called proved he was settling in beautifully with his father.

'I asked you a question, dammit.'

Jill's eyes closed tightly. She'd never seen this side of Harris before. It increased her guilt, because everything was her fault. 'I can't answer it, Harris, but I do know that tonight has to be goodbye. Please forgive me.' She opened the car door and got out.

'Jill—'

'There isn't anything more to say.'

Harris was in pain, but she couldn't do anything to alleviate it because her own pain was too great.

She shut the door, then rushed toward the house with the realization that all her bridges were burned now. The idea of teaching school in Ketchikan no longer held any appeal for her. She was tempted to break her teaching contract. If she did, it would sabotage her career, but maybe that was for the—

'At last.'

She came to a complete standstill on the top step of the porch. Her head jerked around. The rugged, attractive, dark-blond man who'd haunted her every thought and dream was here in Salem, looking very much alive dressed in a dark suit with a white shirt and a tie.

'Zane!'

'You remember my name. That's a start.'

She could hear his suppressed anger, and leaned against the door because her legs would no longer support her.

'Wh-What are you doing here? Where's Kip?'

'With my parents in Bellingham. He'd rather be

here, of course, but I told him that this was one trip I had to make on my own because this was big people stuff.'

Jill couldn't breathe. Her heart was pounding too hard. 'He sends his love, by the way. Every other sentence that comes out of his mouth is Jilly this and Jilly that. His prayers are full of you.

'*So are mine*,' he added in a husky tone. 'Come back with me, Jill, and we'll call it quits for you deserting me in my greatest hour of need.'

She didn't know where to look. 'Kip seemed so happy with you—I wasn't worried about leaving. I—I felt it was for the best. There are many women who'd make a wonderful housekeeper and n-nanny for Kip.'

'I'm not talking about Kip. I'm talking about *my* wants, *my* needs.'

He moved toward her and there was no place to run. In the next instant his hard, male body held hers prisoner. She could no more deny his descending mouth than she could deny air to her lungs.

After a week's deprivation, her hunger could find no appeasement. Neither could his. Jill forgot everything except the thrill of being loved like this, of giving him back kiss for kiss until she was a trembling mass of need.

'I love you, Zane,' she cried out against his lips. 'It's too soon to say it, but it's true.'

'Sometimes love happens this way. It bursts in on you full-flowered. We're some of the lucky ones who can do something about it. I love you, Jilly. Let's not waste any more time, darling.'

'I agree.' She half sobbed her happiness. 'As incredible as this may sound, I want to be your wife.

I've discovered that my life is meaningless without you. I knew it long before I drove away from Kaslit Bay.'

'Thank God.' He moaned the words before desire engulfed them once more. And as she gave herself up to longings which were begging for release it began to dawn on her that he'd come for her because he couldn't help himself, because he loved her.

The joy...

'Your parents seem delighted at the prospect of being grandparents to Kip, and are prepared to come to Bellingham to meet my family whenever you say.' He spoke again, covering her face with kisses.

She was incredulous. 'You've already told Mom and Dad?'

'Of course.' His enticing mouth broke into a smile that lighted up her world. 'They said they were glad I'd come because I was the only one who could provide the cure for what was ailing you.'

'You are!' She cried out once more, from too much happiness.

'Then let's get married as soon as possible. Kip has already suggested a substitute teacher all the kids will like while we take our honeymoon.'

'He must mean Mrs Taft,' she murmured, almost incoherently because she couldn't get enough of his mouth.

'Of course, there's no one like Jilly—but my son didn't have to tell me that.' His voice shook. In the next breath he lifted her chin, the better to see into her eyes. 'I knew it before we ever left the pier to drive to my house.

'You reminded me of a Christmas angel, all gold and white and incredibly beautiful on the outside, full of excitement and sunshine and goodness within. I thought that mortal as I am, with my many faults, if I could be so lucky as to find the key to your heart I'd never want for anything else in life.'

His words transformed her. 'I already loved your son. All it took was meeting the father who'd helped to create such a perfect child.

'When you took the risk of inviting us to your home to wait out the storm because you suspected Kip *might* be your son, I knew then I'd been blessed to meet the kind of rare, marvelous man who maybe comes along once in a lifetime.' Tremulously she whispered, 'How I envied the woman who would win your love. I still can't believe this is real.'

'It's real, all right,' he muttered emotionally. 'And, as our son would say, it's going to get realer and realer.'

'That's exactly what he'd say, darling,' she murmured amidst tears of joy and gentle laughter, before passion took over with its promise of a glorious future.

Coming in August 1997!

THE BETTY NEELS RUBY COLLECTION

August 1997—Stars Through the Mist
September 1997—The Doubtful Marriage
October 1997—The End of the Rainbow
November 1997—Three for a Wedding
December 1997—Roses for Christmas
January 1998—The Hasty Marriage

COLLECTOR'S EDITION

This August start assembling the
Betty Neels Ruby Collection. Six of the
most requested and best-loved titles have
been especially chosen for this collection.
From August 1997 until January 1998,
one title per month will be available to avid
fans. Spot the collection by the lush ruby red
cover with the gold Collector's Edition banner
and your favorite author's name—Betty Neels!

Available in August at your favorite retail outlet.

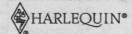

HARLEQUIN®

WANT WESTERNS?

Harlequin Historicals has got 'em!

In October, look for these two exciting tales:

WILD CARD by Susan Amarillas
A lady gambler wanted for murder falls for a handsome sheriff

THE UNTAMED HEART by Kit Gardner
A dashing earl succumbs to a reckless woman in the American West

In November, watch for two more stories:

CADE'S JUSTICE by Pat Tracy
A schoolteacher heals the soul of the wealthy uncle of one of her students

TEMPLE'S PRIZE by Linda Castle
Two paleontologists battle each other on a dig, and uncover their hearts

Four new Westerns from four terrific authors! Look for them wherever Harlequin Historicals are sold.

Harlequin®
Historical

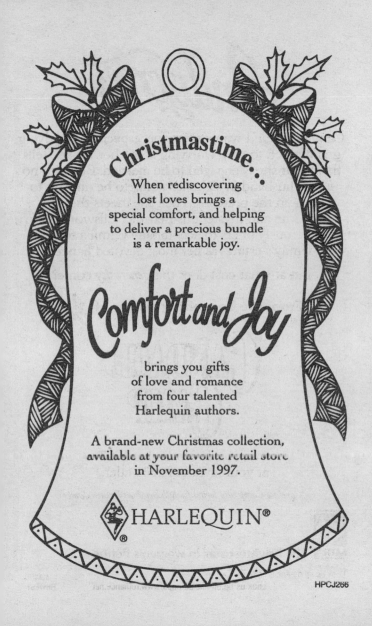

Indiscreet

Camilla Ferrand wants everyone, especially her dying grandfather, to stop worrying about her. So she tells them that she is engaged to be married. But with no future husband in sight, it's going to be difficult to keep up the pretense. Then she meets the very handsome and mysterious Benedict Ellsworth who generously offers to accompany Camilla to her family's estate—as her most devoted fiancé.

But at what cost does this *generosity* come?

From the bestselling author of *Impulse*

CANDACE CAMP

Available in November 1997
at your favorite retail outlet.

"Candace Camp also writes for Silhouette® as Kristen James

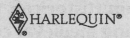
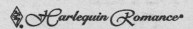

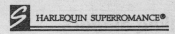

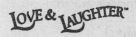

**Harlequin Historicals presents
an exciting medieval collection**

THE KNIGHTS OF CHRISTMAS

With bestselling authors

Suzanne
BARCLAY

Margaret
MOORE

Debborah
SIMMONS

Available in October
wherever Harlequin Historicals are sold.

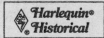

Harlequin® Historical

WELCOME TO *Love Inspired* ™

A brand-new series of contemporary inspirational love stories.

Join men and women as they learn valuable lessons about facing the challenges of today's world and about life, love and faith.

Look for:

Promises
by Roger Elwood

A Will and a Wedding
by Lois Richer

An Old-Fashioned Love
by Arlene James

Available in retail outlets
in October 1997.

LIFT YOUR SPIRITS AND GLADDEN YOUR HEART with *Love Inspired* ™!

Steeple
Hill™

LI1197

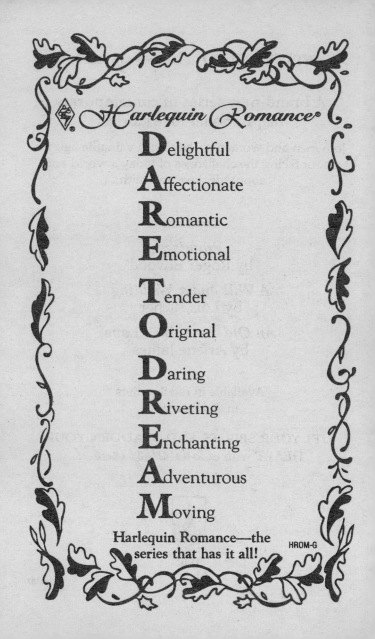

Harlequin Romance®

Delightful
Affectionate
Romantic
Emotional

Tender
Original

Daring
Riveting
Enchanting
Adventurous
Moving

Harlequin Romance—the
series that has it all!

HROM-G